RETALIATION

RETALIATION

AKIO REVELATIONS™ BOOK TWO

CHARLES TILLMAN

MICHAEL ANDERLE

DISRUPTIVE IMAGINATION

LMBPN Publishing
PMB 196, 2540 South Maryland Pkwy
Las Vegas, NV 89109

First US edition, July, 2020
Version 1.01, August 2020
eBook ISBN: 978-1-64971-025-3
Print ISBN: 978-1-64971-026-0

DEDICATION

*To my Wife Danette, thank you for being behind me while I did
this.
A huge thank you to Michael Anderle who let me come and play
in his world.
There are also two others who worked hard to help me bring this
to you:
John Ashmore, Alpha reader extraordinaire
Tracey Byrnes, Alpha reader and first pass editor who kept me
and my sentence structure on track. I couldn't have done it
without you.
And most of all thanks to you the Kurtherian Gambit Fans for
reading.*

—Charles

*To Family, Friends and
Those Who Love
to Read.*

May We All Enjoy Grace
to Live the Life We Are
Called.

— Michael

THE RETALIATION TEAM

Thanks to our Beta Readers

Kelly O'Donnell, Micky Cocker, Daniel Weigert, James Caplan, Rachel Beckford, Larry Omans

Thanks to the JIT Readers

Dave Hicks
Mary Morris
Misty Roa
Diane L. Smith
Tim Bischoff
Veronica Stephan-Miller
Jackey Hankard-Brodie
Peter Manis
Kerry Mortimer
Dorothy Lloyd
Angel LaVey
Deb Mader
Jeff Goode
James Caplan

If we've missed anyone, please let us know!

Editor
Skyhunter Editing Team

CHAPTER ONE

Acheng, China, Destroyed Research Laboratory

Miko regained consciousness in total darkness, his throat dry and his body weak. He groggily tried to sit up but was stopped abruptly after only rising centimeters off the ground. He reached out and touched the obstruction, a rough, unforgiving surface that it took his addled brain a few seconds to realize was stone.

He struggled to get his thoughts in order, and suddenly, the memories from earlier came back to him. The seemingly abandoned base, the smell of smoke, the kitchen filled with.... His eyes shot open wide in the darkness as he remembered the dead cook, lying on the floor in the kitchen and him trying to get to the stairwell in the hangar to call back the Weres. That was the last conscious memory he had, but judging from the current predicament he was in more had gone wrong, much more.

He assessed his situation and determined that he was on his back and buried under an indeterminable amount of stone. Luckily, he had ended up in an area where the

1

hangar had collapsed in a way that left him sheltered in a small opening.

He felt around to get an idea of what surrounded him. When he didn't touch anything, he pulled his legs up to worm himself forward. The slight movement of his right leg caused a shooting pain through his calf. He froze when the movement caused a shift and small rocks and dust fell around him, holding his breath and hoping that his small shelter wouldn't collapse.

When the dust settled, he tried cautiously to move his leg. The pain increased until it felt like his leg was in a hot fire, causing him to stop and reassess his options. He twisted his body as far as the tight confines would allow and carefully felt down his leg until he encountered the problem.

A piece of stone with a sharp point was sticking into the muscle of his calf just below his knee. He ran his hand over the area and soon discovered that he was unable to reach all the way around it or to dislodge it from his flesh.

Well, this is not good, he mused as he continued to search for a remedy. *At least the stone isn't all the way through the leg, hopefully I can pull my leg off it without causing the rocks to shift again.* He moved his left leg to the side as far as he could and clenched his teeth against the pain he knew was to come. *Here goes nothing.*

The pain radiated through his body as he pulled his leg off the jagged stone one agonizing millimeter at a time. He saw bright spots before his eyes and felt his consciousness start to slip before he finally felt some relief as the stone pulled from his leg.

Not an experience I care to repeat, was the first thing

through his mind once the pain had subsided to a dull ache. Now to see about getting out of here before the whole thing comes down.

He wriggled his body forward, his hands stretched out, feeling the way, until he encountered another blockage. He felt around and found that he was sealed in. He pressed against the obstruction, but all he accomplished was to cause more dust and small rocks to fall into his prison. He reversed direction and pushed himself back at a snail's pace, weak from the injury and loss of blood, his body healing but at a much slower rate than normal. He painfully snaked his body through the narrow space, one agonizing millimeter at a time until he was stopped by another obstruction. Unable to escape, he closed his eyes and allowed himself to fall to sleep, hoping his body would heal and regain enough strength to allow him to escape.

"The sun will rise shortly. You must go now." He pushed against the body snuggled beside him. "I won't be the cause of your death, and you have told me that you can't stay with me during the day countless times."

The form moved and a dark figure rose beside him, the features indistinct other than the dark hair that was mussed and sticking out in all directions.

"I know, but it is hard to leave you," the figure mumbled as strong arms wrapped him in a tight embrace.

He pushed against the body and laughed. "I'll be waiting here when you can return. Now go, before anyone discovers you missing. You know that would be dangerous for both of us, and I have no intention of losing you." He reluctantly pulled out of the embrace and sat up in the bed, then slid out from under the covers and sat up, turning to put his feet on the floor.

He started to stand and a noise distracted him, a rhythmic metallic scraping. He turned to his lover, but before he could speak, the scene faded, and he found himself surrounded by darkness.

The sound was louder than before he woke, the dream fading as he became alert, aware that he was still trapped under tons of stone in the remains of the destroyed lab. His senses became more focused, and he could feel vibrations accompanying the noise. Someone was digging close by.

The vibration of stone sliding against stone brought a cascade of dust and rocks into the shelter that had imprisoned him as he felt a breeze blow across his body. The scraping continued, and a moment later, he heard someone breathing hard as they slithered toward him. He lay still, not breathing or daring to move as he heard the noise getting closer. A scent blew in on the breeze, *Human,* his mind supplied as the noise slowly worked its way into his shelter.

The minutes stretched by with agonizing slowness as the enticing smell of fresh blood assailed his nostrils. His fangs extended on their own, and his body was on fire as the blood it craved came ever closer.

After what seemed like forever, a hand brushed his leg. A sharp intake of breath followed, and he heard the person start to scramble away.

No! his mind screamed. What he needed was so close.

An involuntary moan escaped his lips, and the person froze.

"Who's there? a voice whispered. "Are you alive?"

Miko let out another low moan, twisting his body a small amount.

"Hold on!" the voice cried. "I'm going to try to get you out."

The person worked their way back toward him, and their hand closed around Miko's ankle. He was pulled across the stone slowly, and his body was worked through a small opening into a larger pocket that had been created when the mountain collapsed. Miko's savior was mumbling to himself, and he was finally able to see it was a man around twenty years old as he crouched in the space at Miko's feet.

"Just hold on. You are injured badly, judging by the blood dried on your clothes. I'll have you out in a moment. Let me check you so I don't injure you more," the man told him as he worked his way up his body, touching him in the dim light cast by a candle burning inside a small lantern. When he touched Miko's head, his eyes opened, and the man jerked back when he saw the red glow in them. Miko caught the startled man by his shirt and dragged him down, his mouth open and his fangs ready to rend the soft flesh to take the blood he so desperately needed.

The young man's scream of terror cut off abruptly as Miko's fangs ripped into the flesh of his throat, his hot blood pouring into his waiting mouth. Miko pulled hard on the wound, sucking the blood down as fast as he could, animal growls issuing from his throat as he cut deeper into the flesh with his fangs.

It was over in moments, the young man completely drained. Miko felt his strength slowly returning as the blood worked its way through his battered body. He lay there, drifting in a semiconscious state as his body healed. When it was done, he was still weak, but all his injuries seemed to be gone. He rolled over slowly, then pushed himself up and crawled on all fours toward the opening the man had come through.

When he finally broke free, he saw stars above him. In his still-weakened state, he felt as if he had traveled a kilometer or more. The truth was that he had only moved about three meters through the maze of shattered stone.

He climbed painfully to his feet, pulling himself up with his arms until he was leaning against a boulder the size of a truck. He looked at the devastation around him. Where there had been a hidden hangar that was fifty meters deep and twenty meters high, there was now a jumble of stone and broken materials from the mountain it was dug into and the buildings above. The deep valley that had once hidden the hangar entrance was partially filled with debris that came almost to the mouth. The double doors that had opened into it were nowhere to be seen.

Miko was dumbstruck by the total annihilation of what had once been a multi-level complex dug out of solid granite. Now it was a cairn to the Weres he had sent below. He slowly started to make his way up to the ridge's top, sliding precariously on the loose rock and debris and losing one step for every three he gained until he finally managed to struggle his way to the crest.

He collapsed there, completely exhausted from the exertion, his body lacking the energy to heal him further.

He lay there unmoving for an undetermined time until he was brought out of his lull by a sound.

Something had furtively moved behind him, a dislodged rock rolling down the ridge making him aware he was not alone. He lay unmoving, his senses extended until he smelled it. Fresh blood.

Miko remained as still as death as the noise of someone taking hesitant steps got closer. He smiled as he felt his back prodded tentatively. His senses searched for others until he was satisfied that his unknown savior was alone.

"Han, what happened? Are you injured? Say something, brother," a raspy voice called.

Miko felt a hand touch his shoulder and pull him over. When his body was rolled over on its back, he struck, catching the unwary villager in a crushing embrace as his fangs extended, seeking more of the lifeblood that his body needed to heal.

He closed his eyes in ecstasy as the hot blood filled his mouth and poured down his parched throat, fueling his body and giving him the energy he so desperately needed. When he was done, he shoved the corpse off the ridge and sat up. He extended his senses to search for dangers and more prey.

Finding none, he stood and looked at the sky—several hours until daylight. *Plenty of time until I need to hide from the sun.* He set off at a ground-eating pace for a bolt-hole he had located several years ago that was perfect for just such an emergency.

CHAPTER TWO

The Palace, Tokyo, Japan

"Wow!" Asai exclaimed. "I can't believe how crazy the past three days have been. We have had a line around the building from before daylight until we closed every day."

"We certainly have been busy," Yuko agreed. "I'm glad I listened to Eve and bought the property next door. Looks like we're going to have to expand sooner than I thought."

"Told you so," Eve chimed in. "With the new simulations I have in beta testing, we will be this busy for the foreseeable future. Bringing Seki and his gamer friends in to test the simulations has really paid off. Some of their ideas for the first-person shooter games are really good and have proven to be extremely popular."

"Plus, Seki gives Asai something to think about besides work," Koda chided with a grin.

Asai blushed and stuck her tongue out at her cousin, causing everyone in the office to burst out laughing.

Koda returned to working on the computer at her desk.

She pushed her chair back, her eyes wide as she looked at the screen.

"What's wrong with you, Koda?" Asai asked. "You look like you've seen a ghost or something."

Koda frowned. "I can't believe what I'm seeing here. It can't possibly be right."

"Well, what is it?" Asai pressed.

"I was going over the revenue for the past three days," Koda told her. "I think I did something wrong."

Eve smiled. "If you have found that we made a great deal of money, you are absolutely correct. The sims did really well, but we made enough from the concession sales alone to pay all the staff expenses, plus most of the advertising we did before the opening."

"Yeah," Koda blurted. "That's what I found too."

Yuko smiled. "At this rate, we should be able to start construction on the new dock at Kume much sooner than we projected."

Asai ducked her head, wiping a tear from her eye. "I still can't believe you did this to help the people at home. It's overwhelming to hear your plans for Kume."

Yuko stood and went to Asai, wrapping her in a comforting hug. "Asai, it's the least we can do after what happened there. If we had caught on to what Isamu and Ogawa were doing sooner, we could have saved so many more."

Asai sniffled. "But we were nothing, just a small settlement on an island that even the government had forgotten."

"No!" Yuko put her finger under the young woman's chin, pushing her head up till she was looking into her eyes. "You were never nothing. You were a group of survivors, going about the business of living until that monster and his minions almost destroyed you all. We were put here to stop that kind of thing before it happened, but we failed. The very least we can do is aid your people in their recovery."

Asai hugged her back, tears running freely down her face.

"My hope is," Yuko continued, "that once construction starts, some of the workers will see the potential of Kume and want to relocate. The island needs a bigger population to thrive."

Asai wiped her eyes and pulled back. "Yuko, would it be possible for Akio to interview potential settlers like he did our employees before they're allowed to immigrate? The local population would not be able to defend themselves if people like the ones who kidnapped Koda go there." She shuddered. "Or beasts like you found in China."

Yuko smiled. "I'm sure Akio would be willing to help with that. Another idea I have is to seek out honest people with military or police experience who would be willing to relocate. Until the island can import and export goods it is not a feasible plan, but I'm sure there are some who would welcome a more rural lifestyle. Provided they had the basic comforts like electricity and running water, that is."

"Hot running water is a definite plus." Asai laughed. "I would probably be willing to stay more than one day if I could take a bath without having to haul water from the fire to the tub."

Koda snickered. "Oh, yes. Asai can't be away from her

bathtub longer than one day. Seki for a few days, no problem, but the bathtub only a short time."

"Koda!" Asai grinned. "You have no room to talk. I've seen how you watch Horst when he happens to stop in. He hasn't even tried the simulations yet since he hasn't made it past the Coke counter."

Koda's face turned red as she shot daggers out of her eyes at Asai. "He's just waiting until the lines go down. He's polite and doesn't want to cut in front of anyone."

Asai guffawed. "Doesn't want to miss a chance to spend time with you is more like it."

Koda looked at her through the hair she had let fall over her face in an unsuccessful attempt to hide her blush. "Well, what can I say? He's polite and has good taste."

"Where is the blond hunk, by the way?" Asai asked.

"He's gone to Germany with Akio, " Koda answered. "They're trying to locate survivors from his old pack."

"I still have a hard time believing he's a wolf," Asai mused. "After the attacks in the rural areas by those tiger men, I have a hard time thinking that Horst, as kind as he has been, is a—what is it again Yuko—a Wetzelbag?"

"'Wechselbalg' is the proper term," Yuko answered. "But they're no different from any other people. There are good and bad."

"I hope Horst can find some of his people. He's really depressed about the loss of his brother. He doesn't blame anyone," she added quickly, "but he really misses him."

"Akio has the location of several groups of Wechselbalg in the area Horst is from," Eve offered. "Though it's been many years, hopefully, one of those groups will be his."

Koda was silent during this exchange, her face showing

concern. She would never say anything, but she had become very fond of Horst in the short time she had known him. He had spent many hours talking to her after her kidnapping and was a big part of the reason she didn't run back to Kume after her rescue by Eve. The thought that he might want to leave if he found his pack worried her.

Yuko noticed Koda's discomfort at the conversation and walked over to where she was sitting, then leaned down and whispered, "Just because he might find some of the members of his old pack, it doesn't mean he will want to stay there. He was a child when he left and has been away for many years."

Koda lowered her head, ashamed that she was secretly hoping he would not find a reason to remain in Germany. "I know, Yuko. I really want what's best for him. He helped me a lot after my ordeal. He helped me understand that there is more good here than bad, and that there is just as much bad outside of the cities as in them. I admit that when Eve saved me, I was seriously considering running back to my father's house on Kume and never leaving. Now I feel I can do much more good by remaining here, as long as I have my communicator." She pulled on a chain tucked inside of her shirt, showing the device, which was firmly attached. "I don't have to be afraid of a repeat of that."

Yuko nodded and smiled. "Akio plans to start training you and Asai to protect yourselves as soon as we get the staff up to speed here. Plus, I don't think you will have to worry about being caught out alone again. Horst seems quite taken with you, and I think there is little danger of him leaving even if he does find others in Germany. With him around, I fear more for anyone who bothers you. Weres are extremely vicious when protecting someone they care about."

"After the damage the Yakuza has suffered from Akio's little *suggestion* to Sero, the most you will have to fear is a random mugger. As long as that man-mountain is with you, there is little danger of that." Eve laughed.

"I still plan to learn all Akio is willing to teach me." Koda's face paled as she thought about her treatment at the hands of Sero's henchmen. "I might even want to learn to use some form of weapon. I don't plan on ever being a victim again," she finished with cold certainty.

CHAPTER THREE

Rasov, Czechia

"I don't think we're going to find anything but trouble here," Horst mumbled as he walked into the village.

They were on their fifth location of the day and had not found any members of Horst's old pack. The current group of Weres they were on their way to see had set up in a small mountain village, and judging by the downtrodden appearance of the villagers, the Weres were keeping the entire population as their personal slaves.

Akio had stayed out of sight as Horst approached each group, a method he assured Horst would at least give him a chance to talk to the Weres instead of them automatically attacking or running away at the sight of a vampire. The first four groups had been unable to give him any answers, and they moved on without Akio making his presence known.

This group would be a different matter, it seemed.

A scarred and muscular Were growled as he came out

the door of the largest house in the village. "What business do you have here?"

"I'm seeking information about my pack," Horst replied.

The Were sneered. "What pack is that, pup?"

Horst stiffened at the insult but held his temper as five other Weres, a female and four males, came out into the street. The males all glared at him with open hostility while the female moved next to the scarred man and leaned her hip against his.

"The Rohr," Horst told them. "I have been gone for many years and am trying to find where they went."

"Never heard of them," the man growled. "Move along now. You have your answer."

The woman put a hand on his arm and licked her lips as she looked Horst up and down, a predatory gleam in her eyes.

"Hold on a minute, Dahl." She smiled at Horst. "I remember them. It's been many years since I've heard that name."

"Do you know where they went?" Horst asked.

"It was shortly before the war ended," she told him. "I was with the Dorfen pack before it was absorbed by another when Allied bombs destroyed our town. A Were came to us with a story that the Rohr had been decimated by Anton for some perceived transgression. He claimed he was the last survivor. I don't remember his name, but he died shortly after when he challenged the Alpha."

Horst's stomach dropped when he heard that. His one dream since he was taken as a young child had been to reunite with his father's old pack. "Anton? Did he say what had happened?"

She squeezed the big man's arm when he started to speak. "Only that Anton came in the night and killed all he found. That one, I wish I could remember his name: Jan, Johann, Jaeger…"

"Jakob?" Horst offered.

She paused for a moment, her head cocked to the side. "*Ja, Ja,* that was the name he gave. He told us he had been away on business in Stuttgart. When he returned the next day, everyone was dead."

Horst remembered Jakob. He was a supporter of his father and had resisted Anton and Heinz running the pack. He was a strong older wolf but not an Alpha, so he doubted that he was killed in a challenge. "You say he died in an Alpha challenge?"

"*Ja.* We took him in, but he chafed against the Alpha's rules. He challenged within a few days."

Horst nodded, keeping his thoughts to himself.

"You have your answer, so you can be on your way now," the gruff male snapped. "We don't need any more mouths to feed here."

The woman cut her eyes up and glared at the man.

Horst stared at him appraisingly, debating whether to let the rudeness go or accept the unvoiced challenge. Before he decided, Akio materialized beside him, causing all the Weres to take a wary step back.

"You." Akio pointed at the Alpha, his eyes glowing red. "You are responsible for the state of these humans."

"What the hell? You bring a vampire into our town! Kill them!" the woman screamed as she shifted. The big male at her side and another shifted seconds behind her.

As they changed form, one of the other Weres grabbed

the remaining two by their arms before they shifted and murmured, *"Nein."* He stepped back, pulling the others with him.

Horst started to shift but froze in place when the dark brown head of the Alpha dropped to the ground at his feet. The body, mid-leap, continued a short distance before it collapsed in front of him, spewing blood.

Horst watched in amazement as Akio expressed his displeasure at their treatment of the villagers. When he was done, there were three dead wolves and three standing slack-jawed in human form.

"Mein Gott!" the sensible Were who'd stepped back exclaimed. "You moved so fast, all I saw was body parts flying and blood. No discussion, no hesitation."

Akio stared at the three surviving Weres, and they all took another involuntary step back from him. "They were the ones responsible for the wrong here: the Alpha, Beta, and the Alpha's mate. As long as the others don't revert to bad practices, I will not return for them. If they do, it will be a death sentence. Am I clear?"

The Weres nodded enthusiastically.

Horst had no doubt that Akio would do exactly as he said. "I think we are done here. If that bitch wasn't lying about everything, there are no more of my old pack left."

The Were who stopped the others from shifting, an older man with streaks of gray starting to show in his hair spoke up. "She was telling the truth about Jakob being dead, but he didn't die in a challenge. She didn't like him and had Dahl," he nodded at the dead alpha, "kill him. Dahl was the Alpha, but Marlana called the shots."

Akio watched the exchange without comment, reading

the minds of the Weres as they spoke. "You three didn't agree with what they did here. Why didn't you leave?"

"Things are very different here now." The older Were shrugged. "Few of the packs welcome strangers and survival without a pack is precarious at best."

Akio continued to look at him for a few seconds. He delved deeper into each one's mind and determined that none of them had harmed any of the humans. "You are free now to go as you like, but I will only warn you once. Try to subjugate or cause harm to humans in any way, and I will come for you."

The old Were lifted his hands in submission and nodded his agreement. "I promise you won't have to worry about that from me. I would rather take my chances alone than face certain death."

The other two quickly voiced their agreement, and all three walked toward the edge of the village. When they were past the last house, they shifted and bounded into the forest without looking back.

Akio looked at Horst with sympathy. "I'm sorry we couldn't find your pack, but know that you are welcome in Japan as long as you abide by the rules Bethany Anne set forth. Besides," he smiled, "I think a certain young woman would hunt you down if you didn't return."

Horst lost some of the sorrow from his eyes and raised his slumped shoulders. "I hadn't decided if I would stay if I *did* find them. I just wanted to know they still existed. A foolish wish after so many years, I know."

Akio patted Horst's shoulder. "There is no shame in wishing for good, there is too much bad in the world as it is."

"*Ja,* that is true. I thank you for accepting me, but I will need some purpose as well, some way to provide for myself. I refuse to live on the largesse of others."

"I'm certain we can find something that fits your skills. Let's go home, and we will face that tomorrow," Akio advised as he called Abel on his implant to bring the Pod down.

Horst was lost in his thoughts, as they boarded the Pod and shot into the sky, headed back to Japan. After a few minutes, he nodded to himself and spoke.

"Koda told me that Yuko and Eve built the Palace to make money to rebuild the docks and make other improvements on her home island. I have degrees in civil engineering and architecture, as well as experience as an overseer on several projects. Do you think the people there would allow me to help with the rebuilding? I know they suffered a great loss because of Isamu and that bastard Ogawa, and I would understand if they didn't want my help."

Akio reflected for a moment before he spoke. "I can't speak for the islanders, but I know that Mayor Yagi is a wise and reasonable man. Perhaps you should discuss it with Koda and Asai. I'm sure if they supported you, the people there would at least listen to what you have to offer."

Horst started to answer but was stopped by Abel's voice coming through the speakers in the Pod.

"Akio, I have received information you need to see from the drones Eve left at the lab in China."

"I'm on my way back to base now. I'll come by as soon as I get cleaned up."

"I'll have it waiting for you when you arrive."

CHAPTER FOUR

O'Donnell Station, Stanley, Australia

Kelly O'Donnell wiped the sweat off her forehead.

A giggle from the next shearing station reached her ears and she turned her head toward the source.

As she already knew, it was Jenni Davies, the thin blonde nineteen-year-old who had been there with her since daylight. Kelly glared at her until a small smile cracked her scowl and she burst out laughing.

"No matter how many times I tell myself I'm not going to do it, I still manage to forget every time," she grumbled.

Jenni snickered. "Isn't forgetfulness a sign of old age?"

Kelly picked up a handful of coarse wool and threw it at the girl's face. She shrieked and tried to move away, but the ball hit her shoulder and puffed out in a cloud that enveloped her. When the fluff cleared, she looked like she was auditioning for the part of the bearded woman in a circus.

"Dammit, Kel! This shit's impossible to get out of my hair," she complained.

Kelly grinned. "Well, you just remember that the next time you call me old, Jenni Davies, and you better watch your fucking mouth. Proper young ladies don't say 'shit.'"

Jenni gave her the best eye roll she could muster and stuck out her tongue. She spent the next minute trying to get the wool out of her mouth while Kelly was bent over, holding her sides in laughter.

"You know, you can be a real bitch sometimes, Kel," Jenni muttered. "That was the last of them. Let's go wash up and get something to eat. We can get this stuff ready to go tomorrow. It's been a long day."

Kelly waved her on. "You go ahead, Jen. I want to talk to the men before I leave."

"Okay, but don't be too long. You know Marge has dinner about ready, and you won't hear the end of it if you get there once it's cold—again."

Kelly waved her hand, acknowledging her. "I won't be long. You'd better not use all the hot water this time."

"No promises," Jenni yelled over her shoulder as she took off toward the house at a run.

"I mean it, Jenni," Kelly called after her. "I'll put a goanna in your bed if you do."

Kelly smiled as she watched her friend run to the house, laughing as she went. It was good to see her coming out of the funk she had been in for the past year.

Kelly had known Jenni all her life. At five years younger, Jenni had been shadowing her since she could walk. The past year had been extremely hard on the girl. First, her father had disappeared on a scavenger trip to a small settlement eighty kilometers north of O'Donnell Station. A short time after that... Kelly's face flushed with rage at the thought of what that arse Hawthorne had done in the very building she was in.

Matt Hawthorne, the forty-seven-year-old owner of Hawthorne Station, which adjoined O'Donnell Station to the south, was a coarse man with hygiene habits that would make a pig blush. When Kelly's father had died in a bandit raid six years earlier, he was one of the first ones to show up seeking her hand—and her farm—in marriage. He'd refused to take no for an answer and became more demanding each time he came around until Kelly finally told him she would shoot his prick off and feed it to the hogs if he ever looked her way again.

He never forgot that and took the threat to heart. Kelly did have a reputation for being quick-tempered and a crack shot. It had been bandied about for years in the local tavern that at seventeen, she had gone alone into the bush and hunted down the surviving bandits who'd killed her father. The talk was that she had killed each of them slowly, the gruesome details growing with each telling. She had actually only found two of them, and there had been nothing slow about the way she'd coldly put a single bullet into each one.

Hawthorne had stopped trying after that, but when Jenni's dad didn't return, he decided to try her instead. Jenni was a gentle soul and tried to see the good in everyone. She was polite to the man, against Kelly's advice, and he took it as a sign that she wanted him, even though she had turned him down on multiple occasions.

Kelly looked toward the rear of the shed, her memories taking her back to the events six months past.

It was getting close to dark, and she was checking that everything was secure for the night. She had done it just like her dad had every night since the day he was killed and she became the owner of the station.

The door to the shed was unsecured. When she was closing it, she heard scuffling and a muted scream from inside. She pulled the old military Browning pistol from its holster and went in to investigate. Jenni was struggling in Hawthorne's grasp, an angry red mark on her face and blood leaking out of her nose where he had hit her. One hand was clamped tight over her mouth to stop her screams and hold her in place while he ripped her shirt off with the other.

Kelly's body went numb when she saw what was going on. "What the fuck do you think you're doing, arsehole?" she yelled. "Let her go!"

What she did next would become legend on the neighboring stations.

His head jerked around at the sound. He released Jenni and started toward Kelly, pulling a large knife from his belt as he did. The leer on his face as he looked her up and down told her exactly what his thoughts were. "I'll do both of you. You think you're so much better. See how you like it when—"

Before he could take another step, Kelly raised the pistol in her hand and smiled coldly at him as she pulled the trigger once. He went down with a scream of absolute agony, his hands holding his groin as blood soaked the front of his pants.

Kelly stalked toward him with slow, deliberate strides, still wearing that same cold smile that didn't reach her eyes as she watched him writhe on the ground. She motioned Jenni to her and pushed her lightly toward the door after the young woman had warily skirted the thrashing man.

His agonized screams continued as two of the men from the bunkhouse ran to the shed, stopping short when they saw Jenni in her disheveled state leaning against the wall outside the door.

They heard Kelly, her voice as cold as death, say, "I told you I would shoot your prick off, you fucking bastard." Then a second shot rang out from inside and the screams abruptly cut off.

When the men rushed in, they saw Kelly, gun in hand, standing over Hawthorne's body. He was bleeding in two places —his mangled crotch, and a single hole in his forehead. Kelly walked past the two as they stared open-mouthed at the carnage.

"Get that rapist piece of shit out of here and burn his fucking body," she snarled as she stalked past them. "That son of a bitch doesn't deserve a proper burial, and he'd probably make the damned pigs sick if they ate him." When she reached the frightened young woman, she put her arm lightly around her shoulders and led her into the main house.

After that day, Jenni had lost some of her innocence and spunk, and she'd become timid and distrustful around anyone but Kelly. It had taken several months, but she was coming out of her shell and starting to act like the vivacious young woman she had been before the attempted rape. She still stayed close to Kelly most of the time, but would occasionally spend time around the fire at night. The other families who lived and worked on the station made sure she felt safe and welcome when she did. The men all treated her like a little sister, even though she was a beautiful young woman who would make a fine wife.

Kelly shook her head to dispel the dark memory and set out to find the workers and thank them for their hard labor before making her final rounds for the night.

Kelly had fallen into bed and was out almost before her head hit the pillow. Sometime later, she groggily woke with a feeling that something was off. The next thing she heard was her bedroom doorknob rattle, followed by a loud *crash* as it slammed into the room seconds later.

She grabbed the pistol she had kept under her pillow every night for the past six years. When a dark figure stormed into her bedroom, she put two rounds center mass like her father had taught her. The figure fell to the floor with a grunt and stayed there.

She slid out of bed, keeping her pistol pointed toward the body as she reached for the oil lamp on her nightstand. One hand felt around for the worn lighter she used. It had been her father's, and he had told her how he'd found it and several cases of fuel and flints shortly after the WWDE. He had only used it to light this lamp. More than twenty-five years later, it still worked like a charm.

The vicious snarl of a wild animal followed by a blood-chilling scream from somewhere outside startled her, and she knocked the lighter to the floor. She bent down, fumbling to pick it up. As her hand closed on it, someone grabbed her hair and jerked her back.

"Shoot me, will you, you bitch?" a harsh male voice snarled in her ear as the person lifted her off her feet.

Kelly screamed as her attacker jerked her back and forth, her gun flying from her fingers as she reached up with both hands to try to ease the pressure on her head. The man laughed as he threw her onto the bed with enough force for her to bounce and slam into the headboard.

She lay there, stunned, as rough hands fisted into the front of the t-shirt she wore and pulled her off the bed, only to slam her down again. This time, he drove a fist into her chest and knocked the breath out of her.

"Owen," a voice called from the hallway, "are you all right, mate? I heard shots."

"Bitch shot me," her attacker snarled. "I'm in the process of explaining how displeased I am. That shit hurt."

"Well, hurry up and bring her. Decklan is ready to move out, and you're holding us up. I know he's your brother, but that won't stop him from kicking my arse." The voice faded as the man walked away.

Kelly was still in the process of getting her uncooperative lungs to take in enough oxygen when she was snatched up by the shirt again.

"It's your lucky night, bitch, but don't think I'll forget this," was the last thing she heard before everything went black.

CHAPTER FIVE

TQB Base, Tokyo, Japan

"Abel, guide the Pod back to storage, please."

"I have the information you requested queued in the command center, or I can route it to wherever you want," Abel replied.

"I need to clean up before I do anything. I had a run-in with some Weres in Czechia and need to get the blood off before I touch anything here."

"Acknowledged, and the Pod is away."

"Thank you, Abel."

Akio went straight to his rooms and stripped out of his bloody clothes. The encounter with the Weres in Rasov had left him with arterial spray splashed across his chest, and the smell was starting to bother his enhanced senses.

The Weres around the world are getting bolder now, Akio mused as the hot water from the strong jets coursed over him, washing away the grime, and more importantly, the acrid smell of Were blood. *If they aren't kept in line, they will be as dangerous to the survival of humanity as the Forsaken.*

Both the Wechselbalg in Europe and the Sacred Clan in China have become empowered without the threat of Michael and his family keeping them in check. I will need to increase the surveillance on both groups, as well as searching out any others who are going down that path.

He dressed quickly and made his way to the command center to see what Abel had found on the sensors he had asked Eve to position around the destroyed lab in China. They had monitored it closely for the first few days, but when all that was detected were humans from the local area checking to see what had caused the explosions and huge cloud of dust, the lab site had been put lower on his list of priorities.

It had been a busy few days, between the opening of the Palace and the Japanese police asking for surveillance support when they went after the Yakuza gangsters Sero had "willingly" turned over. Eve and Yuko were both spending a good deal of time with the opening, and Yuko had asked Akio to work with Inspector Yonai to use their drone technology to locate and take down the criminals. The information had allowed Yonai's Special Investigations Unit to capture or kill numerous high-ranking criminals without exposing the team to any unnecessary dangers. There had been no fatalities and few injuries to the police teams, thanks to this help.

"What do you have for me, Abel?" Akio asked as he walked into the command center.

Abel had a video feed paused on the main screen. It showed a shot from the valley where the hangar had been. The video started, showing a lone figure making their way up the side of the mountain. Akio stood watching as they took several steps and then slid back on the loose rock.

The figure struggled, apparently injured or ill, as it made its way slowly to the ridge above. When it reached the top, the figure collapsed in an exhausted heap.

"Abel, please zoom in."

The feed switched to another view, this one at the top of the ridge. The focus zoomed in until the screen showed the dirt- and blood-covered face of a man. It was after midnight in China on a moonless night, and too dark to make out any of the features.

"Enhance lighting," Akio instructed.

The picture slowly became lighter. The face was undeniably that of a man, but the angle showed only the blood-covered side. His head turned slightly, bringing the other side into view.

Akio's legs went weak, and he slumped into a chair as he stared at the screen. He looked like he'd seen a ghost. His mouth worked, but no words came out. He finally croaked, "Kenjii?"

Akio felt numb all over as he watched the video. He saw another man approach from out of the camera angle, and his shocked expression never changed as he watched the unsuspecting man turn the body over after prodding it. His eyes widened as he watched the attack and how the body was callously disposed of when it was drained. When the vampire walked out of the frame, Akio blinked several times, a red trail running down both cheeks from them.

"When...when was this, Abel?"

"This was recorded this morning at 2:43," Abel replied. "The feeds from here as well as several other sites that have been deemed low interest are on a scheduled data dump each day. This one wasn't flagged, so I handled it with the routine data."

"Is there any more footage available?" Akio asked. "Did a drone continue tracking?"

"There was one more sighting of this individual as he left the area," Abel confirmed. "The carriers have been recalled, and there are only a dozen drones around the complex now. They are set to record and report but are not tasked to track anything at present. Eve removed that requirement when we discovered we had been tracking local humans who were just curious about the destruction.

"What direction was he headed when he left?"

"Southwest. Is this person of particular importance?"

Akio was silent for almost a minute before he answered. "He was at one time." He called Eve over his chip.

"Yes?" she answered.

"Do you have a drone carrier ready to deploy?"

"Not now," Eve told him. "I can have one ready in a few hours. I'm still at the Palace with Koda and Asai. We have a minor glitch in the new sim that's launching tomorrow. I will be back at the base in about an hour unless you need me sooner. What's wrong?"

"No, that will be fine," Akio assured her. "I need the carrier sent to the area around Acheng. Abel found something, and I would like to see if the drones can locate someone in the area."

"I'll take care of it soon as I get back," she promised.

"Thank you, Eve."

"Abel, when Eve gets the carrier ready, I want the

drones deployed in this area." He touched his finger to the screen and drew a cone-shaped area on the display that extended roughly fifty kilometers out and widened to one hundred kilometers at its end. "From the way he was moving, he is not at full strength. I would like to locate him before he kills again."

"Understood," Abel replied. "I will set the drones to report any contacts to me immediately. If he is still there, I will find him."

"It's very important to me to locate this person," Akio told Abel. "Keep a Pod in stationary orbit above us and call me as soon as you locate him."

CHAPTER SIX

Ning Jing Temple, Dabie Mountains, China

Peng Kun made his way through the dimly lit cave, his steps sure as he trekked down the same path he had traveled daily for many years. His bare feet made no sound on the stone floor worn smooth by centuries of feet taking the same path through the Ning Jing Temple; first Buddhist monks and then Peng Kun's subordinates and students. The clash of steel on steel echoed down the hand-carved cave as Kun came into an area where the light grew brighter. He turned through an opening covered by a heavy canvas curtain into a torchlit room that had been painstakingly chiseled out of the solid granite mountain in centuries past.

When Kun entered the room, a monk in black robes called out a sharp command. All the combatants stopped where they were and went to their knees, lowering their bodies until they were prostrate in supplication to the Master.

Kun nodded at the gray-clad monk and another

command rang out, causing all the supplicants to rise and resume their battles. Kun walked to a raised dais at the end of the room and climbed the three steps to the top, where he lowered himself into a lotus position on a thick cushion. He smiled as he settled, reveling in the softness. It was a perk he allowed himself as a nod to his position as Grand Master of the Serenity Temple, which was a holdover from the days before the Communist takeover when the Chinese government had evicted the Buddhists.

The training area was filled with one hundred pairs of black-robed monks engaging in multiple forms of combat. Some used swords, staffs, or weighted strings, and others fought with bare hands and feet. The combatants reminded Kun of dancers, each move mirrored or countered by their partners. He watched them in silence for about a quarter-hour, evaluating each pair and the gray-clad instructors who moved among them making corrections as needed, which were very few that Kun saw.

Kun slowly unfolded his legs and stood. Just as he reached his full height of one hundred sixty centimeters, the same gray-clad monk as before called out to the combatants. All of them froze in mid-move and dropped to their knees again.

He slowly paced across the first step of the dais, looking at the students with a calculating gaze. His eyes flitted from one to another, like a lord weighing the worth of his prized stock. He cleared his throat and began to speak.

"You have all worked hard to arrive here today, some of you for many years, others for less. Today you stand before me not as acolytes, but as warriors. Each of you came here for your own reason, some because of family tradition and others for the honor of serving the Clan. No matter your reason, the day has arrived where each of you will go out into the world as forerunners to what has been prophesied for centuries by our most Sacred of Masters. Today the ascent of the Sacred Clan to its rightful position in the world begins in earnest!"

As he said the last word, his body morphed, and the sound of ripping cloth followed. Seconds later, where a bald monk of average height had stood was a giant of over two hundred centimeters. His body was covered in short orange fur with black stripes, and his heavily muscled arms bore razor-sharp claws on the end of each finger.

He was silent for a moment, then in a deep guttural growl roared, "For the honor of the Clan." That was followed by the sound of ripping cloth throughout the room, and where the monks had knelt, the room was filled with huge, sleek, black and orange tigers.

All of their eyes, like their master's, looked alarmingly human.

Kun leapt from the dais, landing smoothly in an open space halfway across the floor. He stood there listening to the roars coming from the throats of two hundred Sacred Clan warriors ready to spread the reach of the Clan first across China, and then the rest of the world. The rumor was that Michael was missing and presumed dead. His strictures no longer applied, and the Clan was ready to take its place as the uncontested rulers of all the world.

Kun raised his hands, and the noise stopped immediately. Only the sounds of excited panting could be heard. "Break up into your teams and prepare to travel, you all leave at sunrise."

The cats silently formed into teams of four and padded from the room, leaving Kun and four other tigers who also stood on two legs alone in the room. When the last team had departed, Kun morphed back into a nude man, followed closely by the other four. "Li Song, attend me. We have things to discuss before the teams depart."

One of them, a young-looking muscular man with long black hair, nodded and followed Kun as he exited through the same curtain he had entered earlier.

"I have received no reports from the advance scouts we sent to the Japanese islands," Kun told him. "All other teams have checked in and reported that it is time for the Clan to rise. Have you been able to make contact with any of the lost teams?"

"No, Grand Master," Li replied. "They all reported that they had arrived and were moving into the remote areas as assigned. Each team is equipped with one of the satellite phones that works through what's left of the Chinese military network. We have heard nothing more, and they do not answer the calls."

"That is extremely irregular," Kun mused. "To lose contact with one or two teams is to be expected, but we sent twenty teams comprised of two to three members each to Japan. To lose contact with all is impossible. Are you certain the equipment is still working?"

"Yes, Grand Master. I personally spoke to one of the advance teams in Korea this morning. Unless the Japanese Government has discovered them or devised a way to block the signals across Japan, we must assume all those teams met with some unexpected mishap."

Kun considered that for a moment, nodding to himself

he continued, "I want you to take your team to Japan. Find out what has happened to our scouts and report back. With your warriors departing on their missions, your duties here will be passed on to Cui Yong. He has done well as the under-master of his group of acolytes, and it is time he expands his role within the Clan."

The tone Kun used told Li that the meeting was done. He bowed low to the Master. "I will depart at first light." He backed out of the room.

Kun called to him before he reached the door, "If you find that the teams were discovered and killed or captured, use your best judgment on how to proceed. I will accept nothing less than your complete success. The Sacred Clan shall rise."

"The Clan rises," Li Song solemnly intoned, completing the centuries-old ritual.

Peng Kun prepared tea on a small stove in his office. When the tea had brewed, he sat on a worn cushion against the wall. He held the cup under his nose, savoring the complex scents of the various herbs and spices that comprised the blend. His thoughts wandered as he relaxed.

The tales he'd heard about vigilante Forsaken running around policing the UnknownWorld might be more than rumors. The disappearance of the teams sent to Japan was alarming. Given the death of their last leader at the hands of that damned woman and her people, he feared that some of the rumors may be true. They'd all thought that with her leaving in that space vehicle and Michael presumed dead, the Clan could move in and none could stand against them.

Li had seen the same reports, so if there was someone doing what they had been told, their time was running out. Li and his team had taken down several Forsaken who interfered with Clan business. This one would be no different.

Kun smiled at that thought before he brought the cup to his mouth and sipped. The flavors exploded across his palate, causing him to groan appreciatively. Soon all the planning and training would pay off. Soon Peng Kun would have his own kingdom to run for the glory of the Clan.

CHAPTER SEVEN

Safe House, Yushu, China

Miko had run hard through the mountains until the sky turned from black to dark gray as dawn broke. He had barely made it to his bolt-hole, an abandoned government research building located on the outskirts of town. It had been partially destroyed sometime in the past and was now surrounded by a new-growth forest that had reclaimed the land when the field-clearing equipment stopped working.

The steel-and-concrete building had been a research lab where scientists studied and altered the crops that grew on the huge government-controlled farms that surrounded it. It was two stories, although the levels above the ground were damaged beyond use. What had made it attractive to Isamu was the nearly-intact level below ground. It was constructed like a bunker and had sustained little damage when the upper levels were destroyed.

The other thing that had attracted him was the ready supply of humans who still lived in the town less than two kilometers away. It only took minutes to find victims and spirit them there.

Isamu had prepared it as a place for him and Ogawa to use when they sought entertainment away from Heinz's watchful eye. Isamu had been paranoid about his place after Kamiko Kana's death and wanted a safe shelter in case Heinz and his wolves ever turned on them. Isamu hadn't been the only one who feared betrayal. Miko had found it when he followed the two of them once when Heinz ordered it.

He wove his way through the maze of broken concrete and steel beams on the first level until he came to an empty box freezer in an undamaged portion of the building. He pushed it down and back until he heard a faint *click* and it smoothly moved aside, revealing a metal door set into the wall.

Miko grunted as he exerted himself to pull the door open. It moved slowly as his muscles strained against its immense weight. When it swung open, a scraping noise came from the darkness below. Miko squeezed through and went down the concrete stairs, making sure not to trip over the taut length of chain that ran down the center of the stairway into the darkness below.

At the bottom, he pressed his shoulder against the chain's anchor, a heavy concrete-and-steel block. The weight ensured no human could move the door if they found it. Miko bent his knees and pushed until it hit a metal bar driven deep into the floor and the chain pulled the door above closed. He grabbed a rope hanging from the ceiling and pulled on it. The mechanism attached to it returned the freezer to its original spot, effectively blocking the door from casual observation.

It had taken him several minutes to locate it the night he'd followed Isamu. If Ogawa hadn't been careless while removing their victim when they left, he wouldn't have. The small smear of fresh blood coming from under the freezer had given the location away. It had taken him several more minutes of prodding and pushing to find the release. The door had been almost more than he could move back then. Now it was much easier, even in his weakened state.

Miko followed his nose to a lantern hung on the far wall. A quick, bright flash lit the room momentarily as he struck a spark to the wick. Seconds later, a warm glow brightened the area to the point he could see. Nothing had been disturbed since he was last here.

A hallway lined with metal doors spaced at even intervals stretched into the dark in front of him. He went to the closest one and pushed it open. A heavy iron bed frame with no mattress leaned against the far wall near a small table containing an assortment of medical and mechanical tools and devices. The floor around it was stained dark with blood. Two cots abutted the back wall with a table containing a partially-burned candle between them.

The smell of old blood and Isamu's and Ogawa's scents made his stomach churn in revulsion. He'd never understood why the two of them had that effect on him, but they always had. He'd written it off as disgust at their depravity, but even dead, they still affected him.

He placed the lampstand on the table between the cots

and laid down. Seconds later, he was up again, ripping the soiled covers from both cots in revulsion and throwing them across the room.

He lay there, slowly recovering as his traitorous stomach settled, and planned his next move while he waited for sunset. He needed to feed soon. Even with the upgrades from Heinz's last serum injection, the two people he'd feasted on earlier had only served to heal the damage from the explosion that had caused his forced slumber. The energy he'd expended in his flight to safety had weakened him more. It would take several more humans to get back to his former strength levels. As he drifted off to sleep, he decided to remain in the area until he was strong again.

Miko was in a dark corridor. Dim light seeped under closed doors that stretched as far as he could see in either direction. He ran from one to the next, pounding on each, begging for entry to escape the faceless thing that hunted him. He didn't know what it was, only that it stalked him, and he couldn't let it catch him. It screeched loudly, making him cringe. It almost sounded like language, but it was too feral for him to understand. He ran again, some unknown sense telling him the entity was right behind him, trying to snag him as he fled.

Miko awoke with a start, his fangs out and his razor-sharp claws extended. He panted for breath, panic running through him as he searched the inky-black darkness for his foe. It took a few moments for his brain to catch up with his body and realize where he was. *Another nightmare. Well, I guess I should call it a daymare since I can sense that the sun hasn't set.*

He sat on the edge of the cot as he contemplated the quickly fading dream. It had been many years since he'd experienced one so terrifying that it woke him early. The last one had come when he'd traveled to Shanghai with Isamu several years back, when Heinz sent them to deal with a self-important People's Minister who'd done something to offend him. It had been a dual lesson since Heinz felt that Isamu could teach Miko how to use the proper amount of pain and terror to achieve the objective.

What Isamu had done to the minister covered both the pain and the terror requirements. Placing the man's abused body at his desk in the Hall of the People during the night evoked sheer terror in his peers and colleagues. The Acheng site had suffered no further interference from the Chinese government after they received that message.

As soon as the sun had set, Miko made his way into Yushu. His hunger drove him to waste no time finding a victim, a man making his way to his squat in an abandoned house. Miko was on him before the hapless man knew anyone was around, his fangs ripping into his victim's neck and releasing the lifeblood down his parched throat in hot, pulsing spurts.

Miko greedily sucked it down, savoring the metallic taste as it poured across his tongue. Other than his mouth and throat, he was statue-still. One arm pinned the struggling man to his chest. His other hand had clamped firmly over his mouth to stifle any cries that might alert other potential victims. When the man's struggles ceased, Miko shoved his corpse into an overgrown ditch beside the road and went in search of another.

CHAPTER EIGHT

The Palace, Tokyo, Japan

Koda looked up from her computer as Yuko entered the office. "Has Akio said anything about when he will start my training?"

Yuko pursed her lips in thought before answering, "No, Akio has been working with Abel the past week on something in China."

Koda pouted. "Asai said Horst mentioned something about that a few days ago. He told her Akio has either been gone in a Pod or closed up in the operations center since they got back from Europe."

"Yes, he told me there is something he has to take care of himself. I respect him enough to trust he will ask for help if he needs it. I find it best not to pry into other teammates' business," Yuko gently admonished with a raised eyebrow.

Koda blushed. "I'm not trying to pry, honest. I am just eager to get started training. Remember? I asked to do that almost the moment I first met Akio-sensei on Kume."

Yuko smiled at the young woman. "I remember, and I assure you Akio will train you. He is a man of his word above all else. He just needs to deal with whatever has his attention first."

Before Koda could respond, Asai burst into the room, dragging a befuddled Horst behind her. "Yuko! Just who I was looking for."

Yuko chuckled at Asai's exuberance. "What can I do for you, Asai? Hello, Horst. It's good to see you."

"I want to go to Kume with Horst," Asai answered excitedly before Horst could respond to Yuko's greeting.

Yuko looked at the pair with a wicked smile and a gleam in her eye. "He doesn't have to ask Yagi-*san* for your hand in marriage, does he?"

Horst froze, his eyes moving from speaker to speaker like he wanted nothing more than to escape from a situation he had no doubt would end up being his fault.

Koda burst out laughing when Asai's face turned bright red as she sputtered, "*What*? NO! Yuko! What kind of girl do you think I am?"

Koda noticed Horst's distress, and her laughter redoubled until she was holding her sides, tears running down her face as she gasped, "Can I answer that?"

Asai turned to her cousin, her face going from embarrassed to angry. "Koda Rii, how dare you!" she snapped. Her voice went cold. "You know I would never. I am with Seki, as you are well aware. Besides, he only has eyes for you."

Koda's laughter cut off immediately when she realized Asai was truly angry with her. "I'm sorry, Asai, I was just joking. The look on your face when Yuko teased you was too good to pass up. Plus, poor Horst looking like he wanted to run away was the funniest thing."

"I was also making a joke," Yuko apologized. "Obviously not a funny one. My apologies to you, Asai, and you as well, Horst."

Koda wiped her eyes and walked around the desk to wrap her cousin in a hug. "Forgive me?" she whispered.

Asai scowled at her and then broke into a smile when she couldn't keep her face straight any longer. "Of course I do." She glanced at Horst. "But does he?"

Koda released Asai and walked up to Horst, she wrapped her arms as far around his muscular body as she could and looked up at him through her eyelashes. "So, my mountain of man. Do you forgive me?"

Horst chuckled, the sound deep in his chest next to Koda's head sounded like thunder in the distance. "When you look at me like that, my tiny beauty, I will forgive you anything."

"Don't fall for that, Horst," Asai warned. "She's been using that same trick on her father since she was six years old and he caught her trying to take his fishing boat out. I just knew he was going to beat her, and all he did was smile and take her with him for the next month."

"Hmph," Koda grumbled. "I wish he *had* beaten me. I had to clean his whole catch for a solid month after that. He worked me from daylight to dark the entire time. I assure you, I never tried to take anything without permission after that."

Yuko cleared her throat. "Asai, getting the conversation back on track, I believe you said something about Horst going to Kume when you came in?"

Asai nodded. "Oh, yes. Horst was telling me about his previous experience as an engineer and project overseer on several large construction ventures. He wanted to look at the site for the new port and see if he has anything to add to the project. Besides, I didn't get to go and see my father and mother the last three times you went. I was too busy here with the opening and everything."

"Koda, are you comfortable running the show here for the rest of the day?" Yuko asked.

"Sure," Koda agreed. "Besides, Asai covered for me for a few days after my Yakuza adventure so I could go home. I owe her for that, and I know Horst is looking for some way to feel productive. I tried to get him to work here, but he said the work didn't interest him, only the manager." She blushed.

Yuko smiled. "Then it's decided. We will head over to the old temple grounds and catch our Pod there. It will only take us a few minutes to get to Kume. We can be there in a short time."

"Don't worry about anything here," Koda assured her. "I have my communicator on me, and Eve is upstairs working on that glitchy sim again. I swear, if Seki and his friends didn't love it so much, I would take it out of the lineup."

"I'm not worried, Koda," Yuko replied. "I know how hard you worked to master the training Eve gave you. I have no doubt that you can handle this."

Koda grinned when she heard the praise. She *had* worked hard to squeeze every drop of knowledge out of the training sims. She was thrilled that Yuko had noticed.

CHAPTER NINE

TQB Base, Tokyo, Japan

"Akio, I have reviewed all the data from the drones, and there is no sign of him on any of the footage," Abel advised. "He must have gone in a different direction from the way he went when we saw him."

Akio sat in the dim command center, where he had spent many hours since he had seen the video of the man he thought was Kenjii. He had focused solely on locating him, neglecting to check the data from the other groups he was monitoring. "This is not an effective use of our time. Send the other two drone carriers Eve has ready. I would like you to deploy them to cover an area one hundred and fifty kilometers around the Acheng site."

"Any specific parameters, or the ones currently in effect?"

"Keep the parameters the same," Akio instructed. "I want coverage in every town and village in the search zone. Also, get coverage on as many roads as you can. Use your judgment for those."

The map that showed the drones' current deployment zoomed out until it included the area requested. Dots appeared, marking all the towns and villages as well as main roads and crossroads. "That will give us a good amount of coverage, but there are still areas that need more. I have contacted Eve and secured the use of two more carriers. Those additional drones will allow any settlement bigger than five structures to have at least one unit assigned to it. She also has some of the larger drones ready, with the enhanced sensors and power they can perform random patrols through the larger towns to expand coverage there."

Akio nodded. "Thank you, Abel. I need to locate him as soon as possible."

The room was silent as Abel continued to update the map, showing the coverage that the additional carriers provided. When it was done, there were marks for over twelve hundred carrier drones plus one hundred of the new style. "Akio, I don't want to intrude, but will you tell me why you are so concerned about one person?" Abel asked when the task was finished. "I understand that he is Forsaken and a danger to humans, but this extensive effort is illogical."

Akio considered his answer before responding, "He was dear to me in the past. I've thought he was dead for over a half-century because of his connection to me. It might seem illogical to you, but I need to find him if for no other reason than to ask his forgiveness."

"Forgiveness? Did you do something to him?"

Akio's eyes unfocused as his mind went to a different time—a short but wonderful period when he was not Akio the vampire, but Akio the man. He shook his head, banishing thoughts best left in the past. "Yes, Abel, I loved him," he answered quietly.

"If he is out there, we will find him," Abel assured him.

"Thank you, now bring up the information on the other areas I've had you monitoring. Start with that group of Weres in Australia."

"Akio?" Yuko called over her implant.

"Yes, Yuko?" he replied.

"I'm taking a Pod to Kume with Asai and Horst," she informed him. "Horst wants to look at the dock site there to see if he has anything to add to the project."

"He mentioned something about that to me when we went to Europe last week," Akio recalled. "I apologize, I forgot about it when we got back."

Yuko thought for a moment before she replied. She had noticed that Akio had been distracted but hadn't wanted to intrude. Abel had told her about the Forsaken sighting but hadn't elaborated. "Is there something going on I need to know about?"

He hesitated a moment. "No. I am trying to run down some leads in China while checking the intel on the groups I have Eve monitoring around the world."

Yuko paused, knowing there was more to it than he had admitted, then decided he would tell her when he was ready. It was not like him to forget something that could affect a project like Kume. "Oh, okay. If I can help, let me know."

"I will," Akio answered. "It's something I am not sure about for now. I will tell you more once I can be positive of what I think I saw."

"Eve is at the Palace with Koda. Know that whatever it is you're dealing with, I'm here when you need me, Akio. Always."

"Is Akio well?" Yuko asked Eve when she was alone. "He has been distracted and cryptic for the past few days. Do you know what it is?"

"He is looking for a Forsaken who survived at Acheng," Eve told her. "Apparently, my pucking technique needs improvement."

"This is an unusual amount of time and resources to spend on one Forsaken," Yuko reasoned. "Do you know why it's so important?"

"Abel told me Akio recognized him and seemed surprised that he was alive. It must be someone from his past."

"I don't want to pry, Eve, but would you keep an eye on him? Something is off here, and it concerns me. His anger toward Isamu was not in character. I fear that this new Forsaken might be part of what happened to Akio that made him kill Isamu in so brutal a manner." Yuko shuddered as she remembered Akio pinning Isamu to a wall with his tanto and torturing him before he finally ended his life.

"I already am," Eve assured her. "He hasn't shared the information with even Abel as to why this one Forsaken is so important, or Abel hasn't told me. I have been watching in the background, but so far all he has done is sift through the feeds on over thirteen hundred drones and redeploy them when he doesn't find what he is looking for. I will notify you if that changes."

"Thank you, Eve. I don't want to intrude, but I do not like to see him like this. In all the years I have known Akio, this is the first time I have ever seen him out of sorts."

"I'm on it," Eve promised. "I also uploaded the files with the blueprints I drew up for the Kume dock project for Horst. I used all the data available to determine what is most efficient for the project but left plenty of room for his input."

"That's kind of you," Yuko told her. "He has been floundering for a purpose since he arrived here. I think this will help him immensely."

"It will help us too if he wants to take on the overseer position," Eve replied. "The contractors I am considering all come highly recommended, but Horst onsite overseeing the whole project will cut down on the chance of corruption and greed being involved. Plus, it gives me more time to develop new sims for us here."

Yuko laughed. "We're going to need an expansion on the expansion before we even start construction if you keep going at this rate."

"The realtor who worked with us on purchasing the property was here with his family yesterday," Eve informed her. "He told me that the property around us has appreciated over one hundred percent since we opened. He has sold several properties his company has been trying to sell for years. This area is the hottest real estate market in

Tokyo now. We will have to build up instead of out when we expand again."

"Hmm, maybe we should see what it would cost to add a few more levels to the new building. It will probably be less expensive to do it now instead of later."

"Already on it." Eve chuckled. "I have started drawing up new blueprints with three additional levels. I'll send them to you when I get them finished."

"You're going to be the wealthiest AI in the galaxy if you keep this up," Yuko teased.

"I'll have you know, I am the richest AI in the solar system already," Eve responded with mock seriousness.

Yuko chortled. "I suppose you are at that."

Eve grinned. "Have fun on Kume, and tell Yagi-*san* I said hello. I need to get this new sim uploaded and run the beta test on it. This is the one with the user feedback Seki suggested. I want to roll it out over the weekend since Monday is a holiday and we are expecting large crowds."

CHAPTER TEN

Ning Jing Temple, Dabie Mountains, China

"Master Peng?" the acolyte called softly from outside the curtained door.

"Enter," Peng Kun commanded.

The acolyte prostrated himself on the floor, his forehead pressed down firmly until Kun spoke.

"Report."

"Master, I have been sent to inform you that Master Li has called. He is arriving in Japan tonight. He wishes to know if you have any further instructions for him before his team begins the mission."

"Tell him to report in twice daily as he searches," Kun ordered, hoping he was being unnecessarily paranoid but wanting to know as soon as possible if Li's team met the same fate as the others.

The acolyte rose to his feet, bowed at the waist, and backed out of the room when Kun said no more.

Kun closed his eyes and settled back into the lotus position he had been in before the acolyte came. To anyone watching, he appeared to be in deep meditation. In truth, he was thinking about the past—how he came to be in this temple and what he had been directed to do. Kun had been born and bred for the Clan, his parents paired as children for the purpose of producing him, just as their parents and their parents before them had been. The Clan had been selecting couples for centuries, cultivating the strongest traits and breeding out the less desirable ones.

Kun was born to be a warrior and leader of warriors. His path was predetermined, and he had followed it his entire life up until that bitch and her people killed the Leopard Empress and her father. His death, coupled with that idiot General Li starting the war that had almost destroyed the world, had changed everything.

The Clan was scattered into many enclaves hidden in monasteries all over China. There were entire villages and towns where only Clan members lived. They had adapted to changing times and were hidden in plain sight. Farmers, tradesmen, doctors, bankers; the Clan had members in every field. By sending their children to universities, getting jobs, and even enrolling in the military, they had infiltrated all aspects of life in China. Peng Kun had been a general in the People's Army when he was sent to take over this facility.

The cover story had been that the Buddhist monks from this temple were spreading sedition. The Communist People's Party was suppressing religion again. A Clan member placed high in the party also ordered that the temple be left intact and occupied as a warning to others who dared to defy the people, and just like that, the Clan had use of the facility.

Kun had been assigned to command the forces left to occupy the temple complex. Over time, he had managed to have Sacred Clan members of the military moved there and the humans reassigned. On the day the world collapsed—the World's Worst Day Ever, or WWDE as it was now called—he'd had a battalion of troops training there, all Sacred Clan members.

Over the years since WWDE, Kun had established contact with some enclaves, but others had not been heard from in many years. Of the ones he had been in contact with, he was the highest-ranking survivor, and by default had named himself Grand Master of the Clan. It was not a position he had been trained for as a warrior, but one aspect of being a soldier was to adapt to changing situations. The deaths of their leaders and the destruction caused by the war was nothing if not a changing situation.

If the Clan had known that General Li was planning his attack, he would have been killed immediately. As it was, with the turn of a key and push of a button, the command code was sent to millions of infected computers around the world. With that simple act, one man had killed billions. The virus had spread, affecting critical systems in every country in the world. Of course, those countries panicked and blamed their enemies, and it was only a matter of time until someone launched a nuke. The virus and the resulting chaos had been all the push needed to make it happen.

It could have been much worse. However, the virus cutting communications off over much of the world meant that the information did not circulate in seconds, it now took days. The United States, Russia, and China still had limited capabilities, as did a number of other countries.

They'd all had plans for just this eventuality. Every commander of a nuclear-capable asset had their orders. No one knew how many missiles were ultimately launched—not all them obviously, but enough to cause even more death and destruction.

Beijing and Hong Kong had been reduced to bombed-out wastelands before it was known that the virus had come from China. When that information was made public, all countries that were still capable attacked. When it was done, China no longer had any large cities that had not suffered damage. Many of the largest were uninhabitable nuclear wastelands, occupied only by the ghosts of the millions who had lived and died within them.

The rural and farming areas were spared the bombs, but without the support they depended on from the cities, manufactured goods—and more importantly, medicines—were in short supply. That had led to the deaths of millions more. The people of rural China had always felt they were apart from the people in the cities, able to sustain themselves. The truth was that the Chinese government had made the whole country interdependent. They had managed to weed out the knowledge of home cures and the basic survival skills the people living outside of the cities had possessed in earlier generations. Even almost a quarter-century later, the mortality rate in the rural areas was still high from disease and the lack of infrastructure.

The pockets of Sacred Clan survivors were much better equipped to deal with the realities of post-apocalyptic China. Weres were not susceptible to disease and could farm or hunt with equal ease, which ensured they were the dominant species in the areas where they lived. That was why Kun had launched the plans for the Clan to take over now, instead of in another century as the founder's plans had called for.

He was brought out of his reverie by the sounds of combat echoing through the temple. He unfolded from his position on the cushions and made his way to the training area to watch the progress of the Clan's next group of operatives.

CHAPTER ELEVEN

TQB Base, Tokyo, Japan

Akio had been going over satellite images of the various groups he had been monitoring for only a few minutes before he noticed something was off. One of the groups he had determined to be a potential problem was gone. The small settlement was still there, but there were no signs that it had been occupied for some time. "Abel, how recent are these images?"

"These images were recorded fifteen days and twelve hours ago," Abel replied.

"Go back to the images taken just before those," Akio instructed.

The screen shifted and showed the same group of buildings, this time with some signs of habitation. Smoke rose from two of the structures, and a couple was seen crossing the street that cut through the center of the settlement.

Akio looked at the image then ordered, "Go back to the images before these."

Again, the screen flickered, and the same area was displayed. This image was taken on a bright day, and there was smoke coming from all the homes as well as numerous figures moving about.

Akio frowned. "When were these images taken?"

"Forty-eight days and three hours ago," Abel replied.

"Now, where could you have gone?" Akio murmured as he looked at the screen.

"Abel, please run a search of all data that has been gathered in this area and see if you can find out what happened. There were close to three hundred Weres living there."

"Search started based on your parameters," Abel's voice intoned mechanically.

Within seconds, Abel spoke again. "Findings inconclusive, additional data required."

"What does that mean?" Akio asked.

"The existing data does not provide enough information to determine the answer to your query," Abel replied.

Akio sighed. Abel was a very competent EI and easy to work with most of the time. Other times he was unable or, Akio suspected, unwilling to extrapolate to provide answers to the questions without literal direction. "Can you define what additional data you need?"

"Without the data, there is no way to determine what data is required," Abel replied.

Akio's lips tightened to hold back the retort that came to him. He remembered similar conversations with Eve in the early years. He thought for a moment before he replied, "Abel, what can be done to obtain additional data that might help determine the answer?"

"I need more images than are currently available. The

existing data shows activity in the settlement forty-eight days ago. Additional images of the surrounding area from thirty-two days ago show a line of vehicles one hundred and twenty-six kilometers away heading southwest. I can determine to within ninety percent surety that the vehicles came from the Were settlement based on three large trucks that match the type and color of vehicles known to be there. That and the data that indicated the Were settlement still had working vehicles and others in the area allow me to be ninety percent certain those are the Weres you are looking for."

"So, what you're telling me is that you need to find their current location to tell me where they are?" Akio asked, already knowing the answer but curious as to how Abel would answer.

"That is accurate."

Akio was silent while he considered, determining that Abel was not ascending to AI status anytime soon. "Abel, what is the best method to obtain the information you need?"

"Ideally, one of the satellites would locate the vehicles in a static state, and they would remain there until the next pass. Otherwise, a drone carrier combined with moving a satellite into orbit over the area to boost the signal for near real-time intelligence. I have queried Eve, and she advises that all the drone carriers currently operational are in China. It will take one day, fourteen hours, and fifty-one minutes to recover and redeploy one of them to this area."

"What happened to the other carriers?" Akio asked, remembering that Eve had deployed more previously.

"Eve has started production on the larger drone units,"

Abel replied. "Some of the materials needed are not currently available, so she recycled the other units to salvage them."

"When will the new units be ready to deploy?" Akio inquired.

"One carrier with two hundred drones will be operational in four days, six hours at the current manufacturing rate," Abel intoned.

"Pull up the map that shows coverage for the China operation," Akio instructed. "Show me a deployment pattern with one of the carriers removed."

The monitor shifted, showing the area requested. First dots disappeared in one section, and then others moved to take their places. The area was large but still had decent if not optimum coverage.

Akio made his decision. "Go ahead and redeploy one carrier to Australia. Determine the most likely destinations the missing Weres could have gone and work back to their last known location using that data."

"Acknowledged," Abel replied.

Kume Island, Okinawa, Japan

Yuko brought the Pod down smoothly on the landing area in the town. All activity stopped, as it always did when the Pod came into sight.

Mayor Yagi was waiting when the door slid open.

Yagi started to greet them when his mouth closed with an audible snap and his eyes went wide.

Yuko glanced back to see Horst straightening up after

ducking his head to exit the Pod. Ducking wasn't necessary, but almost.

Asai stepped out behind him and waved happily to her father. "Father, this is Horst. He wants to help with the port project."

"*Oof.*" Yagi grunted when Asai wrapped him in an enthusiastic hug. "Careful Asai-*chan,* I break easily." He chuckled as he kissed her on top of her head.

Asai grinned and lightly poked him in his stomach. "With all this additional cushioning, I'm surprised you felt it." She snickered.

Yagi feigned anger as he turned to Yuko. "See what I have to put up with? Not home five minutes and already sounding like her mother. I work hard every day," he lamented. "Yet the women in my life begrudge me a good meal."

Asai laughed. "Mother and I don't begrudge you *a* good meal. It's the multiple good meals you eat each day that we are concerned about."

Yuko grinned at Yagi as he shifted to the side, one arm wrapped lovingly around Asai. "Well, now that we are capable of tending the fields, along with the supplies Yuko-*san* and Akio-*san* bring us, I am making up for the lost ones. We all are."

Asai looked at him lovingly. "I don't begrudge you any of them," she murmured. "You were the glue who held the survivors together during the dark times."

He blushed, always uncomfortable when his wife or daughter praised him. He didn't feel he had done nearly enough to protect them, no matter that he would have died if he had resisted Isamu and Ogawa. "Who is this rather healthy young man, Asai?"

Asai smiled. "Father, I would like you to meet Horst. He is my friend and Koda's very good friend. Horst, this is my father, Mayor Suzu Yagi."

Yagi raised one eyebrow as he heard this, giving Horst an appraising look.

Horst had remained a few paces away, giving the two space for their greeting. Now he stepped forward, his hand extended in greeting. "Hello, Mayor Yagi-*san*. It's nice to finally meet you. I have heard a lot of good things about you from Asai and Koda."

"Thank you, Horst-*san*. Welcome to our humble island."

"Not humble much longer, Father," Asai enthused. "We are ready to start building the new port ahead of schedule. The Palace has done exceedingly well since it opened."

Yagi started at her announcement. He knew the plans Yuko had for rebuilding but didn't expect it to happen for quite some time. "'Port,' Asai? I believe the word you meant to use was 'dock,' my dear."

Asai's grin got even bigger. "No, Father, I meant what I said. Horst has looked at the original plans and believes they are not enough to handle what Kume needs."

Yagi glanced at Horst and then at Yuko for confirmation. Yuko nodded and raised her hand toward Horst in an "it's his story to tell" gesture.

Yagi shook himself visibly. "Come, let's go inside. Ono will skin me alive if she thinks I kept you here too long without offering proper hospitality."

"Maybe not skin you completely, but she would make

you feel it," Asai joked as she pulled her father toward home, her arm still wrapped around his waist.

When they entered, Ono was just putting a pot of water on and already had her special tea service laid out on the table. Asai let go of her father and rushed into her mother's open arms.

"Asai, my daughter. You are looking well," Ono said as she held her at arm's length. "We were concerned for you when Koda told us of her experience at the hands of those," she hesitated, not using the first word that came to mind, "criminals."

"Mother, I never saw a criminal," Asai assured her. "Except the ones on the news when the police arrested them all."

Ono shook her head. "There is no way they got all of them. The Yakuza is like an *Orochi*. There are many heads, and another pops up as you cut one off."

"I know Mother, but I am cautious," Asai told her. "I seldom have the time or need to leave the Palace, and when I do, I'm not alone."

"I know you are cautious," Ono conceded. "I just worry about you and Koda, is all."

Asai kissed her mother's cheek, then looked at her with an impish smile. "I think if anyone decides to try *anything* with Koda again, it will end badly for them." She nodded at Horst, who was standing sideways in the doorway, his shoulders too wide to enter the house otherwise.

Ono released Asai and looked where her daughter indicated. Her mouth dropped open as she stared at the giant of a man. She closed her eyes briefly, and when they opened, she bowed to Horst. "Forgive me, I didn't realize Asai had brought company. I am Ono Yagi, wife of the Mayor and ashamed mother to this rude child who failed to properly introduce us." She spoke with mock seriousness, her eyes giving away the lie as they danced with restrained mirth.

Horst didn't miss a beat as he bowed deeply. "It is my pleasure to meet you, Ono-*san*. I'm sure you taught her properly. The fault is not yours."

Asai looked at the two, her face flushed and her mouth opening and closing as she tried to speak.

Ono burst out laughing and was joined by Horst, Yagi, and Yuko as Asai still stood with her mouth opening and closing like a fish's.

"Oh, I like this one, Asai," Ono told her daughter as she walked to Horst and shook his hand.

Ono then turned to Yuko. "Forgive me, Yuko-*san*. I was so shocked by Horst-*san* coming through the door and then having a laugh at Asai's expense that I failed to welcome you properly."

"Think nothing of it, Ono-*san*," Yuko told her with a grin. "It's been, oh, let me see, two hours since I have seen Asai at a total loss for words today," she finished with a chuckle.

Asai found her voice just then. "What is this? Did someone declare today was official Pick On Asai Day and not tell me?"

The indignant look on her face as she protested brought on another round of laughter from around the room.

Asai maintained her serious look for a few more

seconds before she joined in, enjoying the fact that her mother could laugh at all.

"This area here, Yagi-*san*," Horst pointed to an area of unoccupied dwellings, "could be cleared and a facility to house the workers could be built. What I have in mind could be repurposed into a hotel when the workers leave."

Yagi looked at the area, trying to picture what it would be like with the building. "How many floors are you thinking? Why would there be a need for a hotel? We are a small community, and I don't see us growing to need it."

Horst shook his head in disagreement. "No, I think with what Eve and I have been researching, you will have any number of people wanting to visit here. Kume was known for its beauty and was a tourist destination for years, correct?"

Yagi nodded. "Yes, but we no longer have the means for people to come here."

"That leads me to the proposition I have for you. I believe people from all over Japan would be willing to come here if travel was easier. I have been talking to Eve, and she has a design for an engine that is much more efficient than what is currently in use. She said it would be easy for her to fabricate one large enough to power ships— ships that are faster than any operating now."

"I still don't see how there are enough people able to travel to support it."

Horst smiled, imagining the future. "Currently, the only

ways to travel between islands are by sailboat, or by securing a spot on one of the few solar-driven cargo ships. What I am thinking is to add Kume as a regular stop on a route for ships that are designed to haul both cargo and passengers.

"Eve has already located and secured four ships that can be fitted with the engine. They will have luxury rooms topside, with ample cargo space below decks, like the large passenger liners that plied the seas early in the last century. They can carry a good number of passengers as well as a significant amount of cargo."

"But why would people come here?" Yagi asked.

"Because we make it the place to go," Horst told him with enthusiasm. "Much like Yuko and Eve did with the Palace, we advertise it as an affordable getaway. With the ability to move cargo and people faster and more comfortably than any other ships, combined with a regular schedule that puts a ship here every four days, I think we could build Kume into a must-see destination."

Yagi was silent as he absorbed the proposal.

Horst recognized information overload in the mayor. "Of course, I will need to do some research back in Tokyo to see if the numbers support it, but I needed to talk to you first. Yuko, Eve, Koda, and Asai have already proven that people are starved for entertainment. They have people walking for days just to see the Palace."

Yagi looked around the site again as he thought. "These homes are all uninhabitable, not that any of the owners are still alive. I see no harm in you checking, but I still have doubts."

"All I wanted was your blessing to check into it further,"

Horst assured him. "If you were against it, there would be no need to do that."

"We already have the castle here. If you can get the tourists to come again, maybe we can heal some of the hurt and make it into a positive thing."

Horst winced as Yagi said that. "Ah, Yagi-*san*, there is something...something I need to confess before you agree to go ahead with this."

"What's that?" Yagi inquired trustingly.

Horst swallowed hard and looked away, not wanting to see the look on Yagi's face. "Isamu and Ogawa were sent here on the orders of the Forsaken who raised me. Until I met Akio and Yuko, I...I was part of the group responsible for what happened here."

Yagi looked at the man, hearing the pain in his voice as he confessed. "Asai has already told me about you, Horst. She told me you not only helped destroy the organization, but that you personally killed the creature who was behind it all." He paused a moment, then continued, "She also told me that you are more than human."

Horst stiffened, not knowing what to expect.

Yagi placed his hand gently on Horst's shoulder, causing him to flinch. "She has also told me how you feel about Koda, and that you believe you need to atone for the evils done here. I tell you now, you didn't send Isamu here, and you are not responsible for his actions. You exacted the vengeance I was unable to, along with Akio and Yuko. If anything, it is I who owes you."

Horst raised his eyes and saw in Yagi's eyes the sincerity of his words. He blinked back the hot tears that threatened to spill. That simple act of kindness from a man he felt responsible for hurting made Horst realize that he was not only free of Heinz but that he could possibly forgive himself for the evils his brother had perpetuated. He hesitated as all that Yagi had said sunk in.

"You know what I am, Yagi-*san?*" he asked warily.

"*Hai*, Horst-*san*. I know that you are an honorable man my daughter speaks highly of. I know that Yuko and Akio have accepted you into their fold. I know my niece thinks well of you. For those things alone, I would be proud to call you friend. Knowing that you lost someone you loved and gave up everything you knew to stop it from happening again makes me want to call you family." His voice cracked with emotion, and his eyes sparkled with unshed tears as he finished.

Horst slowly reached for Yagi's shoulder. He swallowed hard, trying to keep his emotions in check. "Yagi-*san*, I, I don't know what to say. I would be honored to be a part of your family."

Yagi smiled at the huge man as he pulled him into a tight embrace.

Horst hesitated only a second before returning it, feeling that he was home for the first time in many years.

CHAPTER TWELVE

Ning Jing Temple, Dabie Mountains, China

"Master Cui." Commander Yimu, the commander of the Clan's scouts, bowed with his hands clasped at his waist while he waited for a response.

Cui Yong had taken over all day to day operations after Li had departed for Japan. The network of scouts ranging through the area was only one of many things that took up twenty hours of his day.

"Report," Cui ordered.

"We have received a report from Yushu that there are bodies turning up in the area," Yimu informed him.

"What of it?" Cui snapped. "Bodies turn up all the time. It is the world we live in."

"These bodies all have similar markings that indicate the same cause of death," Yimu expanded. "They appear to have been killed by a Forsaken."

Cui's eyes widened at this revelation. "A Forsaken? We haven't been troubled by them for years. Are you certain?"

Yimu nodded. "The scout reports that he has located

five bodies in the area. All have bites on their necks and have been drained of a significant amount of blood. He also reported that the bodies were poorly hidden, and in one case, was left beside a road with no attempt at concealment."

Cui thought for a moment. If a Forsaken was in the area and not concealing its kills, it could cause a panic. Although the government had collapsed, there were still pockets of the Party scattered around the country. They operated more like ancient warlords than the formal government of before, but each commanded large numbers of troops. If they started actively searching for a vampire, they could cause trouble for the Clan.

"Has the scout located the Forsaken?" he inquired. "Is there more than one?"

"His last report indicated that he was still searching for it," Yimu replied. "He also reported that it appears to be a single Forsaken operating there, based on the look of the bites and the scent on the bodies."

Cui nodded. "Thank you. Advise the scout who found this that Master Peng will be notified of his diligence."

A short time later, Cui met with Peng Kun. "Master Peng, Commander Yimu has brought information that there is a rogue Forsaken killing humans near Yushu. One of his scouts has found several bodies, not hidden, that bear the marks of a vampire bite."

"That cannot be allowed," Kun stated. "The last thing we need at this stage in our plans is to deal with a Forsaken causing trouble. Has the scout located where he is hiding during the day?"

"Not when the report was sent," Cui replied. "It took a few days for it to arrive using the runner network."

"We need to put this Forsaken down before he draws attention to us, and *especially* before he creates any more of them. It has been many years since we were troubled by vampires, Li and his team killed the last one in this area six years ago."

"I propose sending a strike team to the area," Cui suggested. "Equipped with one of our remaining satellite phones, they will be able to flush it out and destroy it."

"How many functional units are left?" Kun asked. "We must ensure we have the means to remain in contact with Li in Japan."

"Three units are still operational," Cui informed him. "The other option is to equip them with the older radios. We have plenty of those in storage, but it will require deploying additional units to relay the messages back and forth."

Kun did the math. "That's roughly two thousand kilometers. Do we have enough working units to cover that far?"

"Yes," Cui replied. "Li saw the need for a way to communicate long distances after the country collapsed. He has collected close to one thousand of the type that do not require a computer to operate or program. We have plenty of spare tubes and crystals, as well as over thirty working base units."

Kun thought for a moment, trying to remember the specifications of radios that were being phased out when he was a newly minted officer. "Those base units require a good deal of power to operate. How do we get around that?"

"Some of the techs have managed to cobble a solar array and batteries that will power them for short periods. They can monitor for several hours but are limited to a few transmissions each day. A bonus of these is that they have boosted the signal strength, so we will only need to deploy four of them."

"Make it so," Kun commanded. "Keep me apprised of any updates."

"You will deploy to the predetermined areas and assemble your units," Cui explained to the communications teams selected for the mission. "Monitor the frequency and relay any updates back here immediately."

"You should all be in position within a week," Pan Xun instructed. "Runners have been sent ahead to assemble Clan members to provide logistical assistance and help with the equipment along the route. That will allow you to run longer distances each day and get into position sooner."

Pan was one of Cui's team. He had assigned each of them to additional duties to fill the spaces vacated when Li took his team to Japan. It was good experience, but they were still finding their way as commanders instead of the sub-commanders they had been before. His idea to assemble transport for the heavier base units showed Cui that he was growing into the position as he should.

"There are teams already on the way with the portable units. They will deploy to relay reports sent back from the strike team to the bases. Since we don't know if the Forsaken will remain in that area, we have sent out enough to maintain coverage over a large section of land."

The team leaders all bowed to Cui and shouldered the special packs each member carried. They were designed to be worn in both human and tiger form to allow for faster travel over the long distances each team had to cover.

Within minutes, the teams were assembled and running toward their assigned destinations. The Forsaken would be run to ground and eliminated soon.

CHAPTER THIRTEEN

Safe House, Yushu, China

The figure in front of Miko was out of focus and blurred. The voices around him—there was more than one, he was sure of it— were muffled and unintelligible. The only thing that was clear was the pain of his arms pulled tight above his head and the agony coming from his chest. Pain shot through him as a sharp instrument was shoved into his flesh over and over. Laughter rang in his ears as his agonized screams echoed through the room.

Miko sat up with a start, his hands curled into claws and a growl rippling from his throat. He was on his feet in an instant, ready to tear his enemy to shreds and feast on his blood.

He looked around, unsure of where he was, the scent of blood strong in his nostrils. He calmed, realizing he was alone in the safe room he had been using for a hideout for the past week. As his breathing slowed, he willed his body to relax. His hands uncurled, and the fangs he hadn't realized were extended retracted into his mouth.

The odor of blood was still in the air, and he saw that the light shirt he had on was soaked with it. He snatched it from the bottom, ripping it in his haste, and discovered he was not bloody and torn as he first feared but was covered in a sheen of blood sweat again. The dream...*No, nightmare,* he corrected, was coming more frequently. Each time he woke to a voice his mind told him he should recognize, followed by screams.

As always, the dream faded fast, and he lost the memory before he could remember who it was.

Another nightmare. I'm not injured. Miko balled up the ruined shirt and threw it aside in disgust. He could tell the sun was just setting, another new experience for him, and an apparent effect of the last serum Heinz had given him. In addition to more strength and faster healing, he had discovered that he could tell in an instant the position of the deadly sun and how long until it rose or set.

He had fed nightly since he'd arrived in the area after escaping the prison he had been trapped in when the lab was destroyed. His body was healed now and he was back to full strength. The dreams were the only thing that had not gotten better. They continued to torment him, like a distant memory that he should be able to recall but was just out of his reach.

He had also discovered that his ability to compel humans to do his bidding had grown stronger. His compulsion had been weak before, barely able to hold a human's mind long enough to feed. The shirt he had destroyed was one advantage of this new ability. He had compelled a young peasant boy to go into the town and bring him new clothes. He'd watched from his hiding place as the boy returned to where he had been told, placed a bundle on top of a pile of rubble, and waited for him as instructed.

He crossed the room, weaving around the items left by Isamu and Ogawa. His lips curled into a sneer of disgust as he remembered what those two had done here. It had been their own personal chamber of horrors, everything a sick fuck torturer and his apprentice could want.

No wonder I'm having those dreams. I'm living in a damned torture chamber.

Miko stopped in the corner and poured a small amount of water into a bowl from an old fuel can he had found. He sponged the blood sweat from his body as best he could, scraping away the spots that had already dried.

Satisfied, he dug through the bag of clothes he had tossed on the floor the day before until he found a shirt that was serviceable. He had discovered that the opportunities for food and clothing were becoming limited in the town nearby. The number of missing people had caused the residents to stay inside at night, forcing him to either risk alerting others if he entered a home, or to range farther each night to find prey.

He had determined it was time to move on tonight. Miko wasn't sure where he would go, but he knew he had stayed here too long already. With several people missing from the local population, there was sure to be a search soon. The last thing he needed was anyone finding him

CHARLES TILLMAN & MICHAEL ANDERLE

asleep here. Not that he was helpless during the day, but he couldn't escape as long as the sun was up.

He had reached the conclusion over the past two nights that he should head for the sea. His plans were incomplete, but he was thinking he would go to Korea or maybe even Japan. Heinz had not had contact with any other Forsaken, and Miko had no memories of his life before he was turned.

Heinz had told him that some, not many, lost the memories of their past life and that he was one of that fortunate number who didn't have the baggage of human memories. Miko had never questioned that, and now that Heinz and everyone else he knew was gone, he found himself without purpose.

He did know that wherever he went, he had to be more careful not to call attention to himself. Heinz had warned him for the last twenty years about a Forsaken who hunted other vampires. Akio, the Bitch Queen's assassin, Heinz had called him with derision when he said it. When word that he was being called the Dark One by members of the UnknownWorld reached him, he went into a rage.

Miko never asked what history Heinz shared with this vampire. He had asked Chang once and was told not to ever mention that name to Heinz. For some reason, he had found himself dwelling on that name recently. It made him feel a strange sense of kinship, a lone vampire against the world, not that he had any intention of seeking him out. One thing that was very clear from all the sources Heinz had: Akio was dangerous and hated all Forsaken.

Miko shook himself, forcing the odd thoughts away as he gathered his few belongings and headed for the stairs.

He pushed against the stone that anchored the door above, straining under the heavy weight. The stone moved slightly and then faster as he pushed until the chain was slack.

He pulled the rope that hung down from above, and a soft click signaled the release of the freezer above as he ascended the stairs. He pushed against the door, and it pushed the freezer that concealed it aside enough for him to slip out onto the heavily damaged first floor.

Miko extended his senses outward—another perk from the last serum—and determined no one was near. He moved some debris to reveal a coiled cable under it. One end of the cable had a loop in it and the other went through a hole in the floor. He grabbed the loop and pulled, straining as he did, and a scraping sound came out of the open stairway door until it was pulled closed from below. He concealed the cable and pushed the freezer back in front of the door until the hidden latch locked it back in place, sealing the room below.

He worked his way around the fallen beams and concrete, careful not to leave any sign that he'd been here in case he ever needed this hiding place again. When he stepped out into the twilight, the sun glowed a faint red over the far mountains.

He turned toward the southwest and started to run.

CHAPTER FOURTEEN

Unknown location, Australian Bush

Kelly came to slowly, her stomach lurching as her head bounced against the hard surface she was on. She pushed herself up on her arms and opened her eyes, a blinding headache causing her to cry out. Her body swayed as the surface under her moved again, and a wave of nausea overcame her. Although she retched violently, nothing came up, but the heaving gave her tunnel vision and made the pain in her head pound harder with each beat of her heart.

"Easy, Kel," a voice called softly as hands gently lifted her long black hair from around her face. "I've got you."

Kelly tensed at the touch and started to lash out until her brain registered that she knew that voice. "Jenni? Is that you?"

"Yes, and don't move around too much. You have a nasty bump on your head, and you've been fading in and out for hours. You scared me, Kel. I thought you were dying."

"What the fuck..." Kelly started, then the events of the

night before came rushing back to her and she realized they were in a moving vehicle. "Where are we going?"

"I don't know where," Jenni told her. "But we're in the wagon we use to trade with the other farms. The men who attacked the station last night herded us in like cattle and covered it with tarps. We've been traveling all night. I could see out a little when it got light but not enough to recognize where we are."

Kelly heard movement and looked up to see several young women from the station, and two others she recognized from a neighboring station. There were a couple of children who were barely out of diapers, but no men present in the tight confines. "So, I take it we're prisoners? Where are the men?"

"Pulling the wagon from what I could hear," Jenni answered.

They traveled all day. The heat in the wagon rose as the day wore on until it was oppressive and hard to breathe, not helping Kelly's queasy stomach or her head. She thought she might have a concussion from the head injury, but she wasn't skilled enough to make an accurate diagnosis.

Any attempt to communicate with their captors was harshly rebuffed. When one of the women pulled the tarp off of the back and tried to climb out, she was violently knocked back, her body sprawling across the legs of her fellow prisoners.

"The next one that tries gettin' out dies," a rough voice yelled into the wagon.

None of the others attempted to escape. They continued to bounce along for the rest of the day and on into the night. They all suffered in silence, Jenni keeping watch over Kelly, who had a walnut-sized lump on the side of her head that she didn't remember how she had gotten.

Apparently, her attacker from the night before had slammed her head into something before he brought her out and threw her into the wagon. Jenni had kept her awake the entire day, nudging her or talking whenever she started to drift off. Kelly fought the urge to lash out verbally as her head pounded and her stomach continued to rebel. The only thing holding her back was the special bond the two shared.

One of the youngsters started crying after several hours in the rough-riding wagon. The poor child needed to relieve herself badly, so Kelly shifted the other captives away from one corner where she knew a floorboard was broken and had been hastily patched. She carefully and quietly worried at the patch until she had removed a section of the floor. The opening was only the width of the planks that floored the wagon, but it let in some air. More importantly, it made a functional opening that could be used as a makeshift toilet. After helping the child use the area, Kelly moved aside, accepting grateful murmurs from several others who worked their way over and around the others to make use of the hole.

When the wagon finally came to a stop, it was dark, and the heat was starting to dissipate. The smell of sweat was stifling under the heavy tarp, but Kelly welcomed the lack of motion. The fresh air that flooded in when the tarp was pulled away was a relief, but it didn't last long. As soon as the tarp was off, men began shouting at them to get out.

The ones who didn't move fast enough were grabbed

and roughly pulled from the wagon, and they were all herded through a gate into a large fenced area.

Kelly shuddered when she saw the crudely painted sign above the gate.

WELCOME TO HELL

Stockade, Adelaide Oval, Adelaide, Australia

Three weeks passed. Three weeks of seeing their captors bring in more people every day, of not being told anything—or worse, being told by one of the guards to wait and see. Something about that held more menace than no answer.

Kelly had wasted no time enlisting the assistance of the few men who'd worked for her and some she knew from neighboring stations to set up a shelter inside the compound. They had made use of some rusted metal sheets that one of the older men told her resembled the skin of an airplane. Whatever it was from, it served to block the harsh sun that hung overhead and provided an illusion of cool in the shade.

Their captors ignored them for the most part, only bringing them meager rations and water every day or so after they had been there four days. The first time they did this, there was a free-for-all as soon as the gates closed—people fighting to take whatever they could. Their captors stood outside, laughing at the pandemonium they had caused. Kelly had spent the next day going to everyone, convincing them that it was in their best interest to work together. The fact that she had six of the biggest men there backing her went a long way toward convincing some of the holdouts it was a good idea.

The next time the food was brought in, Kelly and her group were the first to approach when the gates had closed. She supervised the distribution and made sure everyone got their fair share. The water container was placed under a shelter, and someone monitored it all day. It was never enough, but her planning made sure no one died.

She made it a point to greet the new people when they arrived from then on, helping them get settled and providing them with food and water while she explained what she could. She couldn't answer all their questions, but the sense of authority she projected kept most of them from causing problems.

A group of five that came in the middle of the second week they had been captive laughed when she explained the process. It was a mismatched group who told her they didn't take orders from anyone, especially a slip of a girl. When one of them grabbed Kelly to kiss and paw at her, much to the amusement of his fellows, two of her men pulled him away from her and tossed him into the rest of his group after a few well-placed punches and kicks. His friends made noise, but they were quickly surrounded when the others saw what was going on.

It would have gone a whole lot further than that if her men had had their way, but she stopped them before any more violence could occur. The next time the gates opened, that same group decided to rush the two teens who brought the food in. What happened next was the reason everyone moved away whenever the call of "gate opening" went out now.

When the five men were a few feet from the two teens, who watched them dispassionately with no sign of fear as they rushed toward them, five huge wolves raced into the enclosure. The screams of the ruffians brought everyone out from under their shelters to see what was happening.

Most wished they hadn't when it was done. The five were all down, either dead or wounded, and the wolves stood between them and the watching people as the teens went to the surviving men and calmly cut their throats one at a time.

The bodies were left there until nightfall the next day when a lone man came through the gate flanked by two huge wolves. He explained that because of the incident the day before, from then on, anytime the gate opened, everyone was to move to the far end of the stockade. Anyone who failed to do so would meet the same fate as the five.

After three weeks, there were a hundred and forty-six people crammed into the enclosure. The captives continued to work at survival as the number of new people coming in dwindled. Kelly made it a point to speak to everyone daily, doing what she could to keep any of them from falling into a funk or worse, something they couldn't come back from.

Adelaide Oval Corporate Suite, Adelaide, Australia

Decklan Walsh scowled from the plush chair he was

reclining on as the man in front of him stammered through his report.

"We, uh, we-went out, like you said, Dee. T-there just ain't anybody l-l-left out there. That l-last b-batch was a f-f-full day's run ou-ou-out from here, and we only managed to catch th-th-thirty."

"Just how many did you flea-bitten shitstains kill, Flynn?" Decklan demanded.

Flynn's face reddened further. "C'mon, Dee. You know they fight back. Hell, Owen got shot by that little black-haired minx on the first run. You saw that for yourself."

Decklan's scowl turned into a low growl as he looked at the man, his patience, which was already thin, almost gone. "Get out and take your men back out into the bush. Don't come back until you have rounded up any other humans within one hundred kilometers of here. Rounded up and *captured*, not killed. *Do you understand me?*"

Flynn blanched, realizing how close the Alpha was to losing it. The last time that had happened, it had taken the poor bloke a week to recover, even as a werewolf. "Yeah, ah, yes sir," he answered as he backed out of the door hastily.

A low giggle from the bar caused Decklan to snap his angry gaze there.

A tall redhead wearing short-shorts and a too-tight halter top grinned over the top of a bottle.

He scowled at her. "What's so funny, Nikki?"

She chortled. "You had poor Flynn about to roll over on his back and piss himself."

He stared at her, an angry look still on his face, and she laughed harder. His grimace turned up into a smile, and he barked a laugh. "Poor Flynn, my hairy arse. He wasted too many on that last run. Besides, I think he did piss himself a little."

"Why does it matter if he kills a few?" she asked. "It's not like any of them are going to live anyway."

"Because I told those idiots I wanted them alive," Decklan told her. "Just because I intend to kill off the vermin, it doesn't mean it can't be entertaining. The more they kill, the less entertainment I have."

Nikki stood up and sauntered sexily over to where he sat. She dropped into his lap and ground her rear against him as she settled in. "Come here, my big, scary Alpha," she cooed. "Let Nikki make it all better.

He pushed his nose into her curly red hair, breathing deeply of the scent of woman and wolf.

CHAPTER FIFTEEN

TQB Base, Command Center, Tokyo, Japan

Akio had spent many hours poring over drone footage in the command center over the past weeks. His search had been unsuccessful so far, so he now had Abel checking everywhere the EI could access for any news from the specified search area.

Although there was still a government presence in China, their working computer systems were still few thanks to Chinese companies using the same corrupted chips they'd sold to the other governments in their own systems.

Akio was one of the few people outside China to know how bad the breakdown in communications there had truly been. His ability to monitor UnknownWorld issues there had been severely limited, along with every other country except Japan. It had taken several years after the WWDE for the Chinese to reestablish an infor-mation network. It had taken Eve seconds to infiltrate it. Even with total access, information first had to be entered for it to be useful. *That* was another problem entirely.

"Akio, I haven't located anything that would indicate Forsaken activity anywhere near that area," Abel reported. "There is a report from Shanghai about a suspicious animal attack. The report indicates it was a large cat believed to be a tiger, but the investigator's notes show that the cat would have been much taller than normal."

"Probably the Sacred Clan again. They've been getting more active in the past few years. Shanghai has a decent port, and many ships destined for foreign lands dock there. Some of the Clan members who came here traveled through there. An isolated attack is not a serious concern. Flag that area and alert me if there are any similar attacks there. If there are more, I will go there and deal with it."

"Shanghai and the surrounding areas, flagged," Abel confirmed.

"What's happening in Shanghai?" Yuko asked as she walked in, a cup of tea in each hand.

"*Domo,* Yuko." Akio nodded gratefully when she offered him one of the cups. "An attack that is probably Sacred Clan-related," he answered after taking a sip. "There is only one report so far."

"Didn't you tell me that some of the Clan members you found here had arrived on ships from there?" Yuko asked.

Akio nodded. "*Hai.* If they're sending out more of those groups, then we will have to deal with them eventually."

"Perhaps it would be prudent to have some of Eve's new toys there to keep an eye on things," Yuko suggested. "The larger ones have proved to be useful in monitoring urban areas."

Akio grimaced, thinking how they had failed to find what he was looking for. "*Hai,* that is worth trying."

Yuko noticed his grimace when she mentioned that and decided it was time to push her friend a little. She respected his privacy, but the more time he spent sequestered, looking through data, the more she and Eve worried. Eve had queried Abel about what was going on, but he couldn't explain why Akio was so fixated on finding one vampire in all of China.

"Akio," she called softly.

"Yes?" He didn't look up from the screen he was viewing. Video streamed across it so quickly that it was a blur if she didn't use her vampire powers to watch it.

"Would you stop for a moment, please?" she asked in the same soft voice.

He paused the video and swiveled his chair to face her with a puzzled look.

Yuko drew a deep breath, hesitant to intrude, but she knew her friend was going through a crisis and wanted to help him. She raised her hand, making a gesture that encompassed the entire room. "You've spent a great deal of time in here over the past few weeks. I am concerned for you. It's not like you to focus so intently on finding one Forsaken, especially one who isn't causing a great deal of harm to humans."

Akio grimaced before he blinked and resumed his normal stoic expression. That small reaction spoke volumes to Yuko. She had lived with him for many years and knew him as well as any person could. He had gone from being distant and closed to close and caring. She had never seen him this...emotional, for lack of a better word, in all that time.

He stared at her without answering. The longer the silence went on, the more his face showed how upset he was about this Forsaken. His mouth moved several times as if tasting the words before he spoke them.

"That Forsaken is someone I knew long ago." He swallowed hard before continuing, "I thought he was gone since I was forced to watch as he died in agony. That he is now Forsaken is my fault," he whispered, a single bloody tear rolling down one cheek.

Yuko placed a comforting hand on his back. He flinched at her touch.

"Akio, I'm here for you." She spoke softly while gently rubbing his back to try to comfort him. "Whatever it is, please let me help you."

Akio's eyes were open and he appeared to be looking at her, but she could tell he saw only memories. A range of emotions rolled across his face. Grief turned to sorrow, sorrow turned to anger, and finally, anger turned to fury. Yuko watched, her hand never stopping as he came to terms inside his mind.

He inhaled—a deep, shuddering breath that was painful to hear—and then he spoke, his voice low and shaking with barely contained rage as the memories he had pushed down so long ago once again burned bright in the forefront of his mind.

"You are aware that I had dealt with Isamu and Ogawa before." He paused and forced his body to relax as he fought down the anger. "You heard the taunts they threw at

CHARLES TILLMAN & MICHAEL ANDERLE

me the night they died, and their digs about my choice of companion."

His eyes developed a red glow. He closed them and again forced his taut muscles to relax. "Do you remember what I told you about them? That Kamiko used them to punish her followers for imagined and actual violations of her rules?"

Yuko nodded, not wanting to speak out of concern that he would stop talking.

"I once was sentenced to suffer at their hands. I had dared to break one of her most sacred rules—love no one but her."

Yuko's eyebrows flew up, shocked by this admission. Akio was far more relaxed around her now than he had been when she accepted her role as Vicereine, but he still kept everyone at a distance, like he was incapable of ever letting anyone inside his personal wards.

Akio continued, "The Forsaken I am seeking, Kenjii, was a kind and gentle soul whose only crime was to care for me—a crime that caused him to spend what I thought were his last hours suffering at the hands of those two monsters. All because Kamiko Kana was a petty, jealous tyrant who allowed nothing less than complete loyalty to her."

He wept unashamedly, tears streaming down his face as he finished. Yuko didn't know how to react to her strong and stalwart mentor still hurting from the experience.

Akio scrubbed his face with his hand and looked surprised to see the bloody tears. He shook his head as if dispelling the memory. "This happened a few years after Kamiko's mother died, while Kamiko was still building her empire. She had her fingers in all manner of things, legal and not, and she used my brothers and me as her eyes, ears, and voice. We dealt with the day-to-day operations, keeping the businesses protected and the criminals productive and in line."

Akio considered the young woman who had been his closest companion for almost thirty years before he continued. "Isamu and Ogawa were Kamiko's pets. We all did her bidding, but they were special. I told you that they were torturers; that is part of the reason Isamu was turned. After that, he petitioned Minagawa, Kamiko Kana's mother and the queen at that time, to turn Ogawa as well. She allowed it, and when she was killed by the American bombs, they became Kamiko's personal enforcers.

"Isamu was a strong Forsaken who inherited several gifts from his creator, Kamiko. She was a fourth-generation grandchild of Michael's child Peter, the man he had charged to monitor Asia and enforce his strictures. She had Ogawa turned as well, and he worshiped her like she was his personal goddess. There was nothing he wouldn't do to please her, no one he would not betray."

Akio paused, his eyes closing and his expression going slack as his mind went to a place many years in the past.

Yuko watched him silently, determined to give him whatever comfort she could.

CHAPTER SIXTEEN

TQB Base, Tokyo, Japan

Akio opened his eyes, looking at Yuko but seeing pictures in his mind from the past. He took a deep, calming breath as he prepared to tell a tale that he had never told another living soul.

He relived the memory as he allowed himself to think back to the fateful day that had started it all. He could almost feel the humid August heat on his skin and smell the odor of rotting fish as he slowly started to speak.

"It was the summer of nineteen fifty-six, and I had been sent to Chiba by Kamiko Kana to deal with a local criminal who needed a reminder that there were things in the night much scarier than he was. Having completed that mission, I was looking to grab a quick meal before I returned. My orders had been to give him a reminder, not a reprimand. Had my orders called for a reprimand, I would have had no need to hunt that night. Reprimands were reserved for when the next in line needed to understand that failing

Kamiko resulted in a sudden and very bloody change in leadership.

"The Chiba docks were always a good hunting ground for Forsaken since a body floating in the harbor with its throat cut wasn't an unusual occurrence there. Kamiko demanded we be careful not to bring too much attention to ourselves or the group when we hunted. She was afraid of catching the attention of Michael or his family since that would lead to a change in leadership faster than with the criminals. Plus, when Michael's family got involved, they did not limit themselves to only removing the one at the top. They had no problem killing the top three or four, or everyone to make their point."

He was silent for almost a minute, his face going through a range of emotions until it finally came to rest on the default stoic. "I was hunting the rough area that housed the dockside bars and brothels when I heard what sounded like someone being beaten in an alley beside one of the seedier establishments the area had to offer. It was a place where cheap sake flowed, so deadly fights were not uncommon. My curiosity led me to slip into the alley with the intention of investigating the commotion at the dead end. I found a group of three toughs surrounding a young man on the ground. His clothes were torn, and his face was battered and bloody from the beating he had received. I started to move on, not wanting to deal with four bodies, when I heard the young man speak.

"'You bastards can beat me. You might even kill me,' he swore. 'And you will have to kill me before I submit to the likes of you.'" Akio smiled. "He spat at the largest of the toughs, defiance in his eyes. That tough's actions and words sealed his fate. He was in the process of unfastening his trousers while he taunted the beaten man."

"What did he do?" Yuko murmured uneasily.

"He called him an *okama* and told him they would all have him for flaunting himself in front of the 'real men,'" Akio answered. "I saw red and felt my fangs come out at that. These bullies were attacking the man because they thought he was a homosexual. I had not felt that kind of anger at a human in almost five hundred years. Human or not, his actions were without honor, and he had to die."

A small movement of his lips caused Yuko to focus hard on him. Her eyes widened in surprise. Was that a smile that almost leaked out? No, it couldn't have been.

"I forced my anger down until my fangs retracted and called out softly to him from behind. I asked if perhaps he would like to try me instead.

"All three of the toughs spun to face me. The loudmouth told me it wasn't my business, and if I didn't move on, he and his friends would do the same to me. To be sure I understood what he meant, he thrust his hips, calling attention to what he held in his hand while his friends shook their fists at me.

"I'm sure if I had been human, it would have been intimidating. As it was, it was pathetic. I stepped closer, and when his friends rushed me, I lashed out and grabbed them both. In one move, I threw them over his head and into the wall of the building at the end of the alley.

"As his friends slid down to the pavement, I closed the distance between us and told him I wanted to give him something instead. I caught him by his shirtfront and pulled him in close. He flailed, screaming that he was going to kill me. He finally landed a blow to my face with his fist, but before he understood that his punch hadn't bothered me, I pulled him closer and allowed my eyes to glow and my fangs to extend. His fear when I pierced him was sweeter than the taste of his blood.

"When I was done, I looked deep into his eyes and snapped his neck for good measure. When he dropped to the pavement, I felt a small sense of pleasure because his trousers had fallen to his ankles as he died. A petty thing on my part, but fitting that he suffered that final humiliation.

"One of the men I had thrown was struggling to his feet, I judged that the other would never get up again when I saw the angle of his head. I took that one too, drinking him dry and reveling in the rush of his terror as I did it. When I was done, I released him and smashed his head against the bricks, shattering his skull and finishing him off as well."

He paused again, and this time Yuko was sure he was smiling.

"I felt my body tingle as the fresh blood rushed through me. I had almost forgotten the young man until I heard him whisper, *'Banpaia. I thought you were a legend, but you are real.'* I looked at him, expecting to see terror and fear, but I saw something else instead—something I had not seen directed at me in almost half a century.

Akio's eyes focused, and his voice pitch changed as he came back to the present. "After seeing the three men so casually killed, he should have been screaming or trying to run away. Instead, he looked at me through the hair that had fallen into his face. His eyes were bright with excitement and something else—admiration."

He paused for a few beats, and then his voice choked with anguish. "That sealed his fate, that moment when I should have killed him and moved on. I justified it at the time by telling myself I was going to find out why he didn't fear me as he should. That I was going to determine who had let him live after he found out about our world and then kill him."

He laughed ruefully. "I was never one to lie, not even to myself, but that was what I did. Not letting humans know about the UnknownWorld was the first and most strictly enforced of the strictures Michael had handed down. Even Kamiko wouldn't disobey that rule, and she hated him. That lie I told myself is one that has tortured me for many decades, the lie that led to the death of the one person I had loved in several centuries. Or so I thought until recently."

Yuko saw the pain in her friend's eyes and the slump in his shoulders when he stopped speaking. Her heart ached for him, and she felt the tears forming in her eyes. "Akio." She stood and moved toward him, both arms open. "If there is any way possible, if we have to travel to China and search ourselves, I will not rest until we locate this man."

Akio watched her warily, still hesitant to have physical contact with anyone. Seeing the earnestness in her eyes and hearing the concern in her voice, he slowly stood, allowing her to hold him and give him the comfort he had denied himself for so long—comfort he was still unsure he deserved.

· · ·

Adelaide Oval, Adelaide, Australia

"Gates opening." The call went through the stockade before the gates started to move. All eyes turned to see two large wolves slip into the compound as the gates swung open.

The wolves stopped a few steps inside and snarled at the people milling about. It started with a scream and a few people running the opposite direction and soon turned into a stampede of humanity running in the opposite direction from the wolves.

Four men entered behind the snarling wolves, laughing and pointing as the frightened people shoved and fought to get as far from them as possible.

"Look at that bloke there." An unkempt man who stood well over six feet and weighed at least two hundred fifty pounds, laughed as he pointed. "He plowed that old duffer down and never looked back."

"He looks to be in good shape, Archie," his companion pointed out. "Keep an eye on him. We'll take him in the first batch."

"I got him, Owen. Doubt he will be much fun, though. Look how he's trying to push back to the fence."

"Just take him. Decklan wants to scare them all with this first match. He's going to let Dustin get his first humans."

"Dustin? But he's only a kid," Archie complained.

Owen smiled. "Exactly."

Callum snorted from behind them. "That's gonna be a hoot. Dustin looks like he's ten years old. Imagine the looks on their faces when the little wanker shifts."

Owen laughed evilly. "That's why Dee said no shifting where they could see you. He wants it to be a big shock."

"Your brother is one sick fuck, Owen."

"You know it, Archie." Owen grinned and rolled his shoulders, "Okay, let's pull out four of the men. Dee gets pissed if he has to wait."

The two wolves had been harrying the people, herding them into a tight group, when Owen whistled once. The wolves pulled back behind the four and waited to see what they threw their way, eager to be done so they could change back to human form to watch the show.

The four men spread out and headed for the crowd, each one zeroing in on their chosen victim.

Archie spotted his man still trying to force his way through the crush and darted in, bowling over any who were unfortunate enough to be in his way. He caught him by his collar and yanked him back, spinning a half-turn and throwing him toward the waiting wolves.

The unfortunate man landed in a heap, his breath rushing out of him as he collided with the broken pavement. One of the wolves moved in and cut him off as he struggled to his feet, heading off his attempt to make it back to the relative safety of the crowd.

Owen looked into the crowd and spotted a young man with a boyish face glowering at him with a cold, hard stare. His original victim, an older man in his sixties, was forgotten. He caught the man by his shirt front and pulled him off his feet. He spun around, releasing the shirt and tossing the man toward the wolves. In seconds he was with the first victim, cut out of the herd.

The others soon had two more men, one an overweight

redhead and the other a lean thirty-something with a scar down one side of his face. They all turned to leave when a voice called from the crowd.

"What the hell do you motherfuckers want with them? Why the fuck did you bring us here, and what are you doing with those gods-be-damned wolves?"

Owen's head snapped around to see who had dared to speak. He was shocked to see a thin young woman with long black hair standing in front of the group, hands on her hips and fire in her eyes—the one who had shot him the night he took her.

"You!" he snarled as his eyes widened in recognition. "You're the bitch that shot me!"

He stalked up to her and stared down at her. She glared at him, hands on her hips and pure hatred in her eyes.

"You want to know why we want these meatsacks?" he growled. "Come on, bitch. I'll show you what we're doing, what we're going to do to all of you." Owen's hand flashed out, caught her by one arm, and jerked. Faster than was humanly possible, he bounced her over his shoulder.

The wind was knocked out of her with a loud *whoosh* by the rough treatment. Kelly fought to force her lungs to expand and ease the burning in her chest. She finally was able to expand her lungs and suck in the oxygen her muscles needed.

Being upside-down over his shoulder didn't leave her many options to fight back, but she took what she could get.

"Put me down, you fucking bastard!" She beat her fists into him as she railed. "I said, put me the fuck down!"

On the third punch to his hip, her body was shaken by a

blow on her arse. Each time she hit him, he spanked her even harder until her body bounced against his bony shoulder each time.

She screamed as she punched him ineffectually again. "Ow, ow, ow! Get your hands off my arse, motherfucker!"

"I can do this all day." He laughed as he smacked her hard enough to cause her breath to catch. "Keep it up, and you may get more than a show. I'm still right pissed that you shot me."

She stopped her struggles, realizing she was not accomplishing anything except making him laugh and inciting bruises on her rear. She decided it would be best to bide her time until she could do some real damage to his arse, or whatever other body parts she could reach.

The four men were driven out of the gates into a fenced enclosure no larger than a barn stall. Once they were all inside, a woman who had been standing to the side closed them in and locked the gate with an old piece of chain and a padlock.

The enclosure was made of chain-link fence with rolled barbed wire all around the top. The end opposite the stockade opened into the old stadium at the edge of the playing field.

The field was littered with piles of debris that looked like they could have come from an airplane and other assorted scrap. There were some piles that rose high into the air and others that were only a few feet tall. They appeared to be randomly scattered throughout with no structure or reason. Directly in front of the enclosure was a pile of rusted and broken farm tools consisting of axes, pitchforks, and even a worn and chipped machete.

When Owen exited the stockade, the woman saw Kelly and anger suffused her features. "And just what in the ever-loving fuck do you think you're going to do with that bit of fluff, Owen Walsh?" she yelled as she rushed over to him.

He growled as he sidestepped her. "Go on, Maggie. This doesn't concern you."

She moved to block him. "Doesn't concern me?" she snapped. "You spend the night in my bed, then drag this human trollop out and flaunt her in my face and…"

She cut off when he slapped her across the face with his free hand.

"First off, Maggie, I don't answer to you or any other bitch in this pack. If you think I do, you better take a look around. I have my pick of any of you whenever I want. Not that it's any of your business, but this is the bitch who shot me the other week. I never finished my talk to her about that. Now, go tell Decklan we're ready for him, and before you say what I see is on your mind, remember I can kill you, and no one will say a word."

He stalked off without looking back.

Kelly turned her head to look at the woman and was surprised to see a murderous look on her face. She was even more surprised that it was aimed at the man and not her.

Maggie noticed Kelly watching and gave her a look that Kelly thought held no small amount of pity before she glared at the man's back again. She shook her head, a disgusted look on her face. "I didn't mean nothing like that," she whined. "I was surprised that you was dragging out a…human, is all." She said it like it was a curse.

Owen stopped and turned just enough to look at her over his shoulder.

She ran her hand across her breast and farther down. "Why do you want that skinny little git of a human when you can have this?" Her voice went from a whine to low and sultry as she tilted her head and looked at him through her hair.

"I'll be havin' it again soon if you don't keep pissin' me off. Now go tell Dee we're ready. This bitch," he smacked Kelly across the rear again, "needs to see what's in store for her and the rest of those filthy humans."

"I'll hold you to that." Maggie walked away, putting extra sway into her hips when she felt his eyes watching her.

"Wow, what a big tough fuck you are," Kelly growled. "Put me down, and I'll fix it so you won't be able to do her any good for a month."

Owen hitched her up, bouncing her off of his shoulder again as his hand slammed down on her butt with a loud *crack*. "Shut your piehole before I give you that chance. Dee will be mad if I rip you to sheds now, but I'll take the beating for it if you keep it up. I hate being shot."

Kelly started to snap back when she realized he had again mentioned being the man she shot the night she was taken. She had hit that man twice center mass with 9mm slugs. If this was the same man, he should at least be sore from the shots.

She was silent as he carried her, bouncing uncomfortably on his shoulder up several flights of stairs. They entered a darkened room, and he unceremoniously flipped her to the floor.

Kelly landed hard on her already bruised bottom. "Ow, what the fuck?" she cried.

"Sit there and be quiet if you know what's good for you. I have to get ready, and then all your questions will be answered." He walked over to an old duffel bag in the corner and started to pull out clothes.

Kelly glared daggers at his back, planning all the ways he would pay for how he had treated her.

CHAPTER SEVENTEEN

TQB Base, Tokyo, Japan

The image paused on the monitor Akio had been watching earlier, then went dark.

"I have located the Weres in Australia you inquired about," Abel announced.

The monitor displayed a satellite map of Australia. Abel zoomed in on the southern coast until it stopped on the marker for Adelaide. "I have located two of the vehicles associated with that group in Adelaide. I repositioned a satellite to obtain real-time surveillance and have discovered unusual activity at the site."

The image slowly expanded until it focused on an open oval-shaped structure and a river that ran nearby. The building had obviously been covered on three sides once upon a time. Now only two sides were covered and both ends were open, one by design and the other from some major damage that had occurred at some time in the past.

"This structure was once a sports stadium," Abel informed Akio and Yuko. "On WWDE, a large jetliner fell from the sky and crashed here." The image zoomed in on the end that was adjacent to an area that still had some signs of paving. The area showed signs of intense heat damage and there were piles of warped, rust-covered metal, and the remains of what could only have been an aircraft.

Akio's lips compressed with anger. A rough stockade made from scavenged materials extended from the crash site around the area of broken pavement and sparse vegetation. Inside that fence was a mass of humanity held in deplorable conditions. Some huddled together in small groups, others had their backs against the fence, warily watching the rest with fear and distrust evident on their faces. All were exposed to the elements and the unforgiving Australian weather.

Outside the fence, rough-looking men walked the perimeter, occasionally lashing out with makeshift clubs when the prisoners failed to move away fast enough. They high-fived and laughed every time one of them made contact as if it were a game to cause more suffering among the prisoners.

As they watched, there was a flurry of activity at the section nearest the stadium. "Abel, focus in on that area of movement," Akio ordered.

As the image shifted, a group of four men flanked by two wolves entered the compound through a gate. The people fled, gathering at the far end of the stockade. The men on the outside took advantage of the crowd shoving and pushing, delivering blows to hapless people unfortunate enough to be caught between the crowd and the fence.

The men and wolves stalked toward the terrified

crowd, approaching slowly to cause the most fear. When they approached the crowd, the four men moved faster than a normal human could, and they each snatched a victim from the mass. The prisoners were thrown into the center of the stockade and the wolves moved in, driving them toward the opening that led to the stadium.

The four men started back the way they had come. One of them suddenly stopped and in the blink of an eye, he yanked a young woman from the crowd, laughing at her feeble attempts to fight him off. He threw her over his shoulder, one arm pinning her legs to his chest while her hands beat against his lower back. He smacked her across the buttocks with his free hand, still laughing as he matched her blow for blow. His victim stopped her struggles after a half-dozen whacks, her body limp as she was carried away.

"What are they doing with those people?" Yuko's voice was shaking, the question one she was sure she wouldn't like the answer to.

The wolves herded the four original victims into a square enclosure made of rusted metal fencing topped with rows of barbed wire, As soon as they were inside, the gate was secured by a thin woman with long red hair. She turned toward the stockade as the man carrying the woman emerged, stopping only long enough to push it closed with his free hand.

When he turned away from the gate, the red-haired woman was in his path, one finger shaking in his face and the other hand curled into a fist and planted on her hip. Words were exchanged until the man lashed out with his free hand, knocking the woman to the ground and walking away as she glared daggers into his back.

Akio's face was flushed with rage, his eyes glowing bright red and his voice low and guttural when he spoke. "Abel, summon a Pod," he commanded. "I have work to do."

"I anticipated your request," Abel replied immediately. "Your Pod is on station five kilometers above us. I will bring it into the courtyard when you are ready to depart."

"I'm going as well," Yuko told him as she headed out of the command center for her quarters.

"Per Eve's orders," Abel answered, "I am unable to allow you to depart on combat operations without her direct authorization."

Yuko stumbled to a halt at the door. "What did you say?" she hissed.

"After your experience on Kume with the Nosferatu, I am unable to allow you to go on combat operations without the direct authorization of Eve each time," Abel clarified.

"Eve!" Yuko called over her chip, her voice laced with anger.

"Yes, Yuko?" Eve answered, her tone dripping with innocence.

Yuko took a deep breath, not wanting to allow her anger to let her say something she would regret. "Would you please explain to me what Abel's..." She paused for a moment.

"Orders," Abel supplied.

"Yes, that. Thank you, Abel. What do they mean?" she finished, her teeth clamped tight to prevent her from saying more.

"It means," Eve clarified, "That you are not able to slip off into dangerous situations without me being physically present with you, or determining the risk is within acceptable parameters for you to go unaccompanied."

Akio walked out of his quarters, his black Jean Dukes armor fitting him like a glove. He had a matched set of Jean Dukes Specials slung around his waist, and his katana sticking up over his shoulder. He raised one eyebrow when he saw Yuko frozen in the doorway. Her voice was calm, but the fierce red glow in her eyes showed that she was anything but. "What's wrong?"

"Eve has issued a directive that I am unable to go on any combat-related operations without her approval," Yuko ground out. "Abel will not allow me to depart without her authorization."

"Horst is in the lobby requesting to see you, Akio," Abel advised.

"Let him in," Akio told him.

"Acknowledged."

Yuko stepped out of the door and stalked toward her quarters, her voice still calm but her body language showing she was about to explode.

Akio had been left out of that conversation and was happy about it. Eve was working out who she was as an AI, but there had been growing pains along the way. Some days she sounded and acted like Bethany Anne on a rampage, and others, she was calm and formal to the point of seeming mechanical and emotionless. The only consistent thing was her fiercely protective nature where Yuko was concerned. That never wavered and could cause her to seem overbearing and restrictive.

The elevator opened and Horst stepped out, raising an eyebrow when he saw Akio loaded for war. "Someone is about to have a very bad day, *ja?*"

Akio nodded and motioned for him to step through the door Yuko had vacated into the command center. "What can I do for you today?" Akio asked as Horst joined him.

"It can wait since you seem to be occupied at the moment." Horst paused for a beat and asked, "Do you need my help?"

Akio's eyes widened as he considered the offer. He had not seen much of the man since their return from Europe. Although he had elected to stay in Japan, Akio had not thought him interested in anything other than building things. Well, to be honest, building things and Koda Rii. "It's a Were problem. Do you want to be involved?"

"Anything like we saw in Rasov?" he asked.

"Worse," Akio told him. "Abel, show Horst the video."

Horst watched in silence as the video replayed. When he saw the Were pull the young woman out of the crowd, a low growl came from deep in his chest. When it was done he was shaking, his face flushed with rage.

"*Ja,* I will help." His voice was low and rough. "Just because they have the power it does not mean they have the right to be monsters. Being here has shown me how much can be accomplished by working together. The Weres should be working with others, or at least leaving them in peace. Those Weres have no honor."

Akio nodded at his response, seeing that Horst was sincere and wanting to live as a member of the Unknown-World that Bethany Anne envisioned.

"*Hai,* perhaps another Wechselbalg being there could

help sway any who are not completely on board with what the leaders are doing. Much like the three who I let live at Rasov."

"I will do what I can," Horst assured him. "But understand that once some get the taste of power, it is like a drug. Weres are submissive to their Alpha, and when they have the same control over others, it is hard for them to stop."

"They stop or they die," Akio told him. "Have you trained with any weapons?"

"*Ja*, but I prefer to fight as a Were."

Akio nodded once and walked out of the command center with Horst on his heels. "I would prefer you didn't fight unless it is necessary. Perhaps these Weres will benefit from seeing us working together."

"*Ja*," Horst answered. "And if they don't?"

"They die."

CHAPTER EIGHTEEN

TQB Base, Tokyo, Japan

"Eve, you can't order Abel to keep me locked up here," Yuko muttered as she opened her closet and started pulling on her armor.

"Yuko, I was designed by ADAM to protect you from all threats, even if *you* are the threat."

"Me? What?" Yuko sputtered. "What do you mean, protect me from myself?"

"You are acting outside the scope of your mission. I didn't interfere when you went to Kume because Akio explained it was part of your training. I am one hundred percent on board with helping the people there as well. The Yakuza had taken our friend, so it was fitting for you to be part of that. But you cannot keep charging into battle."

Yuko took several deep breaths to calm herself before she responded, "But you can't allow Akio to go off alone to deal with these situations. He needs my help."

"Needs?"

"Of course!" Yuko exclaimed. "He shouldn't have to risk himself alone when I can help him."

"Yuko, think about what you just said," Eve told her quietly. "Akio has been dealing with everything by himself since the earthquake buried his team. Has he needed any help so far?"

"I wasn't ready," Yuko pointed out. "I was not enhanced until recently."

"That's not what I asked," Eve told her.

Yuko paused to consider what Eve had said. "No." She slowly sank to the floor as the realization set in, "He didn't need my help."

"No, he doesn't need your help to fight. He needs you to be the Vicereine, the diplomat, the one who takes care of the UnknownWorld beings who honor Michael and Bethany Anne. Akio needed you to be competent to protect yourself should that need arise, not to be a warrior."

Yuko was silent as she remembered the words Bethany Anne had spoken the night ADAM had introduced her to Eve. Though it had been more than a quarter-century, she heard her Queen's voice in her head.

"First, you can't police the world. Don't try. Whatever they do, let them! Your responsibility is to the UnknownWorld. Akio is responsible for taking care of any Forsaken, and you are responsible for taking care of those who would honor Michael's family or me."

Before she could reply, Eve continued, "I see how your heart aches after every mission you go on. You are not a killer, even though you have killed and unfortunately will likely have to again. Yuko, part of you dies each time. I can't allow you to become something you are not out of a wrongheaded sense of need."

"What about Akio? If he were to be injured, I would not forgive myself."

"Akio is a centuries-old warrior, enhanced by Kurtherian technology to the point that he is practically invincible. He has the experience and the enhancements to survive pretty much anything he encounters, either by killing it outright, or regrouping until he has the advantage. What he can't do is your job. He is a warrior, not a diplomat."

Yuko sat on the floor of her closet, her armor half on as she stared into nothingness. Her mind replayed the events at Kume and her fight with Chang. She was angry about what Heinz and Chang had done to the people of the island, but she still felt a pang in her stomach. She had put up a front, seeming eager to do battle, when in truth, she wished there was a way to redeem all those who were killed.

A light tap outside her closet brought her out of her reverie.

Eve stood there, her android face devoid of emotion. She raised her arms toward Yuko and stood silent, waiting for acknowledgment.

Yuko nodded and patted the floor beside her. Eve approached her and slowly raised her hand to brush a tear from Yuko's face.

Yuko's eyes widened in surprise. She hadn't realized she was crying.

Eve gently wrapped her arms around her, and it was

like a dam burst. Tears flowed as she returned the gesture, holding onto Eve.

"Oh, Eve." She sniffled as the tears slowed. "You're right. I was trying to be what I thought was needed, but it killed me a little each time. I didn't realize until now how much it took out of me each time I took a life. What am I to do? Akio might need me."

"If Akio needs you as a warrior, the situation will be beyond bad, and we haven't encountered anything so far that was even close. Plus, now that I have unlocked the additional code ADAM left me, I have accepted that it is not against my directives to take a life. I can puck 'em up now."

Yuko choked as she tried to laugh in mid-sniffle and started to cough. Eve patted her on the back until she stopped. "So what you're saying is you are bloodthirsty enough for both of us?"

"No, not exactly." She paused, considering her words before she continued, "Remember the Yakuza scum who kidnapped Koda and put her in that cage?"

Yuko grimaced, and her eyes briefly flashed red. "Yes, you permanently injured his hand when you rescued her instead of killing him."

"Exactly. I had him in my sights after I had disarmed him with the drone. I was about to kill him when Koda stopped me. That was when I realized that though I could take life, it should always be the last resort. I can kill out of necessity, but I will not kill for revenge."

"Oh, I didn't hear about that."

"I requested that Koda not tell you how I behaved," Eve admitted. "Had it not been for her, I'm afraid I might not have reached the same conclusions. All life is precious and should be preserved whenever possible. If I had executed him in vengeance, it would have been wrong, and it would have changed me. His life was Koda's to take, and she chose to let him live."

Yuko hugged her friend, thankful she had come to her and helped her rediscover herself. She still felt the need to help Akio, but she knew that Eve was right, and he didn't need her to be a warrior. He needed her to be Yuko, his friend.

"Akio," she called over her implant.

"*Hai?*" he replied.

"I don't believe you need me to accompany you to Australia," Yuko told him. "I will remain here and assist you from the command center if that is acceptable."

"That is acceptable. Horst requested to accompany me and help. I will see if he can convince any not completely in agreement with what the pack is doing to step away. If not, I will give them Queen's Justice."

"May they have the wisdom to choose life. Good luck to you both," Yuko murmured as she closed the connection.

CHAPTER NINETEEN

Gotsu Harbor, Gotsu, Japan

"Li," Wu moaned as the ship limped into the calm waters inside of Gotsu Harbor. "Kill me now and end my suffering. I think I puked my liver out that last time."

Li Song looked at the stricken man with a grin on his lips, having no sympathy for his plight. "Wu, we have arrived. It would be a waste to kill you now. I should have done it two days ago, or let Shao do it when you puked on his bunk."

Wu covered his eyes with his hand, reliving the embarrassment of his traitorous stomach causing him to spew its contents on his teammate's bed. "Tigers do not belong on the sea," he moaned. "I should have stayed in the mountains. They don't move."

"I have never seen one of us suffer from seasickness, you are unique among our Clan. Embrace it proudly," Li chided.

"You do know that if there weren't two of you standing there, I would beat you now," Wu grumbled.

Li clapped his friend on the shoulder as he laughed, "Good thing I have a twin, then. We will rest in the town a few days before moving on. That was a hard trip for all of us."

The ship had encountered a freak storm that damaged the solar collectors three days into the journey. With no way to charge the batteries and the winds blowing too hard for the crew to deploy the sails, they had been at the mercy of the currents for several days. By the time the crew was able to cobble a makeshift collector together, the choppy seas and unpredictable twists and turns had even Jin, the stoic of the group, ready to shift and kill them all.

"If we find that the teams sent here are not dead, I swear I will kill them myself," Wu grumbled as his stomach churned again.

"I hope that there is a simple explanation and all is going as planned." Li shrugged. "I fear they have met with an unexpected obstacle, though. The teams sent here were some of the most dedicated to the Clan. They would have to be dead not to have found some way to make contact."

Wu nodded, knowing Li was right. After all, they had trained the teams tasked with Japan personally. That thought made his stomach tense for a reason other than the epic sea sickness he was dealing with.

"Here, Wu, drink this. The barman swears it will cure you of the aftereffects of the sickness," Shao Hua told him as he returned to the table they had taken in the corner of a restaurant and bar next to the inn Li had secured.

Wu eyed the glass suspiciously. He sniffed it warily before he shoved it away, his nose wrinkling in disgust. "Smells like the inside of a chamber pot in the summer," he complained.

"I told the barman the same thing." Shao grunted as he slid the glass back in front of Wu. "He swears it will settle your stomach and stop the floor from moving under you."

Wu watched him through slitted eyes, unsure if he was being truthful or if it was payback for his bunk. He glanced at the barman, raising the glass, and received a smile as the man nodded and motioned for him to drink.

He grabbed the glass and slammed the contents back, trying to get them down without having to taste the vile-smelling mix. His eyes shot open wide as he gasped. "That shit tastes worse than it smells," he croaked.

Shao grinned as he answered, "He may have mentioned that. I forgot."

Li and Jin burst out laughing at the look on Wu's face, disgust with a big dose of mayhem thrown in.

"If you are lying, I promise I will kill you slowly and painfully," Wu growled. "If this vile brew doesn't kill me first."

Shao held his hands up, mock fear in his eyes as he chuckled. "See, you're feeling more like your old murderous self already."

Wu glared at his amused friend and realized he was feeling better. "It seems the barman might have been correct. That doesn't mean I don't want to kill you, but I might let you live until we find those missing numbnuts."

. . .

Sunrise Inn, Gotsu, Japan

Li rapped the table the team was gathered around with his knuckles to get their attention. "We were originally supposed to land in Niigata and travel overland to Onuma, where Won and Lee were ordered to establish a base. We are now some six hundred kilometers from there due to the damage to the ship, so I have decided we will go to Aida first."

"Wasn't that where Sun and Ling were sent?" Wu asked.

"No," Li replied. "Sun and Ling went to a small town near Wajima to secure a port facility. Huan and Lim were sent to Aida. Well, a small settlement in the mountains six kilometers west of there."

Wu waved a hand, motioning for Li to continue.

"We will make our way there overland today and try to locate them," Li explained. "Failing to do that, we will try to find out if anyone has seen them. If we have no luck, we will move on to Wajima and do the same."

"What if we can't locate them or any word?" Jin asked.

"We will go on to Onuma," he replied. "If we don't find anything there, I will contact the Master and get further instructions. Before we departed, he discussed us establishing a base here to coordinate additional teams."

"If we find they were taken or killed, is it safe to assume we will get them back or take vengeance on the ones who did it?" Hua asked. "Won Ling is my cousin, and if he has been taken, I will rescue him. If he is dead, I claim blood right to exact vengeance."

Li nodded. "If our people are captive, we will bring the might of the Clan against whoever has them—any of them. If they are dead, blood will spill."

"As it should be," Hua agreed.

"Gather your things," Wu ordered. "We leave in fifteen minutes."

The group all stood and headed for their rooms. One way or the other, they would find out why they lost contact with the teams.

CHAPTER TWENTY

Adelaide Oval, Adelaide, Australia

Decklan was on the field when Owen arrived. He glared at his brother and did a double-take when he saw him dragging a human female along. When he reached him, Decklan pointed to the woman. "What you doing with her? Trying to get Maggie to kill her for you?"

"Nah, me and Maggie already had that talk, and she understood after I knocked her on her arse. This is the bitch who shot me and the one who has been organizing the prisoners. She wanted to know why we wanted those four." He nodded at the men in the cage. "So I figured I'd give her a good close look."

"I saw her face." Decklan chuckled. "You know Maggie's gonna bite something important off if you aren't careful, right? I always told you not to date anyone crazier than you are. One of these days, you might listen."

While they were talking, they looked at the seats. Everyone in the pack had come to see the show. Decklan had only shared his plans with a trusted few. The rest of the pack had no clue what was planned. They only knew the Alpha had commanded them to be there, and there they were.

Decklan shook his head. There was no talking to Owen about his women. He was sure his brother was in for some hurt down the road and hoped he survived it. "Maggie's going to be fine. If she ain't fine, she can either get over it," he waved at the stands, "or one of the other bitches will take her place."

"Well, let's get this show started." Decklan faced the crowd of over one hundred Weres. "Pack members, I've got bonza news for you all. Our efforts to clean out the human scum have been successful." His statement brought a half-hearted smattering of applause from the crowd.

Decklan continued, not bothered by the lack of enthusiasm. He knew that many in the pack didn't agree with his plans. He would show them. Once all the humans were gone, Adelaide would be the first of many Were-only cities in Australia. His plan was to spread the pack throughout the country until it was without humans or Forsaken. They might not understand his genius, but someday they would recognize it. Until then, he was the strongest and the Alpha, and they could just do what he fucking said.

"Today, you will see that humans have no place in our world. The strictures of the past have kept us down for too many centuries. Today we throw off the vampire Michael's yoke of oppression and take our places as the rulers of this new world." He threw his arms in the air when he finished and glared at the pack members until all were applauding.

"Today, you will see one of your own, a young wolf barely grown, demonstrate why Wechselbalg are the superior race." He motioned for a blond youngster who appeared to be barely into adolescence to come forward.

Decklan growled. "Put on a good show. I want the humans to know true fear when you are done."

Dustin grinned at him, a manic gleam in his eyes. "Yessir." He moved onto the field and stood, head cocked to one side as he studied the four in the cage.

Decklan addressed the caged men. "What you see in front of you is one of our youths. All of you were easily captured, but in the sense of fairness, I'm gonna give you a chance at freedom. If any of you can beat this child in open combat, I'll allow you and another of your choosing to go free."

The four looked at him warily, not understanding what his game was.

"In front of you are weapons, and you may use them if you like. The only rule in this contest is to survive." Decklan smirked. "If you can."

He stepped to the side, and Maggie pulled the rope that raised the gate that led from the cage to the field. The men slowly came out, expecting it to be a trap, but when nothing happened, they went to the pile of tools.

"Liam, is this guy serious?" Kane whispered.

"I don't know, but I'm willing to see if he is," Liam replied. "I'm tired of being locked up, and those bastards killed a lot of my friends. If all I have to do is take out that little wanker to leave, I have no problem with that."

The others nodded agreement as they chose their weapons. Liam grabbed the old machete and tested its weight with a few swings.

Dustin stood watching with a bored expression as each

of them settled on a weapon. When all were armed and looking his way, he sneered as he raised one hand palm up and curled his fingers in, taunting them to attack.

Liam growled and rushed toward the arrogant youngster, the machete held out to the front intending to stab him and then cut him down as quickly as possible. When he was only a short distance away, the blond youngster seemed to explode in front of his eyes.

Bits of cloth were still floating in the air when a tawny wolf sprang forward and caught Liam by the throat. His terrified scream was reduced to a gurgle when blood sprayed into the air from his torn-out throat.

"Fuck!" Kane yelled as he tried to back away.

The wolf locked eyes with him, and he almost wet himself when he saw intelligent human eyes looking back. The rake he had chosen for a weapon dropped from his shock-numbed fingers, forgotten as the wolf slowly stalked toward him.

The other two ran the opposite direction. Kane stood frozen in fear, unable to move as he waited for the wolf to end him.

Pod, Over the Northern Territory, Australia

"Horst, when we arrive, I would like you to call out to the Weres and tell them if they resist, they will die. I will take the Alpha first, so the pack should listen to you."

"What makes you think they will listen to me?" Horst asked. "I'm not their Alpha, and I have no desire to be," he added quickly.

"No, you're not their Alpha, but you are *an* Alpha, and a

strong one at that," Akio assured him. "They should sense that when they are able to think again."

"What do you mean, think again?" Horst asked. "Losing the Alpha might anger them, but that is the extent of it."

The corner of Akio's mouth quirked. "I will be using a power that is unique to a few. Bethany Anne, Michael, and the Queen's Bitches have the ability to project fear: deep, dark, bone-chilling, debilitating fear. When that clears, the ones who are not wholly on board with the Alpha should be open to listening to you."

Horst nodded his understanding. He wondered how powerful Akio was to have an ability that was, according to rumor, wielded by only the Patriarch.

Akio started to say something else when he was interrupted.

"Akio," Abel called over the Pod's speakers. He was using them because Akio had directed him on the trip to Rasov with Horst to handle general communications that way. Since Horst didn't have an implant, it didn't leave him out of situations where he may have some input. It also served to make him feel like part of the team, something Yuko and he both wanted.

"*Hai?*"

"I'm picking up activity in Adelaide. I think they are about to start killing the humans they put in that cage."

"How far out are we?" Akio asked.

"One minute, twelve seconds until you arrive at the stadium."

"Nothing we can do now? Are we running at top speed?"

"No, top speed was limited by Eve's orders several years

ago. She analyzed the wear and stress generated by running at top levels and determined the effective life of the Pods would be extended by twenty-two point three-five-six percent if the maximum speed was set lower."

Akio pursed his lips, aggravation showing on his normally calm face. "Was there a valid reason other than maintenance issues for this?"

"Affirmative."

Akio waited for a moment until it was obvious Abel wasn't going to continue. "Please tell me what other considerations were figured into this decision."

"The lack of proper materials and the inability to manufacture some components with currently available resources."

"If we went to maximum speed now, how would that affect our arrival time?"

"By six-point-eight-four seconds."

He closed his eyes, contemplating the probability of being able to strangle the EI, or perhaps his creator. "Will we arrive in time to prevent them from harming the humans?"

"Probability is low," Abel replied. "The cage has been opened, and the humans are selecting weapons now."

"ETA," Akio ground out.

"Twenty-three point four three seconds."

"Bring us in fast," Akio commanded. "Remove the dampers when we come into the stadium."

"Removing the dampers will result in loss of stealth capabilities," Abel warned.

"I am aware of that," Akio replied. "Open the door and

make some noise. Horst, you might want to shield your ears. This is going to be loud."

Horst looked askance until Akio mimed sticking his fingers in his ears. He nodded and got them in just as Abel announced, "Arrival in two-point-nine seconds. Damping field dropping on my mark. Mark."

The Pod had been losing altitude fast for the last thirty seconds. Horst looked around Akio. He could make out the tops of trees and buildings, blurred by the speed at which the Pod was passing over them. At Abel's mark, Horst felt a change in pressure as the inertial damping field dropping was followed by a loud boom.

Akio stood in the open door of the Pod, one hand braced against the frame and his Jean Dukes Special in the other. He jumped out of the Pod as it slowed and fired his weapon as he hurtled toward the ground. The hypervelocity pellet struck the wolf at the base of his skull as he leapt at his helpless victim and his head exploded, covering the ground and the man in gore as the lifeless body struck him and knocked him to the ground.

Akio landed hard, one knee bending slightly, his fangs extended and his eyes glowing red. He saw the human woman from earlier swaying numbly on her feet, and the Were who had grabbed her from the crowd in the enclosure with one hand wrapped around her wrist.

"Horst, get their attention," Akio ordered. "Any who do not fight will be given the opportunity to live. If they fight, their lives are forfeit." He turned toward the massed Weres in the stands.

"*Ja*," Horst answered.

CHARLES TILLMAN & MICHAEL ANDERLE

By the time Horst was unstrapped, and on his feet, the Pod had settled three inches above the ground in the center of the stadium he had seen in the video earlier. The first thing Horst saw when he exited the Pod was a dead wolf with its head blown apart lying on top of an unmoving man. He couldn't tell if the man was alive, but farther on, he saw the remains of another man, and there was no doubt that one was *very* dead.

There were two other men climbing to their feet near the Pod, apparently knocked down by the blast. In the stands were over a hundred Weres, all suffering from the pain the sonic boom inside the confines of the stadium walls had caused them.

Akio was walking toward a Were in human form, sword in his hand at the ready. The Were shifted and started toward Akio when Akio turned on the fear.

Horst experienced the most mind-numbing sense of terror he had ever experienced. His mind was telling him to run, but his body had other plans. He managed to stay on his feet, swaying as he fought to do so. He retained the presence of mind to notice that many of the Weres fell to the ground, clutching their heads and retching as the fear overloaded their ability to function.

As fast as it started, it was gone. One moment, Horst was fighting the crippling sense of fear, and the next, it was a fading memory. He stood still for a few beats as his mind processed what had happened. He had been warned it would happen, but he'd had no reference to imagine how bad it would be. One thing he was certain of was that he hoped to never experience that particular ability of Akio's again. The power of a Queen's Bitch to strike terror into the heart of any who stood against him was beyond comprehension.

Akio was ready when the Were launched toward him.

Horst watched in wonder as Akio's form blurred, then appeared with a dead wolf at his feet. Horst was thankful once again that he'd had the survival instinct not to challenge him the night they met.

CHAPTER TWENTY-ONE

Adelaide Oval, Adelaide, Australia

Kelly watched in shock as the boy stood there, calmly waiting for the much larger men to come for him. She wondered how the leader could order this, like he expected the lad to be able to overcome four grown-arse men. She stared as the boy not only acted unconcerned but motioned for the men to attack him. She winced when Liam rushed forward, expecting it to be over quickly. Her eyes went wide in shock when the boy seemed to explode and a large dog—no, a wolf—stood in his place. Liam never stood a chance.

She slumped in Owen's grip, her legs unwilling to work as her mind overloaded from the unbelievable and gory sight.

Owen's voice sent chills down her spine when he whispered to her, "I'll be the one you face, bitch. I might even give you your little toy gun back to make it more fun."

Nausea settled in the pit of Kelly's stomach at his words. Her stomach turned and she was about to be sick when a tremendous *BOOM* from above made her sway on her feet. She almost fell when Owen unexpectedly released her.

His hands covered his ears as he fell to his knees, his face twisted in pain.

When she looked at the field, she saw a black object hovering inches above it. That was shocking, but what caught her attention next was something she would remember until the day she died.

It was a Japanese man dressed in some type of all-black uniform. He held a large pistol in his hand, and when he looked her way, his eyes were glowing bright red.

Kelly didn't have time to notice anything else before a wave of fear washed over her. It was pure terror, stronger than anything she had ever felt. It sank deep into her very core, causing her to fall to her knees and curl into a ball. Her stomach heaved again, threatening to expel its meager contents.

The fear seemed to go on forever , then stopped as suddenly as it had started. She slowly opened her eyes and saw the man coming toward her at a steady pace. As he got closer, she could make out a patch on his right shoulder: a blood-red background with a woman's head in white. She focused on the patch he wore to distract herself from the nauseated feeling. It wasn't a woman's head at all, it was a skull with long flowing hair and fangs protruding from the top jaw.

A vampire's skull.

Decklan was enjoying the show from the sidelines, his attention focused on Dustin as he quickly took down the first man and moved to kill the second.

Then everything happened at once.

A huge explosion shook the stadium, causing him to cover his ears in pain as the noise assailed his sensitive hearing. Then Dustin jerked in mid-leap and crashed into the man, and they both fell to the ground.

Movement on the field caught Decklan's eye, and he turned to see a being of legend. A daywalking vampire stalked toward him, his eyes glowing like embers. Decklan fought the sudden panic that ran through him and shifted to wolf form in the blink of an eye. Seconds later, his huge black wolf snarled a challenge at the vampire and rushed to meet him. He only made it a few steps before he froze, overcome by a feeling of terror so deep he had to fight not to fall to the ground in submission.

The fear continued to beat down on him, and when it stopped, the vampire was before him.

Akio looked down at Decklan, disgust on his face when he spoke to the Alpha. "You have disobeyed the strictures set forth by Michael. Worse, you have acted without honor and disobeyed the orders of Queen Bethany Anne. Your sentence for these crimes is death."

Decklan shivered involuntarily. He snarled as he warily watched the vampire and crouched as he prepared to attack. He took one mighty leap toward him, intent on ripping the vampire to shreds. Decklan Walsh wasn't fast enough to know he'd already died.

Akio brought his katana down in an arc, separating the Were's head from his body with one powerful swing. The headless body lay at his feet and Decklan's blood sprayed across the sparse grass.

Akio recognized the young woman on the ground from the video. He walked over to her and offered his hand, one eye on the Were still curled up in a ball on the ground. "Are you injured, young one?"

Kelly stared, her mouth open as she shook her head from side to side in response.

"Good. Stay here; all will be made right soon," Akio told her as he turned to where Owen was climbing to his feet, blood running from his nose and ears.

Owen surged to his feet and grabbed Kelly, yanking her behind him as he faced the vampire. He crouched and put up his guard.

Kelly didn't hesitate when she saw him focused on the red-eyed man, who eyed Owen with a contemptuous smirk. This arsehole had taken her from her home in the night, held her prisoner for weeks, and then not two minutes earlier threatened her life. Seeing him with his back to her in such a vulnerable position was too much for her to resist.

She took a step toward his back and screamed her rage at him.

Owen shook his head as he removed his hands from his sensitive ears. Whatever had caused the blast, it had overwhelmed his senses and knocked him to the ground. He felt a trickle of blood running from his nose, and his ears were ringing loudly. Although he healed faster than a human, he took longer than many other Weres. He squared off with the man, preparing to shift and end him, whoever he was, for daring to take what was his.

Kelly moved like a woman possessed. She took a fast step and cocked her rear foot, her eyes locked on her target.

Owen stopped himself from shifting when he heard a muffled sound from behind through the ringing in his ears and saw the man in front of him widen his eyes in surprise.

"Mother—" Kelly screamed as her foot came up to crash into the V at the top of Owen's spread legs, *"FUCKER!"* she finished as she slammed her foot into his balls.

Owen was trying to figure out what was wrong when the pain hit him like a runaway train. Even though Weres recovered quickly from injuries, a swift kick to the jewels still hurt. He turned, intending to kill her on the spot, but he should have maintained his situational awareness. He learned that when he was yanked back by his neck and slammed to the ground.

"Bad wolf. Stay." Akio chuckled. Seeing the human woman deliver a blow to the man who had wronged her made him smile. Well, after he'd winced.

Owen shifted on the ground, and a large wolf jumped up in his place. He darted at Akio, so enraged that he didn't realize what he was. His intent was to hamstring him and then kill him slowly.

Akio lowered his sword.

Owen saw it too late, just before the tip sank into his eye.

Akio shoved the blade so it exploded out the back of the wolf's head, then twisted and pulled the blade out, spinning as he brought it up and around. His body was a blur as the blade whistled through the air to impact the back of Owen's neck. Akio froze, his blade held point down as the wolf's head spun end over snout and landed with a solid thump on the ground.

Kelly's eyes went wide as she saw what Owen was and how easily the strange man in front of her had dispatched him. She took a step back when he looked her in the eye.

He shook his head. "That man was not honorable."

Before she realized it, the first thought through her mind came rolling out of Kelly's mouth. "Fuck him. Son of a bitch had it coming."

Akio quirked one eyebrow up and then nodded. "Yes, you are correct."

He looked behind her and then pointed toward a giant bearded man standing by the strange black box. "Go to Horst; he will keep you safe. I still have work to do."

He was gone in the blink of an eye. One second he was in front of her, the next he was gone, and all hell was breaking loose in the stands. She sprinted the short distance to where the man stood, and when she turned back, there were no words to describe what she saw.

"He's killing everyone," she whispered.

"*Nein*," the man behind her murmured. "Not all. Only the guilty."

.

CHAPTER TWENTY-TWO

Adelaide Oval, Adelaide, Australia

Kelly watched in awe as Akio moved among the people and wolves in the stands. It was pandemonium, with most trying to get away while others attacked. He was moving faster than her eye could follow, one minute standing in one place, the next several rows away. Whenever he stopped for a split second, his sword flashed and another body crumpled to the ground.

The huge blond man behind her was yelling repeatedly, "Do not fight. Stand down, or you will die."

To Kelly's surprise, a brown wolf stopped running, and seconds later, a nude woman stood in its place. Kelly watched as she sank to her knees, head bowed, and the swordsman passed her and struck down a man she recognized as one of the guards who had walked the perimeter of the enclosure with a club. He never saw the blade that took him in the back of his head.

It was done in moments. Where over one hundred people had been sitting and watching the field, now a quarter of them lay dead, and the rest knelt submissively like the woman had.

The man was covered in blood and gore as he slowly walked through the crowd, stopping twice and looking into the eyes of first a red-headed woman and then a skinny man with a scar down one side of his face. Each time his blade flashed and the person died.

"What is he?" Kelly wondered out loud.

"He is a Queen's Bitch," Horst explained. "The most dangerous being you could ever meet, as well as the best friend an innocent person could have."

Kelly turned and stared at the bearded man behind her, his eyes focused on the scene in the stands.

He continued, not looking away, "When the things that go bump in the night misbehave, he is the retribution. His name is Akio, and I am proud to call him my friend."

Kelly turned back to the stands and saw him approach an older man with gray streaks in his hair and stare into his eyes. She was surprised when instead of lashing out with his sword, he offered the man his hand and pulled him to his feet. He said something too soft for Kelly to hear, and the man nodded shakily and made his way down to the field.

He walked to them and nodded to Horst respectfully and then to her before he addressed Horst. "I'm Henry Smythe. Akio told me to come here and wait for him."

"Horst." He nodded as he held his hand out to the older Were.

They continued to watch as Akio went through the crowd, sparing many but cutting down others with no hesitation.

"How's he deciding who he kills?" Kelly murmured.

"I have no idea," Horst lied.

"He's only killing the ones who supported that arsehole, Decklan," Henry growled. "Good riddance to the lot of them."

"How does he know that?" Kelly asked. "I recognized a few of them from the guards I've seen around the stockade, but he just arrived. And why have they all stopped running?"

Horst shrugged again, keeping his own counsel about Akio's abilities. One thing he was sure of was that anyone Akio killed deserved it.

Akio was done in a few moments, and there were now two distinct groups in the stands: the terrified live ones and the ones who knew no fear, the dead. Akio made his way down the steps and out onto the field where the others waited. He eyed Henry Smythe long enough that he started to sweat visibly. After almost a minute, Akio nodded once, pulled a cloth from one of the many pockets in his shirt, and started cleaning his blade.

Henry Smythe took a deep breath and shivered when Akio broke the intense eye contact. He didn't know how, but he knew he had been judged by the deadly vampire. Whether he had passed remained to be seen.

When Akio was done cleaning the blood from his blade, he sheathed it and spoke. "You did not agree with what happened here. Neither did the ones who still live. Why did you allow it?"

Henry's eyes shot open wide. "How? What? No." He stammered to a stop when Akio tilted his head with one eyebrow raised.

"What I meant to say was," Henry took a deep breath as he gathered his thoughts, "Decklan was crazy. Not just a little bit, but murderous-rage fucknuts-crazy if he felt he was being challenged in any way. He wouldn't just kill the person he thought was against him, their entire family suffered."

Horst growled. "Those are not the actions of a true Alpha."

Henry winced, his mind going back to what had happened to the last Were who questioned Decklan, as well as his wife and both his children. "No, he wasn't a true Alpha, but with the followers he has, um, *had*, nobody dared challenge him after the first time."

"Other than murdering these people, what were his plans?" Akio asked.

"He wanted to take over and have an area that was Weres-only, no humans allowed. He planned to start here and spread his poison across Australia. The ones who followed him thought the same."

"Why here?" Kelly interrupted.

Henry looked at her and then to Akio who nodded once. "We've been living in a small town about five hundred kilometers to the north since shortly after the world ended. It was a hard life, but we were in the mountains and able to survive. The human population of the town was wiped out by one of the bugs that went around after the electricity stopped. We moved in and had a working community. Farming and hunting kept us fed, and everyone was given a job. Like I said, it was hard, but we were happy.

"It was a place of safety, and we took in any others who

found us. There were a few small farms in the area still run by humans, and we traded with them while keeping our nature secret like the strictures required."

Kelly cocked her head to one side. "Strictures?"

"The rules that forbid us from revealing ourselves to humans." He glanced at Akio. "On pain of death."

Akio held up a hand to stop Kelly from interrupting. She bristled, not accustomed to being shushed, but before her mouth could get her in trouble, Henry continued.

"Decklan and his brother Owen came to the town about two years ago. Decklan was always talking about a land for Weres and how humans were parasites, using resources we needed and not giving anything back. Most of us knew it was a lie, and our Alpha Robert ordered him to stop spreading his hate or leave. We had nothing against humans. We coexisted peacefully, each group providing things the other needed.

"Decklan did as he was told, but he had a following, most of them newcomers like him who agreed. When two of the stations we traded with were attacked and burned, Robert suspected Decklan and his band. When he challenged him about it, Decklan killed him.

"Robert was a smart leader and we all respected him, but he was old. Once Decklan had established himself as Alpha, the first thing he did was send his men out to kill all the remaining farmers and burn their farms.

"He ordered everyone to prepare to move, and when the beta questioned him, we learned what he was capable of. He killed him and ordered his men to kill the entire family. Only the daughter was spared, and truth be told, she would have been better off if they had killed her too.

He only spared Maggie because Owen wanted her." He nodded at a red-haired young woman watching fearfully from the stands, the same one who had confronted Owen earlier when he was bringing Kelly out.

"She didn't have any choice in the matter if she wanted to live. Owen forced her to go on raids and threatened to kill her at every turn until she gave in and acted like she was on board. I was one of the few who knew the truth, that she hates Decklan and Owen. She wanted nothing more than to see both of them dead. She wasn't strong enough to do it herself and couldn't get any support from the town. We were all too scared of Decklan and his gang."

He took a deep breath and let it out in a long sigh. "After a few months, Decklan informed us that we needed to move here. He said that Adelaide didn't have much of a human presence and was the best place to set up so we could have a Weres-only country. He loaded everything he could into a couple of old trucks we had managed to get going with some homebrew fuel and made sure there was nothing left for anyone to survive with if they stayed. He sent an advance group straight here to secure this area and force-marched the rest of us here in one week.

By the time we got here, the advance group had killed every human left in the town, not that there were very many. As best I could tell, some disease went through here and killed most of them about a year ago.

He nodded at the stands. "Decklan had his group kill all the humans for ten kilometers around. Things got real crazy after that. He made us build that damned holding pen and sent out raiding parties to bring you folks in from the outlying areas. He wanted every human within fifty kilometers either captured or dead. We just found out today what he had planned for you."

Kelly's face paled as she listened. Planned genocide to take over the land was crazy to her. There wasn't anything left that was worth it.

While her mind was still processing everything, Akio spoke. "Henry, you are a man who knows honor, but your fear has caused you to act in a manner that was without honor, and you must atone for it."

Henry lowered his head in shame, knowing he had allowed fear to make him behave in a dishonorable manner. He stood silently, his head bowed, waiting for his death. When it didn't come, he raised his eyes slowly until he faced the black-clad angel of death before him.

Akio continued, "You and your pack need to atone for the harm you have caused these people. You will work with them, help them recover, and together create a place that is safe for all. The humans are resilient and capable of doing great things, and the Weres are strong and are capable of ensuring the area is protected from any who wish to cause harm."

Henry's eyes widened in shock, not only that he was still alive but that this vampire had just ordered him to break the strictures.

"But…the strictures."

Akio cut him off, his eyes holding a hint of red. "The strictures have been revised by Queen Bethany Anne. Those who will act with honor and work with humans may do so with her blessing. Those who do not and cause harm to them will be dealt with accordingly." He nodded at the bodies scattered throughout the stands.

Henry was silent for a moment before he nodded. "But why tell me? I'm not the pack leader?"

"You are respected by the remaining members, and they will listen to you. You were afraid to challenge Decklan openly, but was it not you who convinced him to provide food and water to the captives? It was you who helped your niece Maggie to cope with her situation, and who counseled her to do what she could to help without revealing her true intent."

Henry took a step back, fear on his face. "How do you know that? You haven't had time to find this out."

"I can see it in your mind, Henry Smythe," Akio told him. "You have no secrets from me."

Henry's body stiffened at the intrusion into his mind, his body broke out into a sweat as fear coursed through his veins.

No, I am not Michael. I have some of his abilities, but there is only one Patriarch. Henry heard in his mind.

"Will they want to work with us?" He looked at Kelly after he got his body back under control.

Kelly had been watching the exchange, unsure of what was happening. She jumped when Henry addressed her, focusing on him and his question.

"I can't speak for them. I understand it was Decklan and his men who were responsible for this, but I'm not sure how they will react to all this." She waved her arm at the watching crowd.

"You have kept them organized and cared for while here. They look to you for guidance and direction already," Akio pressed. "If you talk to them, I am sure they will listen to you, as Henry's pack will listen to him."

"I'm not the Alpha," Henry argued.

Akio cocked his head to the side for a moment before he faced the apprehensive crowd in the stands. Had it not been for the compulsion he'd placed on them as he had gone through reading each member as he decided their guilt or innocence, they would all have fled.

He motioned for the others to follow as he walked to the edge of the field. He stopped and addressed the group. "You have seen what happened to the ones among you who caused harm. You live now because you did not willingly follow the Alpha and were not active or willing participants in his madness. You now have a choice: you can leave and cause no further harm to humans, or you can stay and try to reclaim your honor by making something good of this."

He motioned to Henry. "This man is known to you, and more importantly, respected by you. He has worked to minimize unnecessary cruelty and has helped many of you cope with your situations. Will those who wish to stay accept his guidance and leadership as you move forward?"

The crowd watched in shock as the vampire who had so easily slain so many earlier spoke to them. Never had they heard of any vampire giving Weres a choice. They came in, killed who they wanted, and told the others what to do. A low murmur went through the crowd as they absorbed his words.

"Speak to them," Akio urged.

Henry took a half-step forward and looked out at the crowd, stopping briefly and nodding to certain members before he cleared his throat and spoke. "You all know me. I don't think of myself as a leader." He was cut off as several in the crowd disagreed. He raised his hands for quiet and continued, "As I was saying, I never wanted to be a leader. I liked living a quiet life. I let what I wanted override what I knew to be right. Yes, I talked to some of you and cautioned others not to do anything prematurely."

He paused and drew a deep breath. "I knew what Decklan was doing was wrong. I lived among humans my whole life until the world went crazy. I don't hate them, and I know you don't either. We all just want to survive in the reality we live in."

Nods and murmured agreements from the group spurred him on.

"Akio," he pointed out, "has given us a chance to change things here. We all looked on as the humans were rounded up and killed and we said nothing. We were wrong, and we owe it to ourselves to reclaim our honor and the honor of the pack. Akio wants us to work with these people to make a safe place for all of us to survive and hopefully do more than that."

"The strictures forbid—" an older woman started before Henry cut her off.

"The strictures have been..." he glanced at Akio, "*updated* to take in the challenges we all face in this new world. Akio assures me that we can work with the humans without fear of reprisal. He also assures me that anyone who preys on others will meet the same fate as Decklan and his crew."

Henry stepped back as the crowd began to talk among themselves and turned to Horst, who shrugged. "What is it, Henry?"

"I was just curious how a Were—and an Alpha, if I'm

not mistaken, though you hide it well—came to be traveling with a vampire."

Horst snorted. "It is a long story, one that there is not enough time to get into now. Suffice it to say that if Akio deems you worthy, no matter what's happened in the past, he means it. I also don't suggest failing to do what you say. He's a bit of a stickler about honor."

Kelly went to the enclosure, where the humans were all pressed close to the gates, trying to see what was going on in the stadium. When she approached, she was met with too many shouts and calls to understand. She raised her hands for quiet and was surprised when the crowd settled.

"We're free," she started. "The people responsible for this are all dead."

Cheers went up from the crowd, and she had to wait a full minute for them to calm down before she could go on. "Not everyone here was in agreement with the bastards who took us. They are willing to work with us and help us all make a better go of it."

"Why the hell would we do that?" a voice called from the crowd. "They sure as hell didn't do a thing to stop it."

"No, they didn't stop it." She motioned for Henry to come forward. "This man Henry Smythe is the new leader, and he's also the one who convinced them to give us the food and water for the past few weeks."

The crowd continued to grumble until a man started pushing through from the back. "Make way, move aside," he called as he urged people aside, some gently and others with a little more force, depending on age and sex.

When he was in front of her, he smiled down at her fondly and winked. "Well, what do you think we should do, Kel?" he asked her in a loud voice.

The crowd quieted, waiting to hear her answer. "I think it might be a good idea. Some things still need to be worked out, but I think it could benefit everyone." She shrugged. "I suppose you lot should decide what you want to do and who you want to speak for you."

The man who had pushed himself to the front, Lukas Hass, turned to the crowd and raised his voice for all to hear. "You heard what the lady said, so what will it be? Work with this Smythe and his folks or not?"

There were a few calls of no, but the majority of the people were swayed by Kelly's willingness to try.

When that died down, Lukas spoke again. "So, it seems most of you want to give it a try. Now, who do you want speaking for you?"

This time there was no dissent; everyone yelled her name.

"Lukas, what the fuck?" Kelly spluttered.

He faced her. "Kel, you have kept this lot active and occupied since we got here. You had me and the boys help you organize shelters and then the distribution of food and water."

She shrugged, "So, what's that got to do with me being the speaker? I'm just a young…"

"Don't you finish that Kelly O'Donnell. You and me both know it's shite, so don't you even think it." He glared at her a moment, then his face broke into a grin. "Besides,

I've known you all your life, and if you *weren't* in charge, you would make life hell for whoever was if you didn't agree with 'em. I'm just cutting out the middleman here."

"Lukas Hass, I never."

A feminine giggle came from the side and Kelly's head snapped to the source. "What the hell, Jenni? You're supposed to be my friend."

"I am, Kel, but you and me both know Lukas is right. Now, why don't you and that hunk of handsome blond bloke," she nodded at Horst, "get this fucking gate open so we can get on with it."

Kelly rolled her eyes in exasperation at her "friends" as she moved aside for Horst to get the gate open. "Watch yer damn mouth, Jenni. I told you before, proper young ladies don't fuckin' talk like that."

"So, let me be sure I understand. You lot are wolves who look like humans?" Kelly asked incredulously.

Henry looked at Horst, holding his hands up in exasperation. "Maybe you can explain it better than me. I seem to be making a right mess of it."

Horst thought for a handful of seconds until his eyes focused on the young woman. "Kelly, we are human. Humans with special abilities that I have recently found out came from aliens meddling with us. We have technology in our bodies that allows us to turn into wolves, but we are still human in our minds even in that form."

"Some are right arses in either form," Henry grimly added. "But they're human just the same."

The three of them were sitting in one of the executive suites discussing how their arrangement was going to work. Horst had suggested that the leaders talk privately first and decide what they wanted from each other.

The first step was to answer Kelly's questions about what she had seen and heard.

"I saw that boy turn into a wolf and kill Liam, then that arsewipe Owen turned into a wolf right after I kicked him." Kelly leaned forward. "How does it work? Does it hurt?"

Horst and Henry both winced, remembering that kick. Henry had already made a mental note not to piss her off. If he did, he would have no trouble remembering to never give her a shot at his package.

"No, it doesn't hurt," Henry answered. "I always thought it was magic, but Horst here says it was aliens."

Horst snorted. "*Ja*, I just found that part out recently. I always knew it was in the blood, just like with the vampires, because of who raised me. The alien thing was a shock, to say the least."

"Wait a fucking minute," Kelly exclaimed. "You're telling me vampires are real, too?"

As if on cue, Akio walked into the room.

Horst nodded at him. "*Ja*, very real."

Kelly turned her head to see what Horst was nodding at, and the memory of Akio with glowing red eyes and fangs came back to her, as well as how he seemed to appear and disappear as he cut down Decklan's followers.

"You, ah, you…" Kelly spluttered.

Akio looked at her and willed his eyes to turn slightly red. "*Hai*, young one. I am what you would call a vampire, but like the Wechselbalg, I am also human."

She looked at the three, her mind turning over the information, which threatened to overwhelm her.

"Do you live off of blood like Dracula?" she asked.

Akio shook his head. "No, I don't need blood to survive anymore."

She latched onto the last word. "Anymore? So, you used to drink human blood?"

"*Hai.*"

"What changed?"

"My Queen, Bethany Anne, gave me back my honor and my life. She fixed what was wrong inside me that required me to take blood."

She hesitated. "So, if I encounter another vampire, I won't have to pull out a cross or something?"

Horst snorted, choking back a laugh.

Akio raised one eyebrow at him. "A cross will not help if you encounter a Forsaken. That is a myth."

Kelly frowned. "Forsaken? What's that?"

"That is what a vampire who refuses to honor Bethany Anne's rule is called. That is the reason I am here: to deal with Forsaken when they harm humans."

"But you came here because of Decklan?" Kelly was lost. "How did you know what he was doing?"

"I have access to technology that allows me to keep watch over parts of the world," Akio informed her. "The Wechselbalg needed to be dealt with. I saw the need and responded."

"I for one will forever be in your debt for that," Henry acknowledged.

"As will I," Horst added.

"This world we live in is hard, and I fear it will be

harder as time passes," Akio stated with certainty. "Humans, especially those with special abilities, need to work together to make it better where they can."

Kelly was thoughtful for a full two minutes before she shook her head, coming to a decision. "How do we make this work?"

Henry answered her. "First we establish trust between our groups. I think we need to bring them together and let them see that we are not so different. We have a town here that is large enough for everyone to live comfortably. There is good land for farming, a river with good water, and the ocean to sustain all of us working together."

"What about our farms and livestock?" Kelly asked. "Assuming Decklan didn't have the animals killed, that is."

Akio contacted Abel over his implant. "Abel, do you have information on the livestock and farms the people were taken from? Are they still there?"

"Some of the structures were destroyed, but the fields and livestock suffered minimum losses," the EI replied.

"Your crops and livestock are still there," Akio told her. "I'm sure that with Henry's help, you can bring most of it here and build a place where all can prosper," he told them.

"Well, Henry, it looks like we have some convincing to do." Kelly looked at the older man. "How are you wolves at herding sheep?"

Henry looked at her, frowning.

Horst started shaking, his face turning red until he burst out laughing. The others watched him as he fought to get himself under control. He took several deep breaths and looked at Kelly, then broke into another round of laughter, unable to form words.

"What the hell's so damn funny, ya big bastard?" she asked angrily.

"Wolves." He gasped as laughter took him again. "Herding sheep," he finally choked out.

Kelly looked at him, her brows drawn into an angry scowl. Then her eyes gleamed, and a smile touched her lips. It started as a small giggle, and soon she was laughing along with Horst.

Henry watched both for a minute before his face cracked and he chuckled. "Well, I guess anything is possible in the world we have now."

Akio stood in the background, watching the two groups as Kelly and Henry addressed them. There were a few who were against the proposal, but the two of them were united as they laid out the plan for them to work together.

When they were done, only a handful from each group remained recalcitrant. They were allowed to go their own way, the Weres with a reminder from Akio that he would be watching if they decided to try to revive the hostilities. After reading each one to ensure they didn't have ill intentions, he allowed them to depart in peace.

CHAPTER TWENTY-THREE

Jilin Province, China

The pain was unbearable. Miko felt like his skin was being pulled off slowly in strips. His throat was raw from hours of screams. He wanted to die and end the pain, but each time he thought he was done, his captor forced his mouth open. A warm metallic liquid was forced down his throat and he would pass out, only to awaken to the burning pain.

The dark figure standing in front of him was in focus. A man was watching him. His face was still indistinguishable, but other features were sharp and clear. His dark hair was pulled away from his face and tied at the back of his head with a cord. It ran down behind his back, but somehow Miko knew it hung to the middle of his back and was as soft as spun silk.

There was another figure this time, this one blurred and unrecognizable. He could just make out the shape from the corner of his eye, but his head was held fast, unable to move. Each time he screamed in agony, the figure would laugh loudly and say something unintelligible to the man standing silently in front of him.

Miko awoke as he had each time he had the dream, covered in blood sweat and ready to fight. It took him a few moments to get his bearings and realize he was safe. It was just the dream again.

He had spent a week working his way through the small towns along some unnamed river. He would run through the night, sometimes one hundred kilometers and others less than twenty. He had no destination in mind other than to reach the sea.

Hunting had been good, and he had found better clothes a few days back in a small village that the humans had abandoned. They were cast-offs, but they were far better than anything he had.

Miko had developed a routine where he would run along the river road, the darkness no obstruction for his vampire sight, stopping briefly outside of the towns when he reached them. He would extend his senses, and if he detected anyone moving about in the open, he would either take them and feed or avoid them and move on to the next town.

His decisions were erratic at best. Some nights he would bypass several towns in a row, and other nights he would stop and feed in each one along the way. He never worried much either way. Taking one or two people and disposing of the bodies was easy enough, and more times than not, the people he found were up to no good anyway and wouldn't be missed.

Every night when it was within three hours of dawn, he would start looking for a safe place to spend the day. He preferred to search out remote spots several kilometers away from the river and its small towns and communities and was always able to find a place that was not occupied.

His refuge for the past few days had been a communal farm. The main house had burned at some time in the past, but there was a grain storage silo that was still intact. It had a steel door he could secure from inside, and there was an elevated walkway high in the top. No light could reach him even if the door was breached, so it made for a perfect hiding place.

The abundance of prey a few kilometers away made him become less inclined to push hard on his journey. He still had no destination firmly picked and was settling into a routine of hunting and drinking his fill until he was almost drunk with power.

The dreams were becoming more vivid each time. There was something familiar about the man he had seen in them, like he knew him very well and should remember who he was. The fact that he was associated with the memory of agonizing pain had to mean something.

The sun had been down for over an hour before he moved from the nest of old cloth grain sacks he had used as a bed. He wasn't hungry, having fed deeply the night before on two bandits who had set an ambush for a young woman as she made her way between two villages.

He smiled as he remembered their fear when he appeared out of the darkness and took them. The fear making their hearts beat fast as he drained first one and then the other, adding a flavor to the blood that was like a well-aged sake as it passed over his palette.

He let the woman pass by unmolested, never knowing

the danger she had been in from the two lifeless bandits he had thrown into a deep ravine.

Tonight I need to move on from this place, he mused as he walked along the gently flowing river with the sounds of the night birds and insects keeping him company.

He had been traveling for several hours, walking along lost in his thoughts. The dream was still on his mind and he was unaware of his surroundings until a voice spoke from behind him.

"What have we here, brothers?" a voice called softly from the darkness.

Miko's head jerked up as he tried to focus on the sound. His eyes darted around, searching for the source.

"A lost Forsaken, it would appear, brother," another voice called from the trees beside the road slightly ahead of him.

His senses extended until he finally recognized the source. Weres. How had he missed hearing them, even in his distracted frame of mind?

"What do you animals want?" he called. "Show yourselves, or suffer for it."

"The Forsaken thinks he is in charge," a third voice laughed from the trees a little to his rear.

"Too bad for him that he is mistaken," a fourth called from behind.

Surrounded with Weres of some flavor—cats if his senses were correct—to the front, rear, and side and the river on the other, Miko snarled a challenge. His fangs extended, and his eyes glowed red.

Miko sensed more than saw the first Were when he leapt at him from a branch above his head. His hand blurred and he caught the tiger by its throat, digging nails that had formed into sharp claws into his furry flesh.

He flung the wounded cat aside as two more landed on him, forcing him to the ground under their weight. Pain exploded through Miko as claws ripped into his shoulders and back. One cat tried to sink its teeth into the back of his neck while the other continued to shred his flesh with its claws.

He pushed off the ground, forcefully shoving his body up as he twisted to the side. The cat's teeth grazed the side of his head instead of getting a purchase on his vulnerable neck. He kicked out, a satisfying shock running up his leg as he connected with one of his attacker's bodies. A loud yowl and the sound of bone breaking were his rewards.

Miko caught the other cat around the neck, pulling its head toward him while he dodged the hind claws trying to eviscerate him. He held two fingers out and spread them wide as he drove them into the surprised eyes of the beast. Pushing them deep into the sockets and then curling them down, Miko grunted with effort as he ripped his fingers free, breaking the orbital bones and shattering the face of the tiger.

He assessed the situation. The first attacker was down in a pool of blood that was spreading out from where his throat had been torn open. The second was gasping for breath on the ground, his chest dented where Miko had kicked him. The third was flopping about in agony, blinded from the damage to his face.

The last was moving toward Miko cautiously after seeing how quickly he had dealt with the first three. Not giving up the hunt, but hesitating to get within reach of what they had assumed was a weak Forsaken.

Miko didn't give him time to think before he blurred forward and kicked one of the injured tigers in the head, shattering his skull as he ran past, then smashed his fist into the shattered bones of the other's face. He didn't slow as he launched himself at the last one, who halted his slow approach, shocked by the speed and ferocity of the vampire.

The cat tried to turn and flee, but his body was unbalanced. Miko slammed into his side, catching him mid-turn. He took the cat to the ground, knocking the breath out of him in the process. When the cat regained his senses and his breath, Miko had him pinned with one hand around his throat.

Miko squeezed, slowly cutting off his oxygen supply as he smiled down at the thrashing tiger maliciously. "You chose poorly, cat. Why did you attack me? Surely you know that no mere Were is a match for a vampire."

The tiger twisted and flopped, trying to free himself from the iron grip that imprisoned him.

Miko loosened his hold enough for the Were to take in one shuddering breath before he tightened it again. "I asked you a question. Why?" He lifted the cat's head and emphasized each word by bouncing his skull against the hard ground. "Why. Did. You. Attack me?" He stopped when the cat's eyes rolled back in his head.

Miko released the cat and stepped out of reach of his claws. When the cat showed signs of coming around, he growled. "Shift back now, or I will take you apart one piece at a time."

One moment a large tiger lay gasping for air in the dirt. The next, a man who appeared to be in his late teens was there instead, blood coming out of his nose and ears.

He continued to gasp, trying to draw in enough oxygen to function. Miko watched him for a moment until he was sure he posed no threat and moved to ensure that the others were dead. When he returned seconds later, the young man was sitting up, his eyes round with fear as he looked at the vampire who had so easily defeated the four of them.

"You will answer my question if you want to live to see the next minute of your miserable existence," Miko told him, his voice laced with menace and his eyes still glowing red with anger. "Why?"

"You have been hunting in Sacred Clan territory." The young man coughed as he drew in more air. "Word of it reached our Master, and he sent us to find you," he managed to croak out in a rush.

Miko sneered. "Sacred Clan? What is that?"

The young man bristled, his eyes glowing yellow.

Miko planted his foot on the Were's chest, cracking his ribs as he forced him back into the dirt. "Respect your betters, beast. You live now only because I allow it."

The fire died in the Were's eyes as he stared into the face of death. "Word that a vampire was killing humans in this area reached our master." His face twisted in a grimace as he wrapped his arms across his body, holding his sides when his healing ribs popped back into place. "You have been careless disposing of your kills, and some of the bodies were discovered. The bite marks on their necks and the lack of blood made it obvious that the deaths were not natural. Our Master sent us to find you before you caused panic and exposed all of us to the humans."

"What do I care about what food thinks?" He sneered. "Are your Clan so weak they can't handle a few humans?"

"You risk bringing the Bitch's assassin here by disobeying the strictures," the young man told him. "He kills without mercy and your carelessness is certain to get noticed. The Master will send others if you continue to bring attention to this area. Get out of Clan territory if you wish to live."

Miko thought for a moment. He could feel his back knitting closed from the wounds, the burning pain was now something he could ignore. Though he could ignore it, he was still hurting and enraged that these Weres had attacked him. "You say this Master will send more of you?"

"Yes, we were only the first," he bragged. "Our numbers are many. The Clan rises."

Miko lunged and caught the battered Were around his neck, pulling him close in the blink of an eye and sinking his claws into the soft tissue of his throat. "I don't know anything about your Clan or them rising, but I do know I don't appreciate being attacked by inferior beings."

He closed his fingers, puncturing the arteries that ran up the neck and twisting his hand as he snatched it away. The Were died in seconds as his blood gushed out of the ragged wound and onto the dusty road.

So, this pompous Were master thinks he can force me to his will, Miko mused. He dropped the body into the dust and surveyed the area. He smiled as he thought of how best to let these cats know what he thought of their daring to threaten or demand anything of him.

He gathered the bodies and arranged them. When he was done, he nodded to himself and smiled. Lying in the middle of the road were four nude bodies. Two laid out head to toe, the heads pointing in the direction he was going. The others had been placed head to head at a forty-five-degree angle to the front body, creating an arrow that pointed the way for the next one who came looking for him.

He had left a message that would be easy even for a stupid Were to understand. He turned back the way he was originally headed, knowing he needed to feed soon to replace the energy that had been used to heal the injuries the cats had caused.

CHAPTER TWENTY-FOUR

Aida, Japan

"Li, I'm not liking this," Shao muttered beside him on the hill they were observing the town of Aida from. They had arrived the night before and decided that Wu and Jin would approach, while they watched for any sign of the missing team.

The townspeople were alert and met Wu and Jin, rifles in hand, before they had made it very far into the town. Li and Shao couldn't hear what was being said, but it was obvious that strangers were not welcome.

"I hope Wu doesn't do anything dumb. You know he has issues when humans challenge him," Shao worried.

"I cautioned him to maintain his calm. It should be an easy in and out," Li assured him.

The speaker for the village gestured sharply with his gun at the two Weres, the other four men backing him stood ready, two muzzles pointed at each of them. Wu motioned with his hands, obviously trying to calm the situation, but the speaker was adamant that they go. Shao sighed in relief when the two of them turned back the way they had come without attacking the townsmen.

"What happened?" Li asked as soon as Wu joined him in the camp they had set up outside of Aida.

Wu scowled. "They wouldn't talk to us beyond ordering us to leave. When I asked why, all the headman would say was Chinese are not welcome there and to leave and not come back."

"That's odd. I know that some in Japan still have hard feelings toward China, but that was a bit extreme."

"There's something else I noticed," Jin told him. "One of the men had a knife sticking in his belt. It looked like the blade was coated with silver."

"Silver!" Li exclaimed. "Are you sure?"

Jin nodded. "I couldn't get close to any of them, but it looked like there was a groove cut into the blade with silver worked into it. Like I said, I can't be sure, but I wanted to mention it."

"Yes, you did well to do so. If the humans are carrying silver-laced weapons, that could pose a problem for us."

Shao had been listening to the report and spoke up. "We need to be cautious if they know to use silver. Those guns could have easily been loaded with it as well. Perhaps we should go to a larger town and see what we can learn. If the UnknownWorld has been revealed here and they already know how to fight us, it will not go well for our plans."

Li nodded. "I agree, Shao. We need to be careful until we know what we're dealing with. We will go to Kobe. It's only about eighty-five kilometers away and has a long-established Chinese presence. We shouldn't stand out there as much as we do in these backwater towns. Once we get there, we can decide how to approach the city and try to get more information. We stay away from humans as much as possible along the way."

The others had broken camp and were ready to travel within five minutes of the order. They set off at a pace that was fast for a human, but not so fast as to attract unwanted attention if they were seen.

Kobe, Japan

"Everyone understands what to do?" Li looked each team member in the eye. Grunts and nods from each indicated understanding. "Remember, take no unnecessary risks, and return here by the end of the day. Good hunting."

They had arrived on the outskirts of Kobe the night before, two days after the encounter with the townsfolk in Aida. Along the way, they'd faded into the brush when they saw humans on the road and had avoided towns along the way. It had been a tough two days spent in human form traveling over terrain that would have been a breeze for a tiger. Li had quashed that idea early on when Wu and Jin had started stripping, reminding them that they were much more likely to be shot as tigers.

Wu grumbled constantly but grudgingly obeyed.

They had found an abandoned garage outside of town. The dust on the small truck inside hadn't been disturbed for years. There was a loft above for storage that provided enough space for all of them to lay out their bedrolls and be comfortable. Li decided to use it for their base while they tried to get more information. There were some people in the area but not enough that they couldn't easily be avoided.

Li set out to find the section of town that he had once heard had a large Chinese presence. He had chosen this area based on it being one of three towns in Japan that had, at least before the world collapsed, a Chinatown area. He hoped that the information still held true and he and his men wouldn't be an oddity.

As he walked along the busy streets, he was amazed at how normal it appeared. Since WWDE, China had lost much of its technology and infrastructure. It was odd to see all the homes and businesses that had electricity and the fact that there were buses and trucks on the roads. Not near as many as before the world went to hell, but more than he had seen in China in over twenty years.

His first stop was a cart selling meat cooked over a small wood-fired grill. The owner, a young Chinese woman, wasn't busy, and he had heard her speaking to the customer in front of him. It was a Mandarin dialect he knew.

"Good morning, how much for a skewer?" he asked in Mandarin as an introduction.

She smiled at him. "Two Yen each, or three for five."

He counted out five yen from the stash he carried. Master Kun had given it to him, along with some small gold coins before he left.

Li took a bite of the meat. "*Mmmm,* this is very good."

The young woman blushed shyly and nodded to him.

He ate the three skewers in silence, watching the woman prepare another order for an elderly man. When she was done and they were alone, he asked, "How long have you been here? You speak with no accent."

"I was born here in Kobe," she replied. "My grandmother refuses to speak Japanese, so we only speak Mandarin in our home. There have been many newcomers here since trade has been restored with China. They like to hear it, and it is good for my business."

Li chuckled. "Ahh, beauty *and* a shrewd business mind. There have been many new people, you say?"

"No, not many but a few new ones each month the past few years. I've never seen you before. Are you a recent arrival?"

Li nodded. "Yes, I came here searching for some family who left China a month ago. I went to the town they were headed to, but I encountered armed men who wouldn't allow me to enter."

She nodded. "I have heard others who have gone out into the countryside voice that same complaint. They say Chinese are not welcome in many places now."

"Did they say why?" Li inquired.

She shrugged. "No, none of the people I talked to knew why they were met with hostility. The people just ran them off. All of them said that they were armed, though."

Li offered her a smile. "Thank you for the information, I will leave you to your business."

"I hope your family is okay. Have a good day," she replied as he turned to leave.

"Li, should we get instruction from the Master with this?" Wu asked after they had met back at the garage. "If we can't go into the towns, there's no way to find out what happened to the others."

The rest of his team had spent the day trying to gather any information, but Li was the only one to have any success.

"I spoke to him earlier when I got back," Li answered. "We will go to Wajima next and see if we can find Sun and Ling. If we have no luck there, we are to go to Onuma."

"In any event, we need to be alert as we travel through the countryside," Shao told them. "If the people in the rural areas have a vendetta against people from China, it wouldn't do to be caught unaware."

All nodded in agreement as they prepared to sleep for the night. It was a long way to Wajima. Hopefully, they would learn more there.

CHAPTER TWENTY-FIVE

The Palace, Tokyo, Japan

"Then she asked him how wolves were at herding sheep." Horst held his side with one hand while he wiped tears from his eyes. "It was the funniest thing I have ever heard."

The room erupted in peals of laughter all around. Asai, Koda, Yuko, and Eve were all gathered at the main snack bar, listening to Horst's recounting of what happened in Australia. He had come to pick Koda up for a trip to the store shortly after they had closed for the day.

Koda snorted, trying to hold back the laughter as Horst continued his story.

"Poor Henry had this look on his face like he couldn't believe what she was asking." He let go with another huge belly laugh. "Then...then she," he gasped, "looked at me confused and asked, 'What the hell's so damn funny?'" He burst into uncontrollable laughter.

As the laughter died down, Asai's face paled. "That had to be a horrifying experience for the people there, to be taken from their homes and locked up, treated like things with no value."

Horst sobered and looked at Koda, concerned he shouldn't have told the story of what had happened where Asai could hear.

Yuko saw the look on his face and spoke. "It was something that should not have been allowed to happen, Asai. The problem with the world now, except for here and a few other places, is that the bad people with power intimidate the good into inaction."

Asai nodded, indicating she understood as Yuko continued, "The end result has the potential to be a positive thing for both groups. The humans can rely on the Weres to protect them from outside danger, and the Weres are reminded that they are still human. Hopefully, the groups will become dependent on each other and realize they are better together."

"As long as Henry and that firebrand Kelly are running things, I don't think that will be a problem. Any of them who give her problems best be wearing protection when they do." Horst grimaced as he put his hand over his groin protectively.

Koda giggled. "I think I want to meet this woman. Anyone who has the guts to do what she did to that ass who was dragging her around is worth meeting."

"Perhaps we can go check on them in a few months," Yuko offered.

Horst nodded. *"Ja,* that would be good. Maybe take them some things to make their lives a little easier."

Eve had a thoughtful look on her face. "Did you get a look at the port facilities there? If the docks are not blocked, we could establish trade with them. That area once produced wheat and barley as well as sheep."

"I didn't look, but that's a long way to go in a ship." Horst's brows knitted as he considered what she had proposed.

Eve grinned. "True, it is around five thousand nautical miles, give or take a few, depending on what the climate shifts did to the routes. I can check that with the satellites with no problem. The fleet of ships being outfitted now will have no problem making the run."

She went on, "They might be capable of running a bit faster than I originally predicted."

Horst cocked his head to one side. "Faster? Just how fast will they go?"

"With the Etheric-powered propulsion and the changes I ordered for the drivetrains and hulls, the cruising speed can exceed fifty-two knots."

Horst paused as he worked out the conversion in his head. His eyes bugged out. That's almost one hundred kilometers per hour." He looked at the ceiling for a moment and then focused back on Eve. "You're telling me those ships will be capable of cruising twelve hundred nautical miles per day."

Eve nodded. "At normal cruising speed, with ease. If we're really in a hurry, it is closer to fifteen hundred. But that speed for a sustained period would cause the bearings in the drivetrain to lose fifteen-point three percent of their serviceable life. Plus, the reinforcement I am having done to the bow of each ship can handle bumps and brushes with flotsam at normal speed. We would have to be absolutely sure of clear sailing lanes at maximum speed."

Horst shook his head as he tried to comprehend the power it took to push one of those huge ships at such speeds. He was still looking lost when Koda took him by the arm and tugged for him to stand up.

"Come on, my mountain of a man. I don't want you to hurt that beautiful brain of yours thinking about that too much. Just accept what Eve says and move on; that's what I have to do—*regularly.*"

Asai snorted as Koda led Horst toward the exit, his free hand moving in front of him as he ran the numbers, mumbling, "unbelievable," over and over.

Yuko chuckled. "You're going to break him if you aren't careful."

Eve snickered. "Oh, he is just getting a small taste now. Wait till I take him down the rabbit hole for real. These ships are older ones being retrofitted for expediency. The ones I am designing will go twice that fast."

Yuko shook her head, wondering how wealthy Eve was going to be when Bethany Anne returned.

And how Bethany Anne was going to react.

CHAPTER TWENTY-SIX

Jilin Province, China

The pain faded as something that tasted metallic was forced into Miko's mouth again. He had lost track of how many times he had been through the cycle of unbearable pain, followed by a period of welcome relief, only to be thrown back into the throes of agony again.

The figure was still there, his face a blur, but other features clearly visible. It was a man with long hair pulled back into a topknot. He wore a loose tunic and pants. The pants legs disappeared into the tops of leather boots that came halfway to the knee. He somehow knew the boots were made of soft, supple leather with a thin sole.

The figure from before was more in focus, and he recognized it was the same one that had appeared earlier. It wore what looked like an old military uniform, the type worn by soldiers on the front lines in the last war. The harsh laughter still followed each time the pain came, causing him to shriek in pain. The same as always, but this time the words were clearer.

"You see what you have done? Because you were so weak, this

human now suffers for it. Our queen has sentenced you to watch your lover as he sings his song of agony to you. Does it bring the same joy to your ears as it does to mine?"

He didn't understand. Who was this person, this queen who could order this? There was no queen here, only a figurehead of an emperor since the war ended.

"Again," the figure beside him ordered.

A third figure, this one completely blurred, came from his left. His foul breath carried the stench of rotten flesh. Then the pain started in his guts and radiated through him again.

Miko came awake ready to fight, his body covered in a sheen of blood sweat. He recognized that it was the dream faster than before. It came to him every time he slept now, and he remembered more details when he awoke—not enough to understand why he was having the dream, but enough to know that he should recognize the people he saw in it.

Miko's mind ran with questions. *Queen? The laughing one mentioned a queen. Who is the person experiencing this? It seems like a memory now more than the dream it was before. Is this a memory from my life as a human?*

He lay on the shoulder of the road where he'd passed out, his mind working to understand the meaning of the dream that had haunted him since the day he awoke in the destroyed hangar. He rolled to the side, and the pull in his back reminded him of his deadly encounter with the Weres earlier.

After the rush from the fight died down, he had felt

lightheaded and weak. His back and shoulder still burned from the injuries he had sustained, and his right leg felt weak. He reached down to the leg and felt a cold wetness on his inner thigh. When he pulled his hand away, it was covered in blood. That was his last conscious memory.

He felt around his inner thigh and discovered a rent in the material just below where his leg joined his body. Probing into the tear revealed that he had a deep cut that was slowly starting to close, but blood still trickled down his leg. He applied pressure to the wound, pressing down to close it and speed the healing.

Even though his ability to heal was better since Heinz had given him the last dose of whatever serum he had concocted, it still took several minutes for the blood to stop and the gash to close. By then, his limbs felt leaden and he swayed unsteadily on his feet. He needed to feed to replenish the blood he had lost soon or risk being caught out in the morning sun.

Miko staggered off with slow, unsteady steps toward the next village along the road. He trudged on through the night, coming upon several small collections of houses, all of them abandoned. He became weaker as the night wore on, his body using everything it had to heal the damage he had taken in the fight.

When the sky began turning the midnight blue that signaled dawn was fast approaching, he gave up the hunt for prey and started searching frantically for a place to avoid the deadly sun when it rose.

He found a hut with a small wooden trapdoor that led to an equally small root cellar below. With the sun minutes from peeking over the horizon, he curled into the earthen hole and pulled the door closed. He wrapped his body in an old tarp he had found in the hut for added protection, hoping he didn't need it but too exhausted to care.

Miko woke slowly, his throat burning with thirst, wishing now that he hadn't left the taunting marker for the Weres to find. He knew he had to find prey soon. If he didn't feed and regain his strength before they found him again, he would be in trouble. Not that he feared Weres, but he didn't relish the idea of having to fight in a weakened state.

No dreams today, he realized. *Either I am more injured than I thought, or they are gone. Either way, I need to feed* now.

He struggled out of the cellar, and after a few moments determined his hiding place was undisturbed. He started walking shakily down the dark road, keeping his senses alert equally for Weres and prey, and hoping the search for prey and the blood his body demanded won out.

He had only been walking for about half an hour when he detected a faint scent on the breeze. His mind was so focused on the simple act of putting one foot in front of the other he was almost on top of a small camp before he registered it.

He froze in the darkness, listening carefully while he focused on the scent. *Human,* his hunger addled mind informed him. He crept closer to the camp, seeing the glow of a carefully laid fire, banked to conceal it from casual observation. A man and a woman huddled together, asleep next to it.

Miko silently entered the camp and looked down at the

couple. The man was curled under a thin blanket and the woman wrapped in an old sleeping bag, both sleeping soundly.

He knelt on the ground behind the man, feeling his fangs extend on their own as the sound of a strong, steady heartbeat called to him. His hands shot out, catching the man by his throat with one hand and covering his mouth with the other. He lifted him off the ground and pulled him away from the fire and the still sleeping woman. She stirred in her sleep but didn't wake as his fangs pierced the soft flesh of the man's neck.

The blood hit his tongue, and he felt his body grow stronger with each pulse that flowed down his throat. A short time later, he pulled away from the still body held in his arms. Lowering it to the ground softly so as to not disturb the sleeping woman, he moved in on her. It was only a matter of seconds until he had her in his embrace, taking the blood and energy from her that he needed to survive.

Kaiyuan, China

Miko traveled for hours after he had drunk his fill from the unlucky couple. He made no attempt to hide the bodies or to conceal how they had died. He wanted the Weres to have no doubt that he didn't fear them in case they'd missed the message from the night before.

He smiled as he entered another town a little after midnight. This one was bigger and in better shape than any of the places he had been in since he'd left Yushu. The sign said he was in Kaiyuan. Miko thought for a moment and realized he had crossed into Liaoning Province at some point.

There was a pungent odor of smoke coming from fish-oil lamps fixed to the old power poles that ran through the center of the town. One building was well-lit, and music drifted out of the open door and windows. It had once housed government functionaries, judging by the bare concrete walls and small windows that comprised it, but now it seemed to be a tavern.

Miko took stock of his bloodstained and tattered clothing. The days on the road, as well as the fight with the Weres, had made him look like a casualty of war. He stepped between two dark houses into an area that had a small garden plot, and more importantly, a line with clothes hanging on it to dry.

He chose a shirt and trousers from the line that appeared to be close to his size and stripped off his ragged clothes. The fit of the shirt was a little snug, but the pants were several sizes too big. He snapped the cord that held the clothes, wrapping the loose end around his waist to measure and broke it again when he had the proper length.

After tying the makeshift belt around his waist and rolling the cuffs up on the pants, he looked presentable enough not to cause others to notice. He left his rags on the ground beside the clothes that had dropped when he broke the line and made his way back to the well-lit street.

He started toward the tavern and froze as a familiar scent came to him on an errant breeze.

Weres!

Miko faded into the shadows across from the tavern when two men exited.

"I tell you, Wun, I smelled a vampire."

The other man snorted. "You are jumping at shadows, Han. Master Kun has over one hundred warriors out looking for that bloodsucker since those drained bodies were left in the open. That vampire is on the run or dead by now."

"I tell you, I smelled him!" Han insisted. "There was a smell of rot in the air and nothing to account for it. Our orders warned us to be wary of such things because they meant a vampire was near."

Both Weres were walking away from the tavern with their backs to Miko and the breeze in their faces as they talked. He stuck to the shadows and followed, curious if there were more and looking forward to sending these Sacred Clan idiots another pointed message. *Don't mess with the vampire.*

The Weres continued to argue as they entered a small house on the outskirts of the town. Just as the door was closing, the wind shifted suddenly, blowing from his back directly toward the house.

Han froze. "Wun, He's here!"

The sound of cloth tearing followed by the growl of a big cat was the response from inside the house. In seconds Han shifted as well, and two orange and black striped tigers stood in the center of the road facing Miko.

"Your Master is a simpleton," Miko told them by way of an introduction. "To think Weres can challenge a vampire is the height of idiocy. I suppose I will need to kill more of you before he understands."

The cats snarled as they stalked toward him. Miko relaxed into a ready stance, arms by his sides with his knees slightly bent. When they were almost close enough to pounce, he rushed forward, a cloud of dust rising from under his feet, and butted his shoulder into the one on the right.

The Were screamed in pain as Miko slammed into him. The sound of bones breaking as the cat was knocked to the ground was Miko's reward. The other leapt at him and he twisted to the side, barely avoiding the razor-sharp claws that whizzed past his head. He reversed direction and jumped, easily clearing the tiger and landing behind him.

The tiger spun to face him as Miko lashed out with his foot, catching him under his chin and closing the jaws with an audible *snap*. The cat's head went back from the force of the kick and Miko moved in, his hands curled into claws.

He swiped the dazed cat across his eyes, blinding him before his body could heal the damage the kick had caused. The cat let out a scream of rage and pain. It was the last sound he ever made. Miko swiped his clawed hand across his throat, almost decapitating him.

The tiger collapsed to the ground, thrashing as his damaged body struggled to heal. It was too much too soon, and in seconds, the tiger stopped moving and let out a shuddering breath as he died.

Miko turned to see the one he had tackled hobbling in the opposite direction, getting faster with each step as his broken bones knitted together. He rushed forward, catching the tiger with ease, and delivered a hard kick to his back leg, snapping the bone like dry kindling.

The tiger went down when his leg stopped working, rolling on his injured side as he fought to catch himself.

Miko was on him in an instant, and soon the tiger's blood stained the dusty road under his still body.

Miko stopped and listened for sounds that signaled other Weres were near. Hearing nothing, he set about the task of leaving another message for the Clan.

Minutes later, Miko walked out of town, chucking softly. Both Weres had shifted back to human form at their deaths, and there were now two nude bodies side by side in the center of the road, each holding the other's severed head in his lap.

CHAPTER TWENTY-SEVEN

TQB Base, Tokyo, Japan

Akio bid Horst goodbye as he dropped him off at the complex that would soon be the location of their new base. They had been at the dockyard, where Horst checked on the progress of the ships Eve was having refitted. The work was going well, and Horst was ready to hire a captain for the first one. He had asked Akio to be there when he interviewed the man he had in mind, the captain who had brought Dieter over from Russia.

Eve had located his ship and determined it would be a week before he was back in Japan, and Horst had decided to walk the area where the Japanese government had given them land for a new base. The ship was a few weeks from completion, so he wanted to get a feel for where they would build the base he and Eve had drawn up.

"Abel, bring the Pod down in the inner courtyard," Akio ordered.

Akio felt the craft shift as it started to descend. As soon

as the hatch opened, he was out of it. "Abel, please place the Pod back in orbit above the base."

"Pod away," Abel intoned.

Akio went to the command center and pulled up the video feeds from China. It had become an obsession for him over the past few weeks.

"Akio, you know that I have programmed facial recognition algorithms into the system. Why do you continue to physically view the video?"

"It seems to be the proper thing to do. Kenjii is where he is now because of my actions. I owe it to him."

Abel huffed. "'That is illogical,' is the phrase Eve would use in this instance."

Akio pursed his lips as he considered trying to explain it to the EI. After a few seconds, he reached the conclusion that he couldn't explain the reasoning to him. "You are correct. It *is* illogical. Sometimes humans behave illogically."

Akio took a deep breath and settled into the chair. Illogical or not, he still felt the need, no the *duty*, to do everything he could to locate Kenjii.

The video started to stream across the monitor as soon as he was seated. He watched for several minutes, seeing humans, animals, and in most cases a whole lot of nothing as he sped through the feed at four times the speed a human could.

He allowed his mind to drift while keeping one eye on the feed.

Chiba, Japan, 1956

Kenjii led Akio down darkened alleys and streets with little to no light, avoiding the crowded, well-lit shopping areas with their multitudes of shoppers and vendors who hawked their wares from stalls and carts set up along the streets.

He stopped at a doorway between an apothecary and a small grocery store and slipped a key into the lock. The door opened to a narrow set of stairs leading up. Kenjii gestured to them. "I live here, above my father's store."

Akio hesitated, warily looking up the darkened stairway, unsure about proceeding.

"I live alone," Kenjii offered. "My father has a home farther inland where he and my sister live."

Akio nodded, still not sure why he hadn't killed this confusing man as was required, and even more baffled by his choice to accompany him home. He stepped through the door, which closed and locked behind him. Kenjii moved around him, their bodies touching briefly, and Akio shuddered as heat coursed through him from the momentary connection.

He followed Kenjii up the darkened stairs that opened into a neatly furnished open area with a couch against one wall and a chair with a small lamp on the table beside it. There was a small kitchen with a stove and icebox to the side and a closed door on the rear wall.

"Make yourself comfortable. It will only take a moment for me to put the water on to boil," Kenjii invited as he moved to the kitchen. In a few moments, he had a kettle on the stove and returned to the living area.

Akio had remained at the top of the stairs, unsure of what to do next. Kenjii reached out tentatively and grasped his hand lightly, using the gentle pressure to urge him fully into the room and over to the couch while looking deep into his eyes. Once Akio sat stiffly on one end, Kenjii settled on the other, not talking but not looking away.

Finally, the younger man spoke. "Akio, are you all right? It's safe here, so you can relax."

Akio leaned back into the cushions, not relaxing but not as rigid as before. His eyes still darted warily as he cataloged every small sound that reached them from the street below. He flinched as the kettle whistled, signaling that the water was ready.

Kenjii stood and prepared two steaming cups of tea. When he finished, he returned and held both out to Akio, allowing him to choose.

Akio looked at the delicate porcelain with cherry blossoms hand-painted on them in fine detail. He remembered what was expected, but his body refused to move for a moment. He shook his head slightly and forced his hands to lift until his fingers met the glazed sides.

Kenjii smiled at him, his eyes sparkling in the light coming from the kitchen. "You act as though you haven't done this in a while," he observed as he resumed his seat on the couch, cup cradled in his hands.

Akio looked up from his tea. "It has been many years since anyone offered me hospitality. Most would run screaming into the night from a monster such as I."

"That would be their loss," Kenjii replied. "I see an attractive man before me, not the monster you describe."

Akio snorted, wondering if perhaps the man suffered from some mental affliction that impaired his good sense. "Looks can be deceiving, young one. I have been a monster for more years than your father's father has lived," he stated quietly.

Kenjii's eyes never wavered from his face. "That you see yourself as such is surely a travesty. I assure you that no matter *what you have done in the past, I saw a good man in your actions tonight, not a monster."*

Akio sipped, tasting the mix of tannin and spices as the hot tea slid across his tongue. It was the first thing he'd tasted—other than blood—since that night so many years ago when he'd looked at the lifeless body in his arms and realized what a monster he'd become.

They sipped their tea in silence, looking at the other while lost in thought. Once finished, Kenjii took the empty cups to the kitchen and busied himself cleaning the small mess he'd made while preparing the tea. Soon, everything had been returned to its proper place. He once again settled on the couch. "Did you like the tea?"

"Hai. It has been many years since I enjoyed that pleasure."

"I would gladly share it with you whenever you like. You intrigue me. I wish to know you better," Kenjii whispered.

Akio hesitated. "That...would be dangerous for both of us. Allowing a human to know of our existence is a crime."

Kenjii sighed, unsure of what to say. "That leads us back to the question I asked earlier. Do I live or die?"

Akio suddenly stood, feeling trapped, and paced back and forth in the small area like a caged animal. The war in his mind raged. He knew what was required. He also knew he couldn't do it.

He made the decision, knowing they'd both pay with their lives if he was wrong. Somehow, he knew with certainty that this human wouldn't betray him. "You must never speak of me to anyone. Do not seek me out, or I will have no choice but to take your life if you do. Never let anyone know what you saw tonight. Do you understand?" His voice was raw with emotion as he used what little compulsion he had to make it an order.

"Hai. I would never betray you. I will do as you say and not seek you out, hard though it will be," Kenjii vowed, unaffected by Akio's minor compulsion powers.

Akio stepped toward the opening to the stairs but stopped when Kenjii called to him.

"Here, take this." Kenjii held out his hand. "Lock the door when you go, but know you're welcome here whenever you choose."

Akio reached out, shocked when the young man handed him the brass key that had opened the door below. He took it, and in seconds was back on the street. He locked the door behind him and stared at the key in his hand, not sure what he should do. After a moment's hesitation, he secured it in one of the many small pockets in his clothes that, in his past life, had held weapons and other items a warrior needed. It now held the literal key to the mystery named Kenjii.

He hurried away, not looking back. It would soon be light, and he would be missed if he failed to report in with the results of his mission. He was trusted and had the freedom to hunt when he wasn't on duty, but all were required to be back in Kamiko's dwelling when the sun rose unless they had been given an assignment that required them to be away longer than one night.

As he ran toward home, he was surprised to feel a rush of excitement, despite breaking a long-established rule. It was another feeling he hadn't experienced since the day he became a vampire.

CHAPTER TWENTY-EIGHT

Ning Jing Temple, Dabie Mountains, China

"Master Cui?" Scout Commander Yimu called down the corridor. "A moment of your time, please?"

Cui finished giving his instructions for the day's training to his team and sent them on to the training area. "What can I do for you?"

Yimu approached, his body stiff and his face flushed. "One of my scouts has reported in from Yushu." He growled. "The team that was dispatched to deal with the Forsaken failed. The scout found them this morning about twelve kilometers southwest of the town. They are all dead."

Cui's lips thinned into a tight line as his eyes glowed yellow. "How did they die?"

"Their throats were torn out, and all had suffered trauma to their bodies before they were killed." Yimu took a deep breath, his fists clenched at his side. "They were found in the middle of the highway. The bodies had been arranged to leave a message."

"What do you mean?" Cui demanded. "What message?"

"They were laid out in the form of an arrow pointing away from the town," Yimu spat.

Cui's face turned red, and his voice dropped several octaves. "This Forsaken dares to taunt us? To disrespect us and desecrate our dead?"

He paused, getting his anger in check before he shifted out of rage. "Is there more?" he asked through clenched teeth.

Yimu nodded tersely. "Yes, the scout followed the scent and found a blood trail leading away from the bodies in the direction indicated."

"Did he find the Forsaken?" Cui demanded.

"No, his radio malfunctioned. He ran to the communications relay base outside of Changchun to report. It took him four hours to make the journey."

Cui nodded, not trusting himself to speak. Yimu was a competent commander, and it wasn't his fault that they were forced to use antique equipment that was fickle at best.

"Thank you, Yimu. I will report this to the Grand Master. Make yourself available should he wish to speak to you," Cui instructed after he finished the screaming tirade that was playing in his mind.

He left to find the Master, wishing for the thousandth time that he could get his claws on that wretch General Li and flay his skin one centimeter at a time.

"Grand Master," Cui called through the closed curtain to Master Kun's private chambers.

"Enter, Cui," Kun called from inside.

Cui entered the room and prostrated himself before his master. Kun did not require this level of deference from him, but he knew that the news he brought would not be well received.

Kun sat up straighter on his cushion, one eyebrow raised. "Cui, I feel that you bring bad news. Stand up and tell me what it is," Kun commanded.

"Master, the strike team sent after the Forsaken has been found dead." Cui paused, unsure of how Kun would react to the next bit.

Kun waved his hand in a circular motion. "Let's have it. What is it you don't want to tell me?"

"Their bodies were left in the middle of a road in the shape of an arrow. He used our people's bodies to point us in the direction where he was going to be."

"Oh, he did, did he?" Kun's grin was feral. "It would be bad manners not to follow his lead. Assemble your students; they will take part in this hunt. I expect you to bring that Forsaken wretch to me. In small pieces if you must, but I want him brought here. The Clan accepts insult from no man or vampire, and it is time this one learns that."

Cui looked on in shock that the Master had taken the news so well. He had a reputation that dated back to his time in the People's Liberation Army for taking his ire out on the messenger who brought bad news.

Perhaps he is changing and seeing the error of his ways, Cui mused as he was backing out to carry out the Master's command.

"Cui," Kun called softly.

"Yes, Master?"

"Your team is to carry out the kill. Inform the students that their job is to observe and report. They are to contact your team for the kill." His voice grew rough as his hands changed into paws tipped with sharp claws. His face sprouted orange hair, and the teeth in his mouth lengthened to sharp-tipped fangs. "Do not fail me in this. It will be your last failure if you do."

Cui swallowed hard, his mouth going dry. "I will not fail, Master."

"Send someone for me once you have them assembled. I will speak to them before they depart."

"Yes, Master," Cui mumbled as he quickly backed from the room.

"We are to make the kill?" Pan Xun bounced on the balls of his feet in excitement. "Li's team is the only one in recent history that has taken down a bloodsucker. This is indeed a great honor."

Yi shook his head. "Idiot, the Grand Master does not do this to honor us. It happened on our watch. He is reminding us of our responsibility in the event we fail."

Cui raised his hands to head off the confrontation that was brewing. "Pan, Yi, we will conserve our energy until we fight the Forsaken. After that, kill each other if you want, but not before I can tell the Grand Master that we have carried out our duty and the Forsaken is dead."

Ren nodded in agreement. "We must remain united in this. The strike team members were young, but they had been on many missions before. We should not take this lightly. That this vampire could kill a team and walk away from the fight himself tells me this is a strong one. I imagine he will not die easily."

"Ren speaks the truth," Cui offered. "Let's give the teams their assignments and get out of here before the Master changes his mind. You know he is not happy when things don't go as planned, and I for one don't want to be sent out alone to kill this thing."

The others nodded agreement, each well aware of how the Grand Master's temper worked.

Kun paced the length of the raised platform as he surveyed the students on parade in front of him. He went first to one end and then the other, making eye contact with different students as he paced back to the center before addressing the group.

"The Clan has suffered a grave insult at the hands of a rogue Forsaken. He has dared to hunt in our territory. He has left bodies where the humans can find them, and he has murdered loyal members of the Clan." He paused for a moment, letting the tension build. "As if these crimes were not enough, he defiled the bodies of our brothers. He used them to create a macabre message for any who found them. He has pointed the way forward, and it is now up to you to follow the path set out and find this vampire, this leech, this vile creature. Find him, report your location, and stand by to assist Master Cui's team as they express mine and the Clan's displeasure at the path he has chosen."

The crowd erupted in cheers, punctuated by snarls and growls as Kun finished.

"Follow your leaders," Kun intoned. "Perform your duties to the Clan. The Clan shall rise!"

"*The Clan rises!*"

The response from the crowd was loud enough to leave Kun's ears ringing for several minutes afterward. He made his way out of the training area and back to his rooms while Cui and Zhi checked that each team had a functional radio issued by Ren and Pan, as well as a map to the location they were to go.

Once the check was complete, the team slipped into the bright sunlight outside the temple.

"Have you decided where we should base ourselves for a rapid response once the vampire is found?" Ren inquired.

"Yes, we need to be in front of him to head him off. We will go north of Beijing. There is a base radio station there where we can monitor the progress of the hunt. We can work from there when he is spotted."

The others nodded in agreement, each shouldering a pack that was designed to be worn in whatever form they were in. They set off at a ground-eating run and were soon out of the mountains and running through fallow fields that had once fed the nation. Now those once-fertile fields were covered in weeds and the occasional tree.

Henan Province, China

Their progress was not as fast as Cui wanted. The road was covered in many places, forcing them to go slowly as they picked their way through the underbrush.

"Are we there yet?" Ren mumbled as he had each time they stopped for a break, eliciting a round of laughter from the others.

Cui shook his head, appreciating the attempt at levity for what it was. "At our current pace, we should be there by the day after tomorrow. Even with the delays, we are able to cover more ground in a day than the Forsaken can during the night."

"The sooner, the better," Pan grumbled as he mashed a biting fly on his forehead into paste. "These flies are as bad as a damned vampire."

Cui motioned and they shouldered their burdens and set out again, maintaining a good pace but not as fast as they had before. The road conditions and insects were sapping their energy, making an already long journey that much worse.

CHAPTER TWENTY-NINE

TQB Base, Tokyo, Japan

Akio roused from his reverie when the video feed stopped. He had been sitting in the command center for several hours and had gone through all the feeds he felt were pertinent to him.

He was becoming frustrated by the lack of success. China was a big place, but he thought that he would have picked Kenjii up on at least one of the drones.

He closed his eyes and allowed his mind to drift off to a time he had spent many years trying to forget. Now that he was actively searching for him, he was, remarkably enough, finding comfort in the memories where there was none before. One corner of his mouth quirked up as he thought back to his next trip to Chiba.

Chiba, Japan, November 1956

It had been three months since Akio's last visit to Chiba, where he had met the human who had confused him so. He had steeled his mind as he had learned to do centuries earlier to keep anyone from picking up his thoughts of that night. That he was second in command of Kamiko's personal guards kept most from attempting it, anyway. Kamiko and her pets Isamu and Ogawa were the only ones he feared would try. He maintained a blank expression and mental presence whenever he was around any of them, as he had for many years with Kamiko's mother and now her.

Isamu and Ogawa were recent additions, but both had limited mental abilities. Although not as strong as their creator, they did have the ability to pick up errant thoughts if someone did not guard their mind around them.

They didn't, however, have the experience to block their minds, so anyone with a weak ability could pick up *their* thoughts.

Akio had discovered that they both had twisted desires that he didn't care to see. Their jobs, in addition to being Kamiko's contacts with her outer ventures, were to act as her punishers. Both reveled in the task and enjoyed their new status, since many she deemed needed punishing were from the UnknownWorld and were much more resilient than the humans on whom they'd formerly practiced their trade.

Their most prevalent thoughts involved inflicting pain on the helpless—not because it was demanded by the queen, but because they both got perverse gratification from the act.

Akio had been sent back to Chiba to see the same criminal as before. It had only taken the man a few months to forget the previous warning. This time, Akio was to deliver a reprimand.

He stood in a darkened doorway behind the rundown warehouse that housed the operations in Chiba. He had arrived unannounced a few hours after dark and found a place to observe in secret.

Voices came to him through a broken window above his location.

"Arima, are you sure this is smart? I don't think this is a good move right now."

"Sen, I've told you that she won't miss a shipment here and there. We can blame it on the other factions in the city and let them suffer for our gain." He chuckled.

"I don't know," he answered slowly. "It's only been a few months since that scary bastard was here. I don't want him coming back."

"Are you afraid, Sen?" Arima chided. "Should I bring another in your place and let you hide behind the whores in the brothel?"

Sen bristled. "I'm simply recommending caution, Arima. That's my job, along with keeping the operations running smoothly. We have a good thing here. The Yakuza leave us alone, and we have more than we'll ever need. I don't want to risk losing it all for a small payday when we already make so much more than that over the year."

Arima laughed. "I know what you're doing, but you can't talk me out of it. Trust me on this. She'll never miss it."

Akio's lips turned up at the corners in a not-quite-smile as he heard the crime boss admit to what had already sealed his fate. Not that it mattered—he was a dead man when Akio received his orders. Kamiko didn't mind if the humans skimmed a little here and there, but she wouldn't tolerate anyone who had the gall to lie to her when questioned. That he had admitted trying to use her to attack other criminal enterprises made it worse, especially since the criminals he had recently blamed were hers as well.

Akio stepped out of the darkened doorway and leaped to catch the lip of the window frame. He pulled himself up and held himself steady while he reached into a concealed pocket and removed a small bottle. He caught the cap in his teeth and pulled out the stopper. The scent of oil filled his nose before he moved it away.

He carefully poured the oil onto the hinges that allowed the windows to swing out. Satisfied, he reached through a missing pane and poured the remainder of the oil on the rust-coated latch. He silently released it and slowly opened the window with careful motions. It rotated out silently on the freshly oiled hinges. That done, he climbed into the warehouse and stopped to listen.

Once assured that no one had heard him, Akio made his way to a set of wooden stairs that ran down the wall to the floor below. He unsheathed his katana when he came to the door at the bottom that led into the office, gripping it lightly as he prepared to deliver the reprimand.

A shadow appeared in the grime-covered glass of the door and stopped.

"Be careful, Arima. I don't like it, but you're the boss, and I respect that. I only hope it doesn't come back to bite you in the ass." The knob rattled as he opened the door.

Sen started through the door while still looking at Arima and jerked back when he caught a motion in front of him. His eyes shot open in shock that turned to fear when he saw Akio.

"Oh, shit," he muttered as he backpedaled into the office, only stopping when he bumped into the desk. He hit it with enough force to move it back a couple of inches.

"What the hell, Sen?" Arima yelled. "Watch what you're doing!"

Sen didn't answer, transfixed by the light gleaming off the exposed blade.

Akio stepped forward and pointed to the side with his katana.

Sen gulped, his face ashen as he sidestepped away from the desk.

Arima's eyes were focused on Sen. He didn't notice Akio until the tip of his sword landed on the desk directly in front of him. Arima tried to push back, but his chair was already against the wall. He surged to his feet and stammered a greeting.

"*Konichiwa*, Akio-*san*. To what do we owe the honor of your..." His words cut off in a gurgle as the sword flashed from resting on the desk to extended out to the side at shoulder level, pointed at Sen.

A thin red line appeared on Arima's throat, followed by a rush of blood as the wound opened, covering Arima's front in seconds and pulsing across the small space. His body flopped back into the chair, his eyes wide as he bled out.

Akio turned his head and looked down the blade at Sen. "That one sought to incite dissention within the organization to promote personal gain. Do better, or I will return for you." He delivered the threat in a low voice, one that

Sen later swore sounded like Death himself pronouncing judgment.

Sen started to answer, but before he could form the words, Akio disappeared. One moment, he'd stood there like a vengeful *oni*. The next, he was gone. Sen wiped his face, surprised to see his hand covered in blood as he pulled it away. He was still there an hour later when one of his men came to check on him because he'd been gone so long.

Akio moved at vampire speed across the floor and up the steps leading to the window. He hung on the frame long enough to close and secure it before he silently dropped to the street below. He was a block away by the time Sen discovered the blood on his face.

While moving, he pulled a soft cloth from his pocket and wiped off the small amount of blood clinging to his katana before sliding the blade into the sheath on his back. He slowed to a walk and pulled a dark cloak over his shoulders to conceal it. He didn't fear anyone who might see him, but it was best not to attract undue attention.

He already knew from previous experience that the superstitious among the criminals would come up with many different theories about Arima's death, each one more fantastic than the other. It served his purpose for them to think he was some kind of *Oni*, a demon from Japanese lore. It made them more cautious about how they conducted their business, and in turn, caused less disruption to Kamiko's criminal enterprises. It was a method that had worked well for him for many years.

He had stayed away from Chiba since the night he had met Kenjii, and had suppressed the memory to keep others from learning about his transgression of allowing a human to know of the UnknownWorld.

Although he had worked to push the memory away, he still experienced moments when heat surged through his body, remembering the brief touch and how warm Kenjii's hand felt in his. Those feelings came at odd times, so he was careful to employ every trick he had ever learned to conceal them. This resulted in him spending more time meditating and working out, two of the normal activities that allowed him to focus on something other than the need to actively shield his mind.

Walking through the streets of Chiba, he soon reached the mouth of a familiar alley. He looked down to the end, half-expecting to see figures standing there, but there was only rotting trash this time. His hand strayed to the hidden pocket in his tunic and caressed the small, hard piece of brass secured inside it.

He started walking again, his mind bringing up memories of Kenjii as his feet carried him through the darkened streets and alleys. He stopped after a short time to get his bearings and recognized which street he was on. His glance swung to the store and apothecary in front of him, his fingers still touching the key. Between the businesses was the door it unlocked.

He stepped into a darkened entryway and looked above the store, where a light shone from a window. It winked out as he watched. He was home. Akio stayed in the shadows, watching and fighting the urge to go to the man. His conscious mind told him it was a bad idea, but his subconscious and his body both pushed him to go.

After a half-hour of fighting the internal battle, his

conscious mind conceded defeat, and he slowly walked to the door. The key went into the lock and turned. A soft *snick* signaled that it had accomplished its task. Akio leaned and rested his head against the door's rough wood for a moment before he stepped back and pulled it open.

The door swung out silently on well-oiled hinges. He stepped inside, closing and locking it behind him. He moved up the stairs, a silent shadow in the night, and stopped when barely inside the dark living room.

The scent he recognized as Kenjii's permeated the air and caused the warmth he had felt before to run through him like fire in his veins. He looked around the darkened area, seeing no sign of the man, but a soft noise from behind the closed door at the end of the room caught his attention.

He made his way to the door on silent feet but froze as he heard muted footsteps from the other side. The door-knob rattled as it turned, then the door swung open and Kenjii stood there, his lean body sparkling with drops of water. He wore only a pair of short pants, and vigorously rubbed a towel over his wet hair with one hand.

He looked up when Akio moved, and his eyes flew open in surprise. He stepped back with a small yelp and stumbled as his foot caught on a loose rug. He was falling to the floor when strong arms went under his lower back and shoulders and he stopped abruptly.

He focused on who held him. "Akio? You nearly scared me to death!" he went on in a rush. "Is everything all right? Your eyes. They are red."

Akio stood, effortlessly pulling Kenjii to his feet as he did. He released him, his arms tingling and the fire rushing through his blood hotter than before. "I should not have come here." He stepped back and turned to leave, then froze when Kenjii reached out and caught his arm in a light grip.

"No, please don't go," Kenjii pleaded. "I have prayed to the ancestors that you were not a dream, that I would see you again. I didn't speak of you to anyone or try to find you, but I begged them to send you back."

He looked down at his hand, still holding Akio's arm. "Forgive me, I shouldn't be so forward. My apologies," he stammered as he let go.

As Kenjii pulled his hand away, a sense of loss surged through Akio, and he felt longing deep inside. Both feelings had become so foreign to him over the past centuries that it took him a few beats to recognize them for what they were. He forced his body to relax and his eyes to lose the red glow that came out when he saw Kenjii fall.

He tentatively stretched out one hand and felt the internal fire ignite again when Kenjii reached out and took it in his, smiling that bright smile which haunted Akio's visions during the times he couldn't make the memories stop.

CHAPTER THIRTY

Wajima, Japan

Li Song stood on a hill overlooking what was left of the city of Wajima on the northern coast of Japan. The earthquakes and tsunamis had left their marks on what was once a thriving coastal city. Now it was little more than a small fishing village made up of houses cobbled together from the debris that the natural disasters had left.

Shao lay in the shade of a tree while they waited for Jin and Wu to return from scouting. It had taken them four days to make the journey from Kobe to Wajima. It was only around four hundred kilometers by the fastest route, but it had taken much longer for the team, given the need to avoid built-up areas and possibly hostile people armed with silver weapons.

A faint rustling below his lookout alerted him that someone was coming. A few moments later, Wu poked his head through the brush and made his way to where Li was waiting.

Li nodded toward the town. "What did you find?"

Wu shrugged. "Most of the men are out fishing today. There were a few women and elders about, but the ones who saw me darted inside and locked their doors before I could speak to them."

Li shook his head in disgust. Not only had he failed to locate the missing teams, but they also couldn't find anyone willing to talk to them. He was not looking forward to his next report to Master Peng if he didn't have any information on the teams.

Jin returned three hours later, carrying a brown bottle. He had a smile on his face.

"What are you so damn happy about?" Wu grumbled from where he had been napping against a tree.

Li kicked the bottom of Wu's boot as he went by. "Leave him alone, Wu."

He met Jin where they had stashed their packs in the bushes earlier. "Well, did you get anything useful, or did you spend the afternoon drinking sake? Not that it does anything to you anyway."

Jin pulled a canteen out of his pack and took a swallow. He swished it around his mouth and spat it on the ground. "This is without a doubt the worst homemade hooch I have ever tasted. I think paint thinner would taste better."

Shao rolled his eyes. "So why are you drinking it?"

"Because, my friend, it was the only way I could get anyone to talk to me," Jin replied.

"Do you have the information?" Li demanded.

All signs of levity drained from Jin's face. "I do," he confirmed. "You and the Grand Master are not going to like it. According to the old man I spoke to, Sun and Ling were here. They had practically taken over the town, if he can be believed. 'Tinpot tyrants' was the description he used."

Li reached for Jin, but he darted away before he caught his arm. "Don't shoot the messenger. My erstwhile friend claims he saw it all. He was sleeping off the night before under a tarp when a black box dropped out of the morning sky directly in front of him."

"A box fell from the sky?" Wu scoffed. "How much of that sake did you drink?"

"Believe me, very little," Jin assured him with a frown. "As I was saying, a box fell from the sky, but it stopped inches above the ground, and a man dressed in all black and carrying a sword got out."

"A sword?" Li pursed his lips. "You expect us to believe that crap?"

"That's not the important or even the most unbelievable part," Jin continued. "This man supposedly walked up to Sun and cut his head off without a word. Then, according to my witness, Ling 'turned into a big-assed tiger' and suffered the same fate."

Wu laughed. "I want some of whatever he was drinking."

Jin scowled at him. "Now comes the part that made me believe what he was telling me, drunk or not. The man with the sword was dressed all in black, and he had a patch on his shoulder. He described it as having a red background with a skull on it."

Li's eyes widened. "A Queen's Bitch? He's claiming that a Queen's Bitch flew into town, killed two Weres, and just left them? They all departed years ago in that damned spaceship."

"Yes, he claims it was a Queen's Bitch," Jin confirmed. "He said he had a picture of that one in a calendar back before WWDE. Says his name is Akio, and he was the only Japanese Bitch. According to the old man, he was quite the celebrity here in Japan."

Wu joined them from his spot against the tree. "What happened to the bodies?"

"This is where it gets strange. The old drunk says two government trucks loaded with soldiers showed up about fifteen minutes later. This Akio talked to the officer in charge while the troops cleaned up everything. They shook hands, and everyone left."

Li's mouth opened and closed several times before he was able to form the words. "The Japanese government is working openly with a vampire. Not just any vampire, but a Queen's Bitch, and they know about the UnknownWorld?"

"Looks that way," Jin agreed.

"Shao, hand me the phone, " Li ordered. "Master Peng must have this information immediately."

"What do we do now, Li?" Wu was looking around as if he expected to be attacked at any minute. "Everything I remember about those guys who were the Bitches is that they are like a force of nature. How do we fight someone like that?"

"With superior intelligence and excessive firepower," Li answered as he pressed the button on the satellite phone, dreading how Kun would react and what reprisal he could expect for delivering the news.

CHAPTER THIRTY-ONE

The Palace, Tokyo, Japan

Horst waved his hand at the data on the screen in front of him. "Eve, how will the ships keep from being torn apart at those speeds?"

"First, because they are large and they have the new reinforced bows. Second, because they won't run at those speeds except when the weather and other conditions are optimal."

Horst wasn't convinced. "Still, there have been a lot of changes since WWDE. What happens if you run aground on an uncharted atoll or the top of a sea volcano that wasn't on the old charts?"

"We would not allow full-speed operation unless we were sure the routes were clear," she assured him. "I have already verified that the way is open to Vladivostok, Shanghai, and Kume. The Japanese Navy has information on other sea lanes that I can obtain easily enough too."

Horst shook his head as he looked over the numbers again. "This is phenomenal. These ships will cut days off the time it takes to move people and goods. I believe we will have more business than we can handle once word gets out."

"My calculations using the current shipping data shows that we can easily handle forty percent of the current business at lower rates than the shippers are paying and still turn a substantial profit." Eve pulled up another screen, this one with a picture of a ship design that was radically different from the ones they were currently using.

"What's this?" Horst inquired.

Eve grinned up at him. "The next generation of Etheric-powered cargo ships. This one doesn't have the total capacity of the four that are being currently outfitted, but they have a significantly higher cruise speed. These ships can go from Tokyo to San Francisco in three days."

"*Mein Gott!*" Horst exclaimed. "That's amazing."

Eve grinned. "I am also looking into manufacturing facilities that can build components. The shipyard we are currently using can handle the assembly; we just need to get the parts to them."

"Is San Francisco still a market?" Horst asked.

"Not at this time," Eve commiserated. "But they are starting to recover. Who knows what the next few years hold? That was just an example. Until there is a market for goods there, we still have enough in this region to keep us busy for years."

Horst nodded. "Makes sense. When will the ships we are working on now be ready for sea trials?"

"The first is scheduled to launch in three months," Eve informed him. "I have already booked the first load of cargo. We will be operational two weeks after the launch."

Horst chuckled. "You don't do anything by half measures."

"Things to move and money to make," Eve told him. "There's no logic in doing it by half measures."

Asai growled as she flopped down in the chair at her desk. "Oh, that man."

Koda looked up from the screen she was reviewing sales numbers on. "What's the matter, cousin?"

"Seki," Asai ground out.

Koda cocked her head to one side. "What about him?"

"We were supposed to go to the Emperor's Retreat, that new restaurant that opened today, and he just informed me that he has a game match with his team." Asai pouted. "*Men.*"

"Team?" Koda was lost for a moment. "The group he plays sims with?"

Asai threw her hands up. "Yes. They have formed teams and are having a tournament. One of the teams dropped out, so he moved the match time to that slot because the sim was already reserved. It is the same time as our reservations."

"He does realize that you have some control over the sim reservations?" Koda asked, her voice dripping with ice.

"He claimed he forgot about the reservations, and his team has already made arrangements to be here. I swear, he and his friends are like small children where their games are concerned."

"I'm sorry, Asai. I know you were looking forward to this. Would you like me to go with you?"

Asai shook her head. "No, I am too angry. I wouldn't be an enjoyable companion. You and Horst take the reservation; it's at seven. I think I will spend the evening in my room. Maybe a good soak will help me to not want to beat Seki when I see him next."

"Are you sure?" Koda asked.

Asai nodded. "Yes, I will make him take me another day. It will be his treat that time."

Koda snickered. "That will be a lesson in itself. They have some expensive dishes if I remember."

Asai nodded as she started to leave.

"Oh, Asai?" Koda called as she started out the door.

She stopped and turned.

"Which sim is it that they are having a tournament in? We might want to look at organizing one ourselves. We could offer prizes like sim time and snack bar credits."

"*Space Station Zebra*," Asai replied.

"Ah, that's a popular one. I guess that's why Seki and his guys pushed so hard for the alien team to be made available as playable characters. I'll look into organizing something next month."

"Eve had some suits made that give them positive feedback for hits and allow for non-lethal hits too. He is like a little kid over that stupid game," Asai grumped as she stalked out the door.

"Takumi," Koda called when she was sure Asai was out of hearing.

"How may I be of assistance?" Takumi replied.

"Pull up the *Space Station Zebra* reservation for Seki Yamagoto's team," she instructed.

"I have the information," Takumi informed her.

Koda grinned. "Increase difficulty level for the player designated as Seki by fifteen percent. Decrease weapons accuracy for that same player by twenty-five percent. Increase player feedback settings by ten percent."

"The level of neural feedback you have designated is within tolerances but will increase the player's discomfort. Do you wish to proceed?"

"Yes, proceed as stated."

"Player Seki Yamagoto's parameters changed and confirmed. Do you have any further changes?"

"No, thank you, Takumi. That should do nicely." Koda chortled. "Oh, and Takumi?"

"Yes?"

"Record player Seki Yamagoto's session and send it to my console when the sim is complete."

"Session is set to record," Takumi replied.

"Thank you."

Bet he will wish he had gone out to eat with Asai when that game is done, Koda thought. *Nobody upsets my cousin and gets away with it.*

Eve was surprised to be interrupted by Takumi. "Is there an issue?"

"Koda Rii has issued override protocols for player Seki Yamagoto in an upcoming simulation," Takumi informed her. "The settings are within acceptable safety levels, but there is an increase in the neural feedback level assigned to that player."

"Was there a reason given?" Eve inquired. "Is she testing some aspect of the game?"

"Negative, she didn't give a reason, but Asai Yagi's biometric readings were higher just prior to the change being made, and there is a ninety-nine-point-six-three-percent certainty that these readings involved Seki Yamagoto's actions."

Eve accessed the video footage and played back Asai and Koda's conversation. When she was done, her eyes narrowed. "What parameters did Koda Rii mandate?"

"Player Seki Yamagoto will experience a fifteen percent increase in overall difficulty, a twenty-five percent decrease in weapons accuracy, and a ten percent increase in neural feedback," Takumi listed.

Eve considered the information for a millisecond. "Administrative override. Increase player feedback to eighteen percent, and increase his adversaries' weapons accuracy by ten percent when targeting player Seki Yamagoto."

"Override settings confirmed. I take it that player Seki Yamagoto is about to get a visit from St. Payback."

Eve chuckled evilly. "Exactly."

"Would you like to be copied on the recording Koda Rii has requested of the gameplay?"

"Absolutely."

CHAPTER THIRTY-TWO

Liaoning Province, China

Pain. Gut-wrenchingly intense agony coursed through Miko once again. His voice was raw from the screams that had been ripped from it as his body was wracked over and over with the pain. The harsh laughter followed each time he was reduced to gasping for breath when he couldn't scream anymore.

He had lost all sense of time. He could have been tied up for hours, days, or weeks. All his mind and body knew was the world of agony followed by the relief brought on when the bitter substance was forced between his clenched teeth, then the cycle started over again. He had pleaded to be allowed to die—anything to stop the burning agony that was breaking his mind. He wasn't even given respite when he passed out, his body driven to its limits.

Each time he was brought back from the brink, he heard the familiar voice taunting another. "You have brought dishonor on yourself through your sick perversions. For that alone, you should be the one under our care, but our queen has forbidden me from treating you as you deserve. She will only allow us to play with your lover while you watch, helpless to do anything to save him. Are you proud of what you have done?"

There was no answer from the figure before him. He stood as he had from the start, unmoving and unresponsive to the voice. The man's features were still blurred, like a bright spot of light obscured his face, only now he could make out something; two lines that ran down his cheeks—lines the color of fresh blood.

"Again!" the voice commanded, and Miko's body jerked involuntarily against his bonds as the pain returned.

Miko was on his feet, his breathing harsh and his heart racing. He felt the now-too-familiar blood sweat soaking through his clothes. The memory of the pain he had experienced in the dream was so real that he still felt it in his semi-awake state.

He shuddered as he fought his way out of the haze. *That voice—I know it. The owner's name is right below the surface. Why can't I remember it if this dream is the memory it seems to be? Who is the man? His appearance is familiar. How do I know that his hair is soft? Who is he, and what is he to me?*

Miko had continued to follow the river as it passed through fallow farmland and eventually into the foothills of a small mountain range. He knew that it would eventually lead to the sea. He had no real plan for once he arrived there; he would decide at the end of his trek across the sparsely settled countryside.

It had been several days since the encounter with the two Weres he had beheaded and left as a warning on the road. He had not encountered any more of them, as the talkative one had promised. He still remained wary as he ran along the river bank each night, stopping frequently to extend his senses out as far as he could, thankful he came up empty each time.

One abandoned house he checked had delivered a cache of clothes that fit him. Nothing fancy, just simple work clothes, but they were in good repair. When he was searching for something to pack the clothes for travel, he had come across an unexpected bounty: a pair of *hudiedao*, or butterfly swords as they were also called, lovingly wrapped in oilcloth at the bottom of a wooden chest.

The swords were well cared for, and the hilts showed signs of years of use. Each blade had been honed to a razor edge capable of cutting flesh with the slightest pressure. The swords now rode his hips on a wide leather belt that held them in plain leather sheaths, the distinctive D-shaped hand guards and short blades ready for use at a second's notice. Miko had never felt the need to carry weapons in the past, but Heinz and Chang had insisted he learn to use swords and other weapons.

He had never practiced with two swords, or any as short as the ones he now carried. However, one of his men had introduced him to Filipino stick fighting, a form he enjoyed using as a workout. The swords were shorter and a little heavier, but he was certain the concept was the same.

He had practiced with a katana against Chang, Isamu, and Ogawa and had become faster and more skilled over time. He could easily defeat Chang and match Ogawa blow for blow to win as often as not.

With Isamu, he had become able to defend himself to some extent, at least until Isamu tired of the exercise and ended it in a manner that fit whatever mood he was in. After Heinz'd had to give him blood to heal a serious wound, he had ordered Isamu to show restraint in their future sessions. The restraint only went as far as not striking potentially lethal blows. It did nothing to stop Isamu from wounding him multiple times until he was too weak to continue.

Isamu, what a sadistic... Miko stopped short, his eyes wide as realization struck. *Isamu; he is the voice in my dreams.*

He continued walking, only to stop again a few seconds later. "Ogawa!" he exclaimed out loud. "It was Ogawa who acted as the torturer's apprentice. He was the one causing the pain!"

He closed his eyes in an attempt to remember every detail, trying without success to recognize the man who was watching his suffering. His lover, if Isamu's words could be believed.

Miko was snatched out of his reverie when a low snarl came from behind him. He turned in time to see a tiger leap from the underbrush and spun to the side, avoiding its headlong charge, only to be knocked to the ground when a heavy body slammed into him from the other side. His back caught fire as sharp claws cut deep into it.

Miko rolled to the side, escaping the clutches of the second tiger. He hit the ground hard, barely avoiding the claws of the first tiger as they came at his head. He surged to his feet as a third tiger came flying at him from the darkness, his eyes blazing red and his fangs fully extended, ready to do battle.

The tigers had planned their ambush well. Miko

snarled as the cats moved in for the kill. He spun in place, searching for a defensive position. The road here curved away from the river, running through a natural cut with heavy growth limiting visibility on the high banks to either side. With his options limited to forward or back and the tigers moving toward him, Miko made the decision to rush the one behind him in the hope of getting to a position where he could face the tigers without offering any of them his exposed back.

He feinted at one of the tigers, spinning quickly to rush back and catch the cat blocking his path by surprise. When he was within a few feet of the crouching tiger he cut to the right, feigning fear, and ran along the edge of the road. Overhanging limbs grabbed at his clothes as he rushed past.

The tiger sprang at him, its jaws wide and claws extended, intending to latch onto him and drag him down.

Miko smirked as he easily changed directions to run back toward the cat. He accelerated to vampire speed, and his hand shot up as the airborne tiger passed over him.

The tiger screamed in pain when the razor-sharp *hudiedao* entered its body below the chest. Miko used the forward momentum of its leap to eviscerate it. He brought the other sword up, blocking a slash by a second tiger before his first sword finished the cut.

His hand stung from the force of the tiger's paw striking the flat of his blade, knocking it to the side. When the tiger sought to press its advantage, Miko brought his other blade around and slashed its face, angling the blade to cross over an exposed eye.

The Were faltered and turned its bleeding head away

from the blade, only to feel the burn as Miko brought the other around in an arc that cut across its back. He was clear of the ambush and turned to face the last uninjured attacker as it rushed toward him.

This one was larger and more cautious than the first two had been. Instead of barreling headlong into him, the cat feinted left and then jumped to the right at the last second.

Miko went down to one knee. The tiger's claws ripped the muscle of his left calf to shreds as it raced by before he could strike it.

He threw himself flat when he felt more than heard the tiger attempt to leap on his back. The cat sailed over him and he rolled several times in the opposite direction to create distance while his leg healed, thankful for whatever Heinz had done to give him faster healing.

The big cat slid across the loose stones and twisted his body, finally coming to a stop facing Miko. The tiger screamed its rage into the night, frustrated that it had missed again.

Miko stood, gently lowering his weight onto his damaged leg to test it. It supported him, but his healing, although faster than before, was slower than he would have liked.

The brief respite ended when the cat snarled and raced toward him again.

Miko crouched, both swords held ready as the enraged tiger charged. He waited until the cat was almost in range, then positioned the lower blade to block and raised the other for a quick slash.

The cat veered off at the last instance, going wide to his left.

Miko turned to follow, not wanting to leave himself open for another slash from the deadly claws. He felt a pressure change behind him right before he was hit from behind by a heavy weight. His damaged leg radiated pain as the partially-healed muscles gave out under the strain. The weight pressed down on top of him, pinning him to the ground as he struggled to move out from under it.

He kicked with his good leg and twisted his body enough to free one arm, bringing the short sword up to stab his attacker in the side. He was rewarded by a grunt, but the Were did not move. A snarl to the side let him know the second cat was back for more.

Miko twisted the blade, sticking it into the tiger that had managed to pin him. He felt it twitch and brought his injured leg up, gritting his teeth against the pain, and pushed. The weight moved slightly, and he managed to wiggle out from under it.

The other tiger's teeth locked onto the arm that held the blade buried in the tiger that was pinning him.

Miko was dragged across the rough road, the stones littering it tearing the flesh from his back and sending another wave of pain through him as his barely healed skin was torn open again. The blade he held was wrenched from his hand as the tiger continued to tear into his arm, dragging him away from the injured tiger.

Miko twisted violently to free himself from the strong jaws that held him. With no way to gain leverage while being dragged, it only served to do more damage to his already battered and bleeding limb.

The cat dropped Miko's arm and moved in to pin him to the ground. Miko was weak from blood loss and crazed by the pain, his fangs extended and his eyes glowing bright red. He felt the cat's breath on his face and brought the *hudiedao* up instinctually to block the fangs coming toward him.

The tiger lurched back, barely avoiding the razor-sharp blade. It gave Miko enough respite to roll over and rise on his knees.

The cat came at him, jaws open for the kill.

Summoning his last reserve of strength, Miko held the blade low in his uninjured hand, knowing he only had one chance to end this. The cat's front paws came down and dug deeply into his shoulders as the jaws went for his throat. Miko screamed his rage as he shoved his broken, mangled arm into the beast mouth, holding the jaws a hair's breadth from his neck while his body took the strain of holding the tiger's weight.

Miko brought the blade up in a swift motion, penetrating the cat's chest hard enough to feel bone snap when the tang met the body. He twisted the blade, hoping to cause enough damage to at least get away if he couldn't kill it outright.

The Were grunted from the impact and snarled in pain as Miko viciously twisted the blade. One paw lifted off Miko's bleeding shoulder as the cat tried to pull back, while the other tore furrows in the skin on his chest.

Miko continued to push and turn the blade, opening the wound in the tiger's chest more with each twist, ignoring the pain of his injury.

Finally, the cat went still, its breath wheezing as blood

sprayed from the wound. Miko shoved it away, barely missing being knocked down when it collapsed onto his kneeling form. He took a steadying breath and pulled his blade out of the wound. Grasping it with the blade pointing down, he drove it into the tiger's skull over and over until he felt it slide on the roadway beneath.

The tiger shifted back into human form, and Miko smirked when he saw the man was missing most of his head. He struggled to his feet and staggered to the one who had knocked him down. It was still a tiger, so he grabbed it by one ear and drove the blade through its closed eye. The tiger stiffened and shifted, leaving Miko holding a nude body.

The third attacker was in human form on the side of the road where it had fallen. Miko started to gather the bodies to leave another message, but he was so damaged that he hardly had the energy to remain standing. He shook his head and started trudging down the road.

Knowing he needed to feed and rest, he went to the first house he came to about a kilometer down the road. Extending his senses, he detected two humans inside. He wrenched the door open and found two men sitting in front of a hearth with a low fire burning.

Without preamble he leapt, knocking the first man to the floor and grabbing the other by his shirt. The man screamed when he saw Miko's red eyes and mouth full of fangs. The scream died in a gurgle as Miko sank his fangs into the man, drinking deeply.

When he was finished, he dropped the body to the floor and turned to the man he had knocked down. He was shaking, a terrified look on his face as he clutched a small knife.

Miko didn't hesitate. He rushed his victim, slapping the knife away and drawing him into his strong embrace. He sank his fangs into the soft flesh, puncturing the man's jugular. The hot blood pulsed into his mouth with each beat of his victim's heart. He held the body close, savoring the rich metallic taste as he felt his body healing the damage. The man's heartbeat faded, getting weaker, and when it stopped, he dropped the limp, lifeless body to the floor and took in his surroundings. Although he was healing, he knew he needed to rest and feed again before he would be capable of fighting off another ambush like that.

The house was a single-room shack with no windows and would not provide the protection he needed. He shook his head, disappointment on his face as he stepped through the doorway.

He walked out into the night, hoping to find a secure place to rest and another victim to feed from before the sun forced him to ground.

Sacred Clan Base, Liaoning Province, China

The speaker on the radio unit crackled with static and then a voice came through. "Team thirty-seven to base."

"This is base," the radio operator replied. "Report."

"We have located team twenty-four, and they're all dead. There are signs of a fight and a blood trail that smelled like a Forsaken leading away. It is over a day old."

Cui Yong motioned to the radio operator for the

microphone. "Were they arranged like the others?" he demanded.

"No, they were scattered about," the reply came. "It looked like he left them where they fell. From the amount of blood we found and the spacing of the tracks leading away, it appears the Forsaken was injured."

"But we have lost another team," Cui growled. "Are there any indications that he knew he was being tracked and ambushed them?"

There was a moment's hesitation where the mike was open but the team member did not speak. "No, it looks like Kang's team set an ambush for him."

"What is your location?"

"We are along the river, about one hundred kilometers west of where we found Han and Wun."

Cui consulted a map stuck to the wall before he responded. "Continue tracking the Forsaken and call in with updates every hour. It appears he has gone farther than anticipated. If you find he has changed direction, call in immediately. I will dispatch other teams to the west of your location to box him in. This Forsaken will be ours soon."

"Acknowledged."

Cui Yong threw the cup he had been holding. It shattered into small pieces when it hit the stones above the fireplace.

The door of the room burst open as Yi rushed in. "What's the matter, Cui?"

Cui took a steadying breath, getting his anger under control. before he replied, "We have lost another team to that fucking vampire."

Yi winced. Cui seldom used profanity of any kind, and when he did, someone was in for a beating. "How did that happen? Did they allow him to catch them unaware?"

"No." Cui growled. "That fool Kang thought he would be a hero and set an ambush for the Forsaken bastard. They paid with their lives, and their failure to follow orders has cost us more time. They were killed over a day ago, but the bodies were only found today."

"Was there anything that can tell us where he is going?"

Cui shrugged. "The team that found them is the same one that reported the deaths of Han and Wun in Kaiyuan yesterday. He is heading west, it seems."

"Should we call in the teams that are east of Kaiyuan?" Yi asked. "Have them come west?"

"I already ordered the twelve teams that were deployed to Yushu to move. They are to report to Chengde for further instructions. I will have the others deployed between Yushu and Kaiyuan do the same."

"We will catch him soon, brother. He can't evade us forever."

"I know, but at what cost?"

Yi shrugged. "Kang always was a hothead. The only reason he was leading a team was because of his family's standing. The other leads are solid and will follow orders."

Cui nodded. "Yes, that is true. I'm going out for a bit. Please ensure that the radio operator receives an answer from each of the twelve teams. I need to think about how I want to report this latest failure to Master Kun."

"I will see it done. I do not envy you making the report to Kun, he is becoming more..." Yi trailed off at a sharp glance from Cui. "Shao and Jen caught fish in the river. They should be ready soon."

Cui waved over his shoulder as he stepped out into the midday sun, his mind already composing the report to Kun.

CHAPTER THIRTY-THREE

The Palace, Tokyo, Japan

"*Konichiwa*, Seki."

"*Konichiwa*, Chiyo. Do you want to admit defeat now or wait until we trounce you?" Seki chided.

Chiyo laughed. "Oh, Seki's got jokes today."

The other ten players laughed as the team leaders talked smack. The group had all helped with testing the Palace's games from the beginning and had been friends for years.

"You guys are going to love this," Seki explained as he pulled on a gray jumpsuit with black stripes running up and down at even intervals all around and down each arm and leg. "Eve has upgraded the sim based on the feedback we gave." He pulled the suit on and modeled it.

"What's it supposed to do?" Eiko inquired as she ran her fingers down one arm.

"That's right, you were out with Mr. Wonderful the day we came up with this idea." Seki laughed as he made kissy faces at her.

"You're an ass," she quipped as she punched him on the arm.

Seki laughed. "Careful, little sister. Eve won't let you play if you break her favorite tester."

"I don't know about that," Eve called as she entered the room. "Us girls have to stick together."

"Eve!" Eiko squealed as she ran over and wrapped her in a hug. Eiko laid an arm over her shoulder and stuck her tongue out at Seki as she released Eve from her embrace. "See, big brother, she loves me more."

Everyone guffawed as Seki feigned a hurt look while placing both hands over his heart.

"I see that Seki has shown you the latest upgrade." Eve pointed at the jumpsuit. "I have calibrated the sim to record hits and misses based on the angle you fire from as well as taking any cover used into the equation. What that means to you is you will feel where the hits land and non-lethal injuries won't put you out of the game."

"So, no more three hits and you're out like we requested?" Chiyo asked.

"Correct," Eve supplied. "If you don't get a fatal injury, you can keep fighting. Your aim and reflexes will be degraded based on the seriousness and location of the injury, just like it would in real life. A hit to your hand could make it where your trigger won't work unless you switch hands. A knee shot out will definitely affect how you move."

Murmurs of approval came from the group. They gathered around as Seki and Eiko handed out the suits to the others.

"How much does it hurt when you're hit?" Kita, a waif

with long black hair running down her back in a ponytail asked.

Eve answered, "The program is set to make you feel an impact in the area affected for a non-lethal hit, and will give you the impact and shut down your ability to continue the game for a lethal one. It is all done through the interface, so it is literally in your mind. There are no lasting effects...under normal settings."

"What do you mean, normal settings?" Seki asked.

Eve only smiled at Seki. "Okay, everyone. Close them up and get into position. The mission today is capture the flag. When we drop into the game, each team will be in a different location on a space station. There are non-player characters in the game. If you shoot an NPC, your team loses points.

"The first team to capture the other's flag wins," Eve explained. "You have to touch the flag to win. Even if all of the other team is incapacitated, you still have to finish the mission."

The players all acknowledged her either with a nod or word.

"As soon as everyone is in position with their interface activated, the game will begin," Eve told the players as they pulled their headgear on. "Good luck, and may the best team win."

When Eve had a positive indicator from each position, she started the sim. "Takumi, record the session from Seki's point of view. I want full audio and video, as well as overwatch of his location."

"Acknowledged," Takumi replied. "With the increase in enemy accuracy, the player designated Seki has a ninety-two-point six percent chance of receiving a fatal hit within three minutes of gameplay. Do you wish to leave his player settings at this level?"

Eve laughed. "Good catch, Takumi. Reduce player damage by sixty percent but leave everything else at current settings. Wouldn't want him taken out too soon. Where's the fun in that?"

"Administrator changes recorded," Takumi announced. "You do realize with the interface settings this high, there is a chance that he will continue to feel this after the game? My calculations show that his mind could be fooled into believing the injury is real."

Eve grinned. "I'm counting on it."

The white screen in front of Seki's eyes darkened as the sim started. As the team leader, he was the first in the game, and within a few seconds, he was on the command deck of a space station. The other four members of his team came into the game in short order.

"Team Red Dragon sync successful. Team Hydra sync successful. Begin mission," Takumi announced over the earpieces worn by each player.

Seki raised his pulse rifle and tested his mobility and aim. The short weapon hung from a tactical strap under his right arm and came into firing position with ease. The aiming reticle appeared in his HUD when he squeezed the handgrip and tracked smoothly as he swung the weapon from side to side. The rest of the team performed their

CHARLES TILLMAN & MICHAEL ANDERLE

weapons check, and when all were satisfied, they lowered their guns and nodded at him.

Takumi continued giving instructions. "Each of you has a grid map on your HUD of the engagement zone. This is the small team scenario, and it is limited to the top six levels of the station. If you go out of the marked area, you will be disqualified, so pay attention to your surroundings. Your teammates are marked with a blue indicator; your location is marked in green. Enemy players will show up red when they are in range."

A cluster of blue dots with a single green one appeared on each player's HUD, showing their location in the simulated space station.

The lights dimmed and came back to full strength with a pulsing red light added. A loud klaxon reverberated through the station.

"Attention all personnel," an electronic voice announced over the station's public address system. "Condition Red. There has been a breach on level five, sector 4-alpha. All personnel to battle stations. This is not a drill."

The system played through the alert message once more before Seki ordered, "Silence alarm," as it started to play a third time.

"Here we go." Eiko smiled. "What are your orders?"

Seki grinned. "Eiko, Okura, you're our base team. Hold the command center against the invaders. If we do it right, they won't get close, but I know Eve has built in some twists that we haven't seen yet. The rest of you with me. We're going hunting."

Eiko and Okura nodded their agreement and grinned at each other as they moved to defensive positions behind the command consoles, using what cover was available to establish a kill zone that covered the entrance to the command center with a deadly crossfire. They had handled defense together several times in the past and were the best team for the job. If the enemy breached the door, they were in for a hot welcome.

Seki nodded at both in approval and moved the rest of the team out of the command center into the hallway. The door closed as the last member exited, and the access panel turned red as the lockdown protocol was initiated from inside. With that in place, it would require brute force to open the door, giving Eiko and Okura ample opportunity to take them down.

"We know where they have breached the station," Seki explained. "Our objective is to stop them and either capture or destroy their ship. Our options for destroying it are limited to our personal weapons and any we find along the way. The scenario has the station's defensive weapons offline until we secure or destroy their ship."

"That's brutal," Ito complained. "Why no station weapons?"

"Eve felt that station weapons would make it too easy for the defenders. She said that this sim is a first-person combat shooter, not a space fleet battle. Though she did mention that she was working on one where the defenders and attackers could have dogfights. It's not ready for testing, but we will get a shot at it as soon as it is."

"Sign me up for that one!" Ito exclaimed. "I always wanted to fly a space fighter."

The others all voiced agreement, their minds imagining how realistic Eve would make that when it was done.

"Pay attention, people," Seki admonished. "We need to focus on the mission. There is no way we're letting Chiyo and his band of misfits beat us."

Eve smirked as she watched the action remotely. Seki was being cocky, and she was looking forward to the after-action brief. "Takumi, monitor player Seki Yamagoto's vital signs throughout the sim. Adjust the levels down if he starts to display readings outside of projected norms and notify me."

"Noted," Takumi replied. "Would you like to be notified when the sim is close to ending as well?"

"Yes, give me a five-minute notice. I want to be here when they come out of it."

"Five-minute notification set."

Emperor's Retreat, Tokyo, Japan

"Oh, Horst, that was the best meal I've ever had," Koda gushed. "The steak was cooked perfectly! The whole meal was like an explosion on my taste buds. The seasoning was amazing, I don't think I will ever be able to eat steak anywhere else again."

Horst rubbed his stomach appreciatively as they walked hand in hand down the sidewalk. "It was the best I have ever had in my life, and that's saying something because I ate in many fine restaurants before the world ended."

Koda squeezed his hand. "Asai is going to be so upset she missed out on this. I can't wait to tell her."

Horst chuckled. "You may not want to play it up too much. Seki is already in enough trouble for putting his gaming above his plans with her. He might not survive it if she gets any madder."

"I assure you that Seki will remember this and think twice before he stands her up again." Koda smiled evilly.

Horst's eyes went wide in surprise at both the tone and the scent Koda emitted. Realizing that she was angrier than he thought when he detected the sharp change in her scent. "Why is that, my tiny beauty?"

She smiled. "Let's just say it is not smart to tempt the fates or to annoy the one who controls the game."

"What did you do?" Horst asked.

"Nothing much," Koda told him. "I might have adjusted the amount of pain that a certain forgetful ass will feel while he runs around shooting things with his friends instead of eating that beautiful meal with my cousin."

"That is..." Horst paused, "truly evil. You scare me sometimes."

She wrapped her arms around him and looked up at Horst. "You have nothing to worry about, my mountain of man," she told him sweetly. "As long as you remember who is important."

Horst chuckled at the thinly-veiled threat. "Always, my love, always."

Koda's face glowed as she pulled him down to her level and proceeded to reward him for his proper response. Her lips crushed his, and they both forgot about Seki and the rest of the world for a moment.

Koda pulled back, her body tingling and flushed. "As long as you continue to make me feel like that when we kiss, you have no worries." She sighed.

Horst cupped her face gently in his huge palm and

pulled her in for another kiss. When he released her, Koda was breathing in short gasps, and her face was flushed even more.

She smiled up at him dreamily, not believing the good fortune she'd had when she found him. After a few moments of staring goofily at him, she shook herself. "Let's get back. I want to see how the game went and tell Asai we made reservations for her and Seki three days from now. He might be over the effects by then."

"Truly evil," was all Horst had to say.

Koda laughed. "You have no idea, but when we are done with Seki and Asai, I will give you the opportunity to find the other side of me. As long as you keep kissing me like that," she murmured.

Horst grinned at this. "Well, by all means, let us hurry so that I may begin the exploration posthaste."

Koda giggled as she snuggled under his arm, and they continued walking home.

The Palace, Tokyo, Japan

"Okay, the ship is down this corridor and to the right," Seki announced.

His team had finally made their way down to the breached level. Seki and Mita Nao, the sister of Okura, who was in the Command Center with Eiko, were the last of his team left. Eve had promised some surprises and she had delivered.

First, Ito had been caught in a sudden gravity shift in the lift tubes and plunged down four levels to his death in the first two minutes of play. Next, Kubo was taken out by a plasma grenade that Machi, from Chiyo's team, had snuck in while using a group of fleeing NPCs as cover. Seki had taken him down with blaster fire but had suffered a leg wound that was slowing him down.

Seki grunted as he limped along, favoring his injured leg. "This is something else. I feel the pain every time I take a step."

"Quit whining. I got hit too, it's not that bad. Do you need somebody to kiss it better?" Mita teased, making kissing noises.

"No, smartass," Seki grumbled. "Besides, if I did, it sure wouldn't be your mug doing the kissing. I just didn't expect the upgrades to be so real. Now pay attention. It's just around this corner."

Seki consulted his HUD and saw the breach outlined, indicating where the enemy ship was. He toggled through the settings to try to locate any of Chiyo's team who were waiting to ambush them. Not seeing anything outside the ship, he dropped to the floor and cautiously peered around the corner. Seeing it was clear, he stood and motioned for Mita to follow.

When he was halfway to his goal, his world was rocked by a sharp pain in his back, followed by another to his chest. His HUD started flashing yellow, indicating he had taken a serious but not deadly injury. He dropped to the floor in an attempt to make himself a smaller target as he fired his blaster blindly down the corridor. He didn't have a target but hoped to at least make whoever was shooting him pause long enough for him to escape the kill zone.

He was crawling backward, still firing at the opening at the end of the corridor when his body was wracked with pain in three different locations. His uninjured leg, his lower back, and then his head all were hit seconds apart. His HUD flashed red twice, and everything went black.

Seki dropped out of the simulation with a shriek. When he opened his eyes, he was back in the gray game room. He grabbed his head with both hands, moaning. The other players were looking at him like he had lost his mind.

"When you get done wallowing on the floor, come and congratulate the victors, loser," Chiyo snarked to the laughter of his team.

"What the hell? Don't any of you still feel the injuries from the game?" Seki complained as he stood rubbing his head.

Chiyo scoffed. "What are you talking about? All you should be feeling now is the utter humiliation of being caught exposed to a three-way crossfire. Noob move if I ever saw one, Seki."

"I'm serious, guys!" Seki exclaimed. "I still feel where I was hit, and my leg still hurts from the first hit."

"Maybe it's your conscience bothering you," Eve offered from the back of the room.

Seki spun in surprise. "Huh? I...uh, what do you mean, Eve?"

"Perhaps it is your subconscious making you feel what you're imagining," she told him, her face devoid of feeling. "You know, for standing Asai up to play tonight."

Eve turned to Chiyo with a smile. "Congratulations, Chiyo. That was a masterful ambush you set up. I was wondering why you had your defenders outside the ship. Well done, creating hides in the ceiling and walls of the station."

Chio bowed to Eve. "Thank you, Eve-*san*. It was a treat to make Seki eat his words. That he whines like a child about still feeling pain appears to be his weak attempt to garner sympathy for his monumental defeat at the hands of the better commander."

The whole room erupted with laughter as Seki stood opening and closing his mouth at a complete loss for words.

The door to the room slid open, admitting Koda, Asai, and Horst.

"Hi, Seki, how was your game?" Koda asked, continuing before he could answer. "I was just telling Asai about the meal we had. Thanks for blowing off your date with her to play tonight. Horst and I *really* enjoyed ourselves."

Horst looked at Koda with narrowed eyes, certain he was missing something but not sure what.

Asai walked up to Seki, both hands on her hips. "Koda was telling me how good the food and service was, and how the staff there are fans of the Palace and rolled out the red carpet for them. I hope you at least won."

Seki's eyes darted between Asai, Koda, and Eve. He looked like he didn't know whether to run or try to salvage what little dignity he had left.

"Wait a minute." He turned to the other players. "None of you are feeling any lasting effects? Seriously?"

"Give it a rest, Seki," Eiko snapped, her eyes blazing. "What is this about you standing Asai up to play tonight? I should kick you! No, Asai should kick you for being such a twit. No wonder you're acting like this."

"I'm serious," Seki insisted. "I still feel every shot I took in the game. Eve, something *must* be wrong with the interface."

"Guilty conscience," Eve repeated as she narrowed her eyes.

"Serves him right," Koda added.

Horst shook his head at the three women and chuckled as he muttered, "Absolutely evil."

Seki watched open-mouthed as the three walked out, leaving him to deal with an obviously angry Asai.

"I swear, Asai," he started but thought better of it when her eyes narrowed. "I mean, I'm sorry I forgot our date. Is there any way I can make it up to you?"

"You get on your knees and beg, idiot," Chiyo offered.

"That's a start, but I think he needs to make serious atonement for this," Eiko added.

"Do you mind?" Seki yelled, eliciting another round of laughter from the teams.

"Asai, can we discuss this like adults?" He swept his arm around the room, taking in the others. "Away from the children."

"I don't know," Asai mused. "It seems to me that the *children* are giving you good advice."

"Please, Asai! I know I messed up. I'm sorry, and I promise it won't happen again."

"I assure you that it won't be a problem in the future," Takumi's voice announced from the overhead speakers. "I have set a subroutine to monitor Asai's calendar, and you will not be allowed in any gaming area in the future when she has plans for you."

"Oh, busted by the overlord." Eiko laughed. "Better get busy, brother, before Takumi puts you on the naughty list."

Seki looked at Asai pleadingly. "Can we please go somewhere to talk?"

Her lips turned up in a slight quirk. "Certainly, Seki, we can discuss your penance now. Know that it includes dinner at the Emperor's Retreat in three days. Koda secured the reservation for us. Your treat."

Seki's face paled as Asai's words sank in. It was going to cost him big, and not just the cost of the meal if he wasn't careful. His mind raced for a suitable response, then inspiration struck. He smiled and bowed with a flourish, one hand behind his back and the other outstretched. "As you wish."

Asai's eyes crinkled, and her lips twitched until a laugh burst out. "No fair using a line from my favorite movie, you cad. Don't you know I'm still mad at you?" she mock-scolded Seki as she wrapped her arms around him in a hug.

Seki winced. "Ow, ow, I still think there is something wrong with that game. I still feel it."

"I can assure you, Seki Yamagoto, the game was operating within established limits," Takumi paused before adding coldly, "For all players."

"What? Oh, never mind," Seki rolled his eyes, realizing he had lost more than once today but was still a winner as he took Asai's hand and led her toward the door.

"Koda, you really shouldn't mess with the game settings," Eve told her as they walked down the hall.

"I'm sorry, Eve," Koda apologized. "I was just so mad at

him, and I wanted him to pay a little for hurting Asai's feelings."

"I fully understand that." Eve looked at her and winked. "You just don't know how high you should set them to get the desired outcome is all."

Horst snickered. "All of you, absolutely evil."

CHAPTER THIRTY-FOUR

TQB Base, Tokyo, Japan

Akio was in his quarters, reviewing the plans for the base that Eve and Horst had designed. Eve had secured the old temple and museum grounds they had been using to land the Pods close to the Palace. The plans called for them to use the spot where the museum once stood for the base. That building had been damaged beyond repair when the earthquakes hit shortly after WWDE. The government had removed all the artifacts that could be salvaged and condemned the site shortly afterward.

The temple had also been destroyed. There had been calls to rebuild it, but the powers that be had determined it was too costly. Eve had negotiated an agreement where TQB assets would be transferred to cover repairs and upgrades to several other properties in exchange for ownership of the land.

The new base design called for a reinforced two-story structure above ground and three levels below. A retractable roof was to be installed that would allow them to land their Pods and the cargo containers inside the structure. The lowest level would have a ten-foot steel reinforced wall and a foundation that sat on shock absorbers to minimize the possibility of damage from any future quakes.

Eve had informed him it was a design that was used by the American military at a place called Cheyenne Mountain. That facility, built deep within the earth, was designed to survive not only earthquakes, but also a sustained nuclear attack.

They now owned the entire area and there would be no innocent people around if they were attacked. The over-engineered building designed by Eve and made comfortable by Horst's additions was exactly what Akio'd had in mind when he'd suggested they relocate.

The addition of the hangar for the Pods, as well as an Etheric power supply, ensured he would be capable of a quick response. That they were not dependent on outside power for their defenses allowed Eve to add a shield similar to the one used at the Australia base where the space station design had been tested.

The defenses Eve had designed were more over-engineered than the base. No one would be able to get close without being covered by several layers of security, ranging from non-lethal to unsurvivable.

"Missile defense pucks, remote-operated rail guns, plus a full array of dual-purpose surveillance and assault drones," Akio mumbled as he shook his head in wonder. "Looks like she is expecting a full-scale invasion in the heart of Tokyo."

"Akio?" Abel called over his implant.

"Yes?" he responded.

"I have been monitoring some unusual radio traffic in China," Abel reported. "There are indications that it concerns the person you have been searching for."

Akio clenched his hands. "I'll be there in a moment."

"What is it, Abel?" he called twenty seconds later as he came through the command center door.

"I have been detecting odd radio signals in several areas throughout China for over a week," Abel informed him. "I was able to get a carrier near one that has been stationary and have isolated the frequency."

"Why do you think it is related to my search?

"The transmissions seem to be following a route that leads away from Acheng."

The screen lit up with a map of China. Acheng was marked with a yellow pin. Akio watched as moving red dots appeared, heading in a southwesterly direction.

"This shows the progression of the remote signals as they were detected," Abel explained. "I determined that these signals originated from low-power mobile units, but I was unable to get a drone to one before it moved. They move in unpredictable ways." A blue dot appeared outside Shenyang. "This is the location of the signal that has not moved. I have managed to seed the area with enough drones to capture the transmissions as they were broadcast."

"And?" Akio pressed.

"I intercepted a transmission about a dead team and an injured Forsaken," Abel continued. "The transmission also mentioned two more deaths east of their location the day before.

"Another drone discovered this yesterday. I believe these are the two they were talking about."

The camera zoomed in on one of the severed heads. The skin was rough and torn, not like it had been cut but had been ripped off with brute force.

"Whatever did this is enhanced," Akio stated.

The map appeared again. A flashing white dot appeared, followed by a red one to the west of it.

"The white marker indicates where the bodies were located. The red marker is the remote unit's location. Based on this information, there is a ninety-five-point-six-percent probability that the Forsaken they are searching for is the one you are seeking."

"Notify me of any further transmissions involving the Forsaken," Akio instructed. "I will be taking a Pod to the area for a closer look."

CHAPTER THIRTY-FIVE

TQB Base, Tokyo, Japan

Akio spent two days traversing the area, with no sign of Kenjii. Abel had maintained surveillance on the base radio and had determined that the signals he had detected were all related to the search. Akio had given up for the moment and was back at the base, waiting for Abel to get any information on a location. A Pod was kept ready in low orbit above the base, ready to transport him when word came in.

His memories of Kenjii continued to torment him. Whenever he wasn't occupied with his duties, the thoughts crept in unbidden. He was currently sitting cross-legged on the floor in his dimly-lit quarters, meditating to try to still his thoughts. Try as he might, he could not stop the memories from coming.

Chiba, Japan, November 1956

They sat on the couch in Kenjii's apartment. Each held a small cup filled with the aromatic tea Kenjii had prepared. Akio held himself stiffly, still unsure of his actions, not knowing why he couldn't resist the power that drew him here.

Kenjii was beside him in a relaxed pose, but Akio heard his heart beating rapidly in his chest. He had again offered both cups after he brewed the tea. Akio thought it was an interesting gesture but chose not to inquire why he'd done it yet. He knew he shouldn't be here, that it was dangerous for both of them, but he couldn't stay away. He wanted to understand why he couldn't resist the desire.

Kenjii shifted on the couch to face him, pulling his bare legs under him as he did. "Akio, what troubles you so?"

"I...I don't understand what is happening to me," he answered a few heartbeats later.

"What do you mean?" Kenjii hesitated briefly. "Two friends, enjoying tea and each other's company?"

Akio turned to face him, noting his quirked lips and how the light caused his eyes to sparkle. "I am much older than I seem. I should have more self-control than I have shown when it comes to you. I shouldn't be here with you since it is not safe for either of us. If what I've done is discovered, we could both die."

Kenjii's eyes widened at that revelation, shock evident on his face. "Why would we be in danger? You mentioned it the first time, but I don't understand."

Akio closed his eyes. "The strictures forbid me to allow a human to know what I am. I should not have revealed myself to you that night, and after I did, I should have ensured you couldn't tell anyone. The penalty is death when it is found out."

"What are these strictures?" Kenjii inquired. "Part of a religious order?"

"They are the laws handed down by the first of us, a powerful being who kills those who break them without mercy. For many

years, he and his family have...governed, I believe is the best word, my kind. It is a hands-off style until someone crosses a line. Then, it is a swift death for the offender, and more often than not, others as well. Not allowing humans to know about us is the first and most frequently enforced rule."

"Then we will not let them know." Kenjii shuddered. "I have told no one about you. I wouldn't do anything you wished me not to. I will do whatever you ask of me."

Akio raised an eyebrow at what he said as well as the implied meaning. He frowned. "You don't understand. There is always someone watching and listening."

"I've already told you that I have not and will not speak of this, and as much as it pains me not to come to you, I will not seek you out."

Akio shook his head, frustration evident on his face. "Speaking is not the only way we could be found out. Your thoughts or mine could reveal us to some. They have abilities you know nothing about. A thought at the wrong time could be all some need to discover what I've done."

Kenjii sat silently for a moment, digesting the information. His eyes shot wide in horror as his face flushed red. "Oh, ancestors! So, you're telling me that you can read my mind?" He placed both hands over his face, the flush spreading down his neck to the bare skin on his chest.

One corner of Akio's mouth curved up in a hint of a smile. "Oh, I can tell your thoughts—some of them, anyway—without needing to be a mind reader."

Kenjii spread the fingers on one hand, peeking out at him between them. "But you can't read my every thought?" he pressed, his voice holding a note of hope.

"No, that power is not strong in me. I can pick up on some

emotions, as well as detect changes in your heartbeat and breathing. I can also cloud a person's mind to some extent—it's called compulsion—but my abilities there are limited as well."

Relief flooded Kenjii's features. He pulled his hands away and stared hard into Akio's eyes as another thought came to him. "You can't, ah..." He hesitated before saying the rest in a rush. "Make me forget about you, can you?"

"No. If I could, this would be much easier in one way." Akio paused. "And much harder in another."

Kenjii nodded and shifted on the couch, moving a little closer to Akio's stiff form. He scrutinized the other man's face, a hint of mischief in his eyes. "Just how much older than you appear are you? I recognize the hairstyle you wear. It is an old one, not seen often in this age." He reached out hesitantly as one would do with a skittish horse, and lightly touched the rawhide strip that bound Akio's hair into a high, flowing tail atop his head.

Akio watched, fighting the urge to move away. To bolt from the apartment and far from this man he felt drawn to before he was lost.

Kenjii's hand shook and his heartbeat raced as he slowly ran his hand down the thick mane of black hair that ended below Akio's shoulders. "So soft," he whispered, his eyes half-closed as he continued to stroke its length.

Akio's eyes closed as the sensations overwhelmed him. It was the first time in many centuries he'd been touched in such a manner, and his body reacted to it like a man dying of thirst coming upon a cool, clear lake. He relaxed, sinking deeper into the couch until his back rested against the cushions.

He was so lost in that gentle touch that he didn't register when Kenjii moved closer. He stiffened momentarily as Kenjii's *soft lips gently brushed his. When he didn't resist or move away, the lips became more insistent. Hungry, even.*

Akio's arms came up of their own volition and embraced Kenjii. He leaned into him, pulling his warm body close as he responded with a passion he had not felt in several lifetimes. His blood ran hot as he allowed himself to succumb to the salvation of connecting with another being.

CHAPTER THIRTY-SIX

Liaoning Province, China

Isamu laughed. "Do you see how your little catamite begs? Does it tug at your heart?"

The pain was back, but somehow, Miko knew this time that he was dreaming. It was as if he were an observer of the events playing out. He still felt it and heard screams he recognized as his own, but his mind was clear.

Ogawa held a glowing piece of metal in the coals of a fire. He pulled the red-hot metal out and smiled as he held it to his face.

"We have saved the best for last," Isamu taunted. "We have enjoyed seeing your pain as you watched his pretty face while his body was slashed and burned repeatedly. Heinz has told us how to keep him alive without turning him, and the blood he took from you made him last beyond what I thought possible. I should thank you for this, this knowledge will make our future times playing with humans much more fun. Now, watch that face you debased yourself over as it is destroyed. Enjoy the pitiful sounds he makes as he dies."

Miko watched as Ogawa held the metal closer to his face. He was stretched tightly on a metal bed frame that was leaning against the wall. The torturer's sadistic grin loomed large as he moved the heated metal close enough for him to feel the heat.

Miko woke with a start, his face burning from the heat. He jumped to his feet, his hand going to his face by instinct, his mind expecting to feel burned and ravaged flesh. The pain disappeared at his touch, and he came fully awake. The memory of what he had seen in the dream was seared into his mind.

Why? Why did they do that to me? Who did they force to watch?

Miko froze as memories came crashing into his mind of being caught in the dark that night by a gang who preyed on men like him, abusing them and killing them for sport. Red eyes. An *oni*. No, not an *oni*, the *banpaia* who had taken their blood and saved him. The apartment over the small store, being there with him. Spending hours just sitting and holding one another, no words spoken but each being content with the other's presence. So many nights of warmth and comfort in each other's arms.

Miko almost sobbed at his loss. The name was just on the tip of his tongue.

"Who are you?" he whispered.

He collapsed to his knees in shock, his body jerking as if it was taking blows as his memories returned, each one stronger than the last.

Kamiko Kana coming to his apartment in the night. Her telling him not to move or speak. Being able to see and hear everything but helpless to do anything when his lover arrived. How she'd called him to her and commanded he kneel before her. His movements wooden like those of a puppet on a string as he obeyed.

Isamu and Ogawa had been there. He recalled how Kamiko told the kneeling man that his punishment was to watch his lover die at the hands of those two.

The memories were broken, like a shattered mirror. Scenes flashed one after the other in rapid succession.

Being locked in a dark room with rats and insects tormenting him while he heard Isamu's laughter as he heaped abuse on someone through the door. Being dragged from the cell and tied to a metal frame by Ogawa. The laughter of them both as he screamed his throat raw from the pain of his body being broken and burned. Having bitter and metallic blood, just a few drops, dripped into his mouth and then the torture starting all over again.

All the while, the man watched, unmoving, his face like stone, not speaking or showing any emotion. Kamiko looked into his eyes several times during the ordeal, telling him to always remember every detail and know it was his fault.

He remembered Heinz arriving after Kamiko had ordered the man to leave. After Ogawa had burned his face for what seemed like an eternity. How Heinz had slit his own wrist and forced it against his burned and battered lips, dripping the bitter blood into him. How he had ordered him to forget what had happened, to tell him anytime he thought he remembered anything from his life before.

Heinz had tampered with his memories countless times over the years.

There were still holes in Miko's memories, blank spots he could almost see. They were just beyond his grasp, like an image seen from the corner of his eye but gone when he tried to focus.

Why can't I remember everything? Who was I before they did this to me? Who was that man? I know him. He was...is someone special.

He knew the answers he sought were not in China. He needed to go to Japan. If he couldn't find the answers in Chiba, perhaps he would have better luck in Tokyo. In any case, he knew that even with Kamiko Kana dead at the hands of Michael's granddaughter, someone should still be there who would have the answers. One way or the other, he had to learn who that mysterious-yet-familiar man in his dream was and if he still lived.

With a plan firmly in place, Miko set out into the darkness with his path clear. First, he had to feed. Then he would make his way to Shanghai and catch a ship bound for Japan.

He had followed the river after the fight with the Weres until he tired of the hard terrain and lack of people. He turned north out of the rough and unpopulated terrain and was surprised that he had only made it as far as Jinzhou in the Liaoning Province.

The journey should have taken him one night to make, but because he'd followed the changing direction of the river, it had taken four.

After feeding on four victims and leaving the entire family on the floor of their shack, he headed south. His plan was to go southwest through the farmlands, avoiding the time-consuming mountain route to Tianjin. He would then head in a southerly direction parallel to the coast until he arrived in Shanghai.

He knew he would be able to get passage on one of the steamships that had started a trade route between China and Japan. According to the reports Chang had shown him, it would take around two days if the weather cooperated. Miko felt Shanghai was a better option than Vladivostok since they had used that port several times before. The chances of whoever had destroyed the Acheng site knowing about their connections there were not worth risking.

Miko ran through the night. An hour before daylight, he was about thirty kilometers from Tianjin, and he stopped at a small cluster of houses adjoining a series of tilled fields. The scents of humans and the water buffalo they used to tend the soil were heavy in the air.

He slipped through the moonless night, his senses alert for danger until he was next to the largest house.

Empty; that's odd. I would have thought the workers would gravitate to the largest. He shrugged and moved on to the next.

That house yielded the same results. He knew there were humans around. He thought it odd that they were not in the houses. Miko was about to move on to the next village when a noise from a barn caught his attention. He slipped through the village, being sure to stay in the shadows until he was at the rear of a barn.

There were noises of people and animals coming from

the barn. A cow lowed from inside as if it was in pain, and he could hear voices inside.

"Just a little more," the strained voice murmured. "You've almost got it, girl. Just a bit more."

Miko slid the door open just enough to see inside. A man knelt in the straw behind a very pregnant cow that was lying on the floor. A woman held a lead rope attached to a halter on the animal, and two teenagers, a boy and a slightly older girl, stood ready with towels and a bucket.

"Here it comes." The man grunted as he delivered the calf. The girl moved in with the towels, and the man took one and wrapped the calf in it. He handed the bundle to her, and she carried it to the side.

Miko watched them for a few moments as they tended to the cow. He was weak from pushing his body so hard, but for some reason, he hesitated. Just as he started to push the door open and take the blood his body craved so badly, a memory crashed into his mind.

It was a warm summer night, and the smell of cut hay surrounded him. He was looking out of an opening at the night sky. His hand held another in a familiar, comforting way. The memory continued, and words came with it.

"Why do we have to hide all the time? You come to my apartment or arrange to meet in seclusion. Are you ashamed of me?"

A soft hand cupped his face and stroked a finger along his clean-shaven jaw.

"No, there is no shame, only great danger. If we are discovered, we will both be killed."

"I don't understand. You are not someone who is easily killed. I saw what you did to the men who attacked me.

That was not the actions of someone who needs to fear anything."

The man beside him pulled away a bit and looked deep into his eyes. He found himself drifting away from the conversation, lost in those deep pools.

"It's true that I am a capable fighter, but the people I speak of are just as capable and more. If we are found out, I would be helpless to resist if my queen ordered it."

"Who is this queen? We don't have real royalty anymore, only the puppet emperor who now answers to bureaucrats."

The figure shook his head. "She is not a human queen. She is like me and controls many more. If she ordered it, I would have no ability to resist, even if she ordered me to kill you."

He drew in a sharp breath, his eyes going round with shock. "Surely you jest. No one could hold that type of power over you."

His lips tightened into a straight line. "She can do that and more. Please, let's enjoy the time we have and not dwell on things we have no power to change. Be happy that I am here now and will return to you as soon and as often as it is safe."

The memory was interrupted by a voice close by. Miko's eyes shot open and he found the man standing in front of him, a wicked-looking pitchfork held in his hands.

"What do you want?" he called, his voice trembling as his body shook. "We have nothing of value. Come into the light so I can see you."

Miko stared at the man as his family moved farther back into the barn. The hunger rose in him as the man's heart rate increased and the smell of fear emanated from his body. He took a step forward, his body moving by instinct before his mind even registered it.

The man stabbed the four sharp metal tines at him. Miko's hand blurred, catching the makeshift weapon and ripping it from his hands. He caught the man by his shirt and pulled him close. Feeling his fangs lengthen, he drew back to strike like a serpent into the soft flesh that held what he needed just below the surface.

His eyes wandered to the other three people huddled in the back and he froze. The woman had pushed both children behind her, the girl still holding the newborn calf close. It was the action of a mother protecting her young, not unexpected in this or any age. What caused him to pause was not the terrified look on her face; that was not unexpected either since he had seen it many times.

What made him pause were the words he heard in the woman's mind. They came unbidden, and he knew they were not his thoughts.

Honored ancestors, please do not let this xīxuèguǐ *take him. Please let him take me instead. My children cannot survive without him.*

Miko shook his head to clear the strangeness. His eyes focused on the woman again as more words came.

He stops. Let him look over and see me. She took a step forward, shaking off the hands of her children as they tried to hold her back. "Yes, look here, see me. Don't take him. Please, take me instead."

Miko pushed the man away and stared hard at the woman. She took his actions as agreement and slowly walked toward him. The look on her face told him she was afraid but determined.

Miko looked at the family and was struck by what he saw: love, compassion, and caring. Things he had not felt in many years, but because of the returning memories, he realized they were something he'd once had.

He hesitated briefly, then nodded once at the woman and disappeared into the night. Though he needed to feed, he believed the person in his dreams and memories would think less of him if he had taken that family.

When that thought came to him, he stopped and almost returned to the barn. It was foolish to not take what he needed because someone from his past who might be dead would disapprove. The frightened woman had been a willing sacrifice, knowing her death would not be as dangerous for her children's survival as her husband's. He could provide for and protect them better than she could.

Miko stood in the darkness, torn between what his body needed and what he felt inside was right. It was a dilemma he had never encountered before in all his memory.

He shook his head, disgusted at his weakness. Then he trudged on, leaving the family in peace.

CHAPTER THIRTY-SEVEN

Sacred Clan Base, Liaoning Province, China

"Zi," Pan called from inside the house where the radio was. "The scouts have found the Forsaken's trail. Where's Cui?"

Zi looked up from his meal and pointed at the hill about one hundred meters distant. Cui was walking around the top with the satellite phone pressed to his ear. "Master Peng called again for an update. Since the report of Kang's team being killed came in, he has demanded hourly updates."

It had been several days since scouts had discovered the dead team, but they were still no closer to finding the Forsaken. They had tracked him into the mountains and lost his trail after he went into a river.

"What have they found? Have they located the Forsaken?" Zi demanded.

"Not yet, but there have been more bodies found." Pan waved a hand. "Get Cui! Master Peng will want to hear this, too."

Zi ran the short distance, and in seconds, he and Cui were at the house.

"What is it, Pan?" Cui asked after setting the phone to speaker mode so Kun could listen in.

"Sir, we just received two reports within minutes. Team Seven found three dead bandits on the road near Linyi. Then one of the teams Grand Master Peng sent out after Team Twenty-Four was found reported another near Funing County. All had bite marks that match the Forsaken we seek."

"He's headed south. Recall all the teams north of Funing County and reposition them south to the coast," Kun ordered over the phone. "I am sending all the fighters left in the temple to join the ones I sent out earlier this week. He is close to the coast, and I imagine he is trying to get to one of the functioning ports to flee our wrath."

Cui motioned to the radio operator who had been listening, and he started transmitting Kun's orders to the team.

"It is being done now, Master," Cui assured him.

Kun didn't acknowledge him. Instead, he continued spewing orders. "Cui, your team needs to go south to stop him. You have seven hours before dark, so use that time wisely. Do not fail in your duty to the Clan."

"Yes, Grand Master. We will leave immediately."

"Good. Our people in the towns have all been warned to look out for the Forsaken. We have a large presence in that area, so he will not be able to pass through undetected like he did before."

"Master Cui," the radio operator called. "The team at Funing just reported that they have found his trail. They are tracking him to the south as the Grand Master said, and the trail is less than four hours old."

"Grand Master..." Cui started.

"I heard him. Get moving now," Kun demanded. "I will go to the site at Lu'an, where there is a base radio. These damned mountains interfere with the signal so much. I will coordinate the search from there."

Before Cui could answer, Kun started shouting orders to people at the temple. He came back on the sat-phone when he was done. "Have your radio operator notify Lu'an that I am coming there and for them to contact the radio-equipped teams in the area to coordinate the hunt. We have over one hundred radio operators scattered across the area, so he can't escape us now."

The phone signaled that the connection was terminated as soon as Kun finished speaking. Cui nodded at the door, and Zi and Pan went out at a run to gather their belongings and collect Ren.

They were all in tiger form and running south five minutes later.

Nishitama District, Tokyo, Japan

Li and his team had been running hard for the past two days. After learning the fate of the team sent to Wajima, Grand Master Peng had ordered them to go to Tokyo. They were supposed to try to contact a criminal boss he had dealt with before WWDE. He didn't know if the man was still alive but thought it was worth trying to locate him.

The address he had given was a grand house

surrounded by a high stone wall. Wu and Jin had reconnoitered the night before and found only two entrances, each obstructed by heavy iron gates and guards carrying military-style rifles. Shao had tried to approach it on foot, but motion-detector-activated lights prevented him from getting close. Within moments of the light activating, there was a group of three heavily armed men at that section of wall and two more looking down with scopes on long rifles from the top.

Li had decided it would be best to approach the house during the day, so the team had found a place to hole up half a kilometer away. His plan was to approach it alone, leaving the team out of sight but close if he needed them.

As Li approached, a black SUV pulled up to the gate. After a conversation over the intercom, the gate swung open and admitted the vehicle. The humans appeared to be focused and alert, more so than guards performing a boring routine duty. They were on edge, like they were expecting trouble.

Li walked up to the box affixed to a pole outside of the gate.

As he was reaching for the button, a harsh voice came out of the speaker. "We don't need any of whatever it is you're selling. Leave."

Li looked at the guard inside the gate with his rifle held ready. It wasn't pointed at him, but it would only take the guard a second to do so. He pressed the button, and the voice came out again. This time it spoke in mangled Cantonese. "We don't want any of what you're peddling. Go away before we call the authorities."

"I'm not peddling anything," Li answered in perfect

Japanese. "I have a message from my master for Sakutaro-*san*."

"What is it? Sakutaro-*san* is a busy man."

"My master said that the message must be delivered to Sakutaro-*san* in person. He assured me that Sakutaro would look upon it unfavorably if it was delivered to any ears but his own."

"Who is your master? Sakutaro is too busy to have his time wasted."

"Tell him my master is an old and powerful friend from the east," Li replied. "I assure you he will want to talk to me. It could be worth quite a bit to him. My master is known for his generosity to his friends."

After a ten minute wait, the guard in the shack set into the wall picked up a phone. He had a hurried conversation with someone on the other end, and after he hung up, the gate started to swing open.

Li smiled at the guard who had been watching him the whole time and walked to the open gate. The guard in the gatehouse held a short black rifle with a long magazine sticking out the bottom.

"Halt," the guard at the gate ordered. When Li complied, he glanced at his partner briefly before he ordered Li to raise his arms. The guard checked him from head to toe. Finding nothing, he picked up a flat wand and waved it over Li's body. When there was nothing found, Li was escorted inside the gates.

The guard led him through the front door of the house. It opened into a high-ceilinged great room with a curved staircase running up each side to the second floor. The place reeked of wealth and privilege.

Li tried not to gawk like a country bumpkin in the city for the first time. He was led through the house to a garden in the back, where there were several more hard-looking guards, each of them with a sidearm on their belt and an AK-47 in their hands. None of them threatened him directly, but it was implied in the way they stared and preened like hard-eyed peacocks.

Li fought down a laugh, secure in the knowledge that he could kill all of them without breaking a sweat.

An older man in a wheelchair was looking out over the garden. "You have a message for me. What is it?" he demanded, his voice clear and strong even though his body was thin and weak.

"You are Sakutaro-*san*?" Li inquired.

The man nodded. "*Hai*, now get on with it. I'm not getting any younger while I wait."

Li stiffened, not accustomed to being spoken to that way. "Grand Master Peng Kun bids you greetings and says, 'the Dragon fades while the Tiger rises.'"

Sakutaro stiffened in his chair and turned his head to stare at Li through rheumy eyes. "Leave us," he ordered the guards.

"Sakutaro-*san*, your granddaughter issued orders that you must have one of us with you at all times."

"My granddaughter worries too much. Tell her I said… Better yet, send for her," he ordered. "If she is here, I won't be alone, and she needs to be here for this meeting."

Sakutaro nodded at Li. "She will be here soon. Would you like some refreshments while we wait? You look as though you have traveled a long way to see me."

"Yes, it was a long trip." Li heard heels strike the wooden floors in the great room.

Seconds later, the double doors burst open, and a stunning black-haired woman wearing six-inch spiked heels stalked into the garden with fire in her eyes. "Who let this man in to see my grandfather? Why wasn't I notified? No one is to bother him."

Li was shocked at the venom her voice held as she dressed down the guard who had refused to leave.

Sakutaro watched her, his mouth a tight line and his face flushed. "I did, granddaughter. I am the master of this house and the ruler of this territory. I see who I want, and you had best remember that. Do not confuse an old man's love for his granddaughter with weakness. You would be wrong."

The young woman's face paled as she cut off mid-tirade. "My apologies, Grandfather. I only wish to keep you from being bothered with trivial matters."

"Who decides what is trivial?" His voice was low and held a hint of menace.

She swallowed hard twice, trying to form the words but unable to.

"Leave us, all of you. My granddaughter and I have business with our guest. Have that kitchen girl bring refreshments." He looked at Li. "Tea? Coffee? whiskey?"

"Tea would be fine, Sakutaro-*san*," Li replied.

A young woman in a servant's uniform pushed a cart laden with cups and carafes through the door a few minutes later. When she started to serve them, Sakutaro stopped her. "Leave us. Granddaughter, you will serve our honored guest."

The young woman stiffened at this but dutifully did as she was told.

Sakutaro watched her with a slight smile on his lips. "What news do you have from my old friend Peng Kun? It's been many years since I heard that name. Is he well?"

Li accepted his cup with a nod. "He is well and will be pleased that you are also. We seek information, which Master Kun thought you could provide."

Sakutaro waved his hand in a come-on motion.

"We seek information on a man called Akio," Li told him.

The young woman jerked when he said that and dropped a fine porcelain cup on the floor, where it shattered into small shards.

"That is dangerous information you seek, my friend," Sakutaro answered. "The last who sought him out died for it, and it caused untold anguish to many of his friends when the government came for them."

"I understand he is dangerous, but my master requires that I obtain the information. Do you know where he can be found?"

"No, not the specific location, but I do have an idea where you may start. Understand that if I give you this information, all debts between Peng Kun and I are settled."

Li nodded his agreement. "I will pass the message to Grand Master Peng."

"A few weeks past, one of my associates became involved with the man you seek. He took someone he should not have and died as a result. It is not just the one you seek who poses risk. He is not alone, and the information I have received on his companions says they are not to be taken lightly, even though they are a woman and a strange childlike creature."

"A creature that is some type of child?" Li mused. Akio also having a dangerous woman as a companion was not surprising to Li. Female tigers were more dangerous than the males.

Sakutaro shrugged. "*Hai.* My sources informed me that the child rescued the person who was taken alone. The damage she caused to the structure alone was extensive. She also killed with some weapons that are like none I have ever heard of. Are you certain you wish to hunt those beings?"

"I do as Grand Master Peng directs. What I want or do not want is irrelevant."

Sakutaro nodded, "As it should be. The one you seek has been seen near the Shinjuku City area of Tokyo. The woman who was taken works at an entertainment facility west of that area. I will provide you with the address."

Li bowed. "Thank you, Sakutaro-*san.* My master and I appreciate your assistance."

"Assistance? I offer nothing further than a scrap of paper with a location on it. You were never here and neither my organization nor I will do anything for you or your," he paused for a moment and looked Li directly in the eye, "Clan from this point on."

Li nodded, understanding that the meeting was done and the crime boss felt the information was enough to settle whatever debt he owed Kun. "I will leave you now with my thanks."

"Granddaughter, escort our guest to the door and return. We have things to discuss."

Li stood and followed the young woman from the room, and she walked him to the door in silence. As he was leaving, she softly spoke. "You are on a fool's quest. This person and the people around him are not human. They are some type of *oni*. Go back to China or die."

Li stood looking at the closed door after she departed, wondering what had happened that made the knowledge, even if it was skewed, of the UnknownWorld not so unknown here. He would need to discuss that with Kun before going any further.

CHAPTER THIRTY-EIGHT

TQB Base, Tokyo, Japan

"Akio?" Yuko called over his chip. "Are you busy?"

"No," he answered. "What do you need?"

"I wanted to talk to you if you have a few minutes."

"I can meet you in the command center if you would like," he offered.

"I'm on my way there now."

Akio turned off the music and pulled on his boots, then made his way out of his room. A short time later, he walked through the command center's door.

Yuko was already sitting there with two cups of tea in her hands. Akio nodded his thanks as he took the offered cup and sat, savoring the dark tea's aroma before sipping.

"Thank you for coming," Yuko started.

"Thank you for the tea," Akio replied, gifting her with a smile. "It is delicious."

Yuko blushed, slightly annoyed that he still had that effect on her after so many years. In many ways, she had grown into the confident, self-assured woman Bethany

Anne had said she would. In others, she was still the star-struck young girl from the day she and Akio first met. She smiled at herself as she recalled her disappointment at finding out he wasn't interested in girls.

That feeling made her hesitate, unsure of how to introduce the subject on her mind. "Akio, I wanted to ask how you are." She rushed on, uncomfortable with the thought that she was prying. "You've been withdrawn since you and Horst returned from Australia. You spend all your time in here or locked away in your quarters. Eve and I are worried about you. Is there anything we can do to help you through this?"

Akio stared at Yuko over the top of the cup until she feared she'd offended him. She was on the verge of apologizing and leaving when he finally spoke.

"I have been dealing with old memories."

Yuko stayed silent, watching his face as he thought about what he wanted to say.

"I have been remembering moments from my time with Kenjii, memories I had made myself forget," Akio confessed.

"I have times when my memories haunt me as well," Yuko offered. "I miss my parents intensely, but I have found that talking about it with Eve helps. Would you like to try that?"

Akio looked at her through hooded eyes. He hadn't shared his private life when human, and his time as a vampire hadn't changed that.

"If it is too painful, I understand," Yuko went on. "I don't want to pry, but it hurts me to see you like this. You have been my rock for many years. I want to be yours if you will allow it."

"Yuko." He closed his eyes, a pained expression on his face. "I don't know how to begin."

She placed her hand on his arm. Her expression—caring, concerned, loving, even—made him turn away. Although he knew inside that Bethany Anne had redeemed him, he still had centuries of experience in believing himself a soulless monster who was unworthy of love.

"Akio, you are my friend, and I love you. Know this: no matter what, that will never change," Yuko assured him.

When Akio next spoke, his voice cracked from the emotions he'd put in a box many years ago and promised never to let out. "Yuko, I told you I thought Kenjii was dead. The reason I thought that was because I watched him die screaming while Isamu and Ogawa tortured him in front of me."

His eyes lost focus as he fell into his memory. Yuko thought he'd finished until he spoke in a flat monotone.

"It was the spring of nineteen fifty-seven. Kenjii and I had spent whatever time I could steal since November of the year before. He knew what I was and accepted me. No, he loved me as a person, not as the monster I felt I was.

"I had feelings I hadn't experienced since before I was turned: happiness, joy, love. Things I thought lost to me forever.

"I would sneak to his apartment in the night. Most times he was already in, but occasionally I would arrive and find the home empty. I enjoyed those nights because I was able to set up the tea service and prepare it for him. If he was home when I arrived, he wouldn't dream of not playing the proper host, but those nights I was able to do that for him. It made his eyes sparkle like the stars in the sky when I surprised him.

"Kamiko summoned me and informed me that the criminal I'd left in charge of Chiba had become greedy. I was to go to their headquarters and kill all of them. I carefully contained the excitement that caused. I couldn't afford to act any different than I had in centuries past. I took my leave and was in Chiba a short time later.

"I went through the warehouse like a man possessed. I didn't feed, I simply killed and moved on to the next. When it was done, I took the time to clean myself up, having thought to bring a change of clothes with me. I was happy as I made my way to his home. The night was young, and I was not expected back until just before dawn.

"When I arrived at his house, the lights were on, letting me know he was home. I used my key and rushed up the steps to the living room, excited to see him." He paused, his lips pursed tight and a pained expression on his face.

"Kamiko Kana was sitting on the couch, the one where Kenjii and I had spent many happy nights. She commanded me to kneel at her feet and remain silent. I tried to fight the compulsion but was unable to do so. My creator had given me to her, and I could no more disobey her than I could harm him the day I was made."

Yuko covered her mouth with a hand, repressing a gasp.

Akio didn't notice, lost in the retelling. "Kamiko forced me to follow as Ogawa took Kenjii from his home, the place where he felt safe. I could only watch as they dragged him past me, terrified by what was happening. His eyes begged me to save him.

"What came next was a horror no one should ever endure, or see. They tortured him before my eyes. Isamu directed it like a maniac conducting a symphony, but instead of beautiful music, he caused the gut-wrenching screams of a person in unbearable pain. The sights and sounds have stayed with me ever since.

"Heinz was there as well. He drew my blood with a syringe and explained his theory to Isamu, who tested it by dribbling my blood into Kenjii when the damage was too much for him to survive. The theory proved to be correct, so they played their sadistic games through the night. Between his screams, Isamu and Kamiko repeated that I was the ultimate cause of his suffering. I would have killed them all had I not been compelled, and Kamiko had to reinforce the compulsion several times that night. I was beset with rage such as I had never experienced, becoming more beast than man. I would have taken both of our lives had it not been forbidden. Anything to make the pain stop."

Silent tears ran down Yuko's face. Still, she listened as Akio relieved the burden on his soul.

"An hour before sunrise, they brought him back from the brink one last time. Isamu made me watch as Ogawa heated irons in a fire and held them to his face time and time again. I watched him die. One moment he was breathing weakly, and the next, he was gone.

"I died for the second time that day. Kamiko ordered me from the room and locked me in the metal casket that she used to punish us when we displeased her. I remained there for six months, growing weaker each day, wanting to die but unable to do even that.

"When she released me, she compelled me never to

forget what I had caused and reinforced the orders that prevented me from taking any action against Heinz or her torturers. She then ordered me to feed and clean myself up."

He chuckled darkly, the first sound that hadn't come out dead and lifeless since he had started. "When I finished the bath and was wrapping the cord to hold my hair in place, the pain of looking at the long hair he'd enjoyed running his fingers through on so many nights was too much. In a fit of grief, I hacked it off.

"I might not have been able to take my life, but I could eliminate that reminder of our relationship. I had worn that style since before I was turned. Since then, I have worn it like this as another reminder of what happens when emotion is allowed to overcome common sense."

Yuko's face reflected her horror. She knew that Isamu and Ogawa were worse than animals, given what they'd done to the people of Kume. This admission made some of what they'd said and Akio's actions on the island that night clearer. He'd told her then that he had an old issue with the two. Now that she knew what it was, she wished they could travel back to that day and do it all over again. Well, maybe she'd skip the Nosferatu in the basement, but she knew now that neither Isamu nor Ogawa had suffered as they deserved. They had died much too cleanly.

CHAPTER THIRTY-NINE

Shandong Province, China

Miko traveled hard through the night, stopping only long enough to feed on three men he found camping just off the road. He had no compunction about taking the lives of bandits who preyed on the local farmers as they transported their crops to the trading post to trade for items they needed.

The fresh blood replenished his energy and allowed him to push on. By the time he felt dawn approaching, he had traveled another hundred kilometers. If not for the coming sun he could have continued.

He found a sign along the road that indicated he was ten kilometers from Linyi. He had managed to make good time on the route to Shanghai. He only had around five hundred kilometers to go, and should be there within two nights. Then he could book passage to Japan and start looking for the answers to his past.

He found an abandoned factory that showed signs of many years of neglect. The roof had caved in, and trees had sprouted around it and grown over the years, breaking the concrete as their roots searched out nutrients.

He worked his way through the broken concrete slabs, moving some out of the way and then back into place behind him as he went. When he found a doorway not blocked by debris, he forced it open.

Inside was a dry, and more importantly, dark, space with no windows. Miko pulled the door closed, wrapped a piece of heavy-duty electrical wire around the handle, and tied the other end to a piece of equipment. Miko had no idea what the machine did, but the heavy metal bolts anchoring it to the floor made it perfect for his makeshift door lock.

He lay down behind the machine, as far from the door as he could get, in case someone found his hiding place for the day. He could function during the daylight hours, although he preferred not to. Being awake when the sun was up had always bothered him on some level. If anyone invaded his space, they would not find him an easy target.

This time when the dream came, his mind recognized it immediately. Isamu and Ogawa were gone, along with the mystery man who was so familiar. Heinz stood over him, talking softly.

"Miko; your name is Miko. You will answer to that name only. No matter what other names you might be called, you are Miko. Do you understand?"

He watched himself answer, his body no longer restrained and bearing no signs of the torture he had endured. "I understand."

"You will not remember what happened before now. If

you are troubled by memories from before this time, you will tell me immediately."

"Immediately," he mumbled.

"You will obey me in all things," Heinz ordered. "You are mine to command. My wants are your wants, and you live to do my bidding."

He watched as his body stood and followed Heinz. They got in a car and a tall bearded blond man drove them to a small airfield, where they boarded a plane.

A few hours later, they arrived at an airstrip in what he recognized as the strip he had used many times over the last few decades, the strip that serviced the lab and base at Acheng.

He woke up for the first time in weeks not primed for a fight and covered in blood sweat. He lay there for a few minutes recalling the dream, or more accurately, the memory. That was the first memory he recalled from the life he had led for the last century.

Miko. Heinz gave me this name. Who was I? Why did he bring me back from death? Surely there is more to this.

More frustrating questions he hoped to answer when he arrived in Japan.

CHAPTER FORTY

Kunshan, China

Yi Zhi kicked the body they had found thrown down an embankment. The twin punctures on his throat left no doubt to his cause of death. "Master Cui, we are still behind him."

All the teams had been recalled to the nine provinces that made up southwestern China. With the men sent out by Grand Master Peng and the other teams streaming into the area daily, Cui believed the Forsaken was as good as found. Cui had run his team hard the day before and well into the night, stopping only for short rests and to check for messages from Kun. They had made the entire journey in tiger form and had put many kilometers behind them in the past day and a half.

Kun had sent messages through the sat-phone each time an update was received. That information allowed Cui to guide his team to the point where they were close on the heels of the Forsaken. The kill Wu had found had been taken shortly after sunset, which put them less than three hours behind him. They were in Kunshan, less than one hundred kilometers from the southern coast, and had been running along the old expressway since early afternoon. That expressway ended forty kilometers south in Shanghai.

Cui had notified Kun of his suspicions that the Forsaken was trying to get to the port in Shanghai to make his escape several hours earlier. Kun had pulled more radio-equipped teams into the area and set up a network that would alert them when he arrived.

The hard pace Cui had set was wearing on his men, and tempers were starting to flare. They were all tired and angry, wanting nothing more than to find and kill the Forsaken who had caused them so much pain.

"We will have him soon, Yi, and when we do, he will not have a fast or easy death," Cui assured him. "The Clan shall be avenged for the disrespect he has shown."

Yi growled. "I will delight in peeling his skin away in small pieces for many days."

Cui flashed an evil grin. "His screams will usher the spirits of our dead to the temple of the ancestors. They will be pleased."

Yi nodded as the four set out at a ground-eating pace once again.

Shanghai, China

Miko had his goal in sight. He had pushed himself the past few days to levels he had never been able to achieve before. He had discovered that in addition to being physically stronger, he now had mental abilities that allowed him to read minds on a limited basis. It required strong emotions in his victim such as fear, but he was able to pick up their thoughts as he took them. He had discovered that the more afraid they were, the easier it was to read them since the experience with the family in the barn. He didn't know if it would continue to get stronger, but past experiences with the serums Heinz had given him had taught him that the effects sometimes did continue to develop over time.

He had passed a sign half an hour earlier that told him he was almost to Shanghai. The past two days had taken a toll on him as he pushed himself ever harder to reach the port city. It was approaching one in the morning, and he was heading down a wide dark street with empty, shattered buildings on each side. The damage was years old, judging from the trees that grew inside of some of the bombed-out structures.

The entire area was devoid of human life. He could sense small animals in the rubble, but humans hadn't lived there in many years. He had fed an hour earlier on a trio of drunks who had passed out after sampling the brew from a makeshift still they had set up in an abandoned supermarket. Miko's body was fully healed from the damage he had taken since leaving Acheng, but he was mentally exhausted.

He had picked up the scent of Weretigers several times since he had woken up. The scents crossed his path, causing him to slow and expend energy searching ahead with his senses. He discovered that he had gained more range than he'd had when he'd started this mad dash across China. He put it down to another gain from the injection and that he was exercising the ability more.

Whatever the cause, he had used it three times in the past hour to go around groups of Weres in his path. It annoyed him to have to avoid them, but he knew they had to be the ones the Were he'd killed over a week ago had said were searching for him.

He froze when he heard a cough in the shadows ahead. He reached out with his senses and found two Weres in human form on the ground floor of a multistory building that was relatively undamaged. The windows were gone, but from what he could see, the building had not been hit by any of the bombs that had damaged so many more.

A feral grin crossed Miko's face. He was tired and angry that these Weres still thought they were equal to a vampire.

He cut down an alley to the next street over, then stopped at the mouth and searched for more Weres. Once he was sure the two he had found were alone, he jumped to the second level, catching the floor where the window was missing and swinging his weight inside.

Miko slowly worked his way through the building, skirting piles of debris left by scavengers who had stripped out anything useable. He entered an open stairwell leading down, carefully dodging the piles of trash dropped there over the years until he was on the ground floor.

The two Weres were still watching the street in front when Miko burst through the open door into the room. He had his butterfly swords in his hands as he rushed across the open space to the first Were, and he swung both swords in a cross sweep, one high and the other low. The first Were was dead before he hit the floor, blood gushing from the wound across his throat, while his hands futilely pushed against his guts where they spilled out of his open abdomen.

Miko allowed his body to follow the direction of the high sword and spun to face the second Were. He had shifted while Miko dispatched the other and was now in the form of a tiger that stood over a meter tall at the shoulder.

The big cat snarled a challenge as he leapt for Miko, who blocked a swipe from one claw-tipped paw with a sword but was thrown off balance when a pile of trash slipped under his foot.

The tiger missed his throat, but the paw slammed into him. His chest felt like it was on fire when the sharp claws gouged four deep furrows across it. The force of the blow combined with the loose material underfoot caused Miko to fall to the littered floor.

The tiger was on him in a flash, one paw on his shoulder, the claws digging deep into his flesh while the powerful jaws moved in for the kill.

Miko brought the razor-sharp *hudiedao* up and slammed it hilt-deep into the tiger's side. The wide blade met resistance when it hit the beast's ribs, but Miko powered it through until the bones snapped.

The cat backed up and yowled in pain, ripping Miko's shoulder as it jerked the claws buried in it back. That was the opening Miko needed to bring his second sword into play. The damaged flesh around his shoulder pulsed, sending a white-hot bolt of agony through his body as he stabbed the tiger repeatedly with the short sword.

The cat fell over with a heavy *thump*, a sword embedded in its side and blood pooling out of the multiple wounds in its chest. Miko rolled onto his back, his breath coming in pained gasps as the flesh on his shoulder slowly knitted back together. As he lay there healing, he heard the snarls of hunting cats echoing in the distance.

The vampire painfully climbed to his feet and listened. The snarls were coming from three different directions, some closer than others, but all were heading toward him. He ripped his short sword from the body on the floor and jumped through the empty window frame. When his feet hit the pavement, he sprinted south, the only direction he had not detected snarls coming from.

CHAPTER FORTY-ONE

TQB Base, Tokyo, Japan

Akio and Yuko were sitting silently in the command center, still lost in their thoughts of the tale Akio had shared.

"Akio," Abel announced over the speakers. "I have located the person you seek."

"Where?"

"He has entered Shanghai," Abel replied as the monitor above the desk came to life. The screen showed a lone figure walking down a dark street lined with debris and shattered buildings.

"Enhance lighting," Akio requested. The picture cleared as Abel adjusted the light. "Zoom in on the person."

The figure on the screen slowly grew larger until his features were clear. He was a sorry sight. His clothes were in tatters, and his bare skin was visible through numerous holes. His tunic was stained with dark blotches, and his hair was matted and filthy.

"Kenjii, it *is* you," Akio whispered.

The figure moved warily, stopping every few meters as though checking for scents.

"I've located another fixed location in Lu'an. The transmissions all concern the Forsaken," Abel continued.

Akio smiled. "Kenjii. His name is Kenjii."

"Acknowledged. Kenjii is now the vampire's designation." The monitor switched from his location to a map of the region. "Here is Lu'an." A blue dot appeared on the screen. "There is a drone inside the facility and a carrier close by to relay the signal." The map zoomed out and multiple red dots popped up. "The pursuers are converging on a single area."

"Do they have him in sight?" Akio asked.

"Negative," Abel replied. "The radio traffic indicates that they know he's headed to Shanghai. They've been following a trail of corpses."

Akio got to his feet. "Do you have drones on more of the searchers yet?"

"Yes," Abel confirmed. "I've attached drones to twenty-three teams throughout the area. I have audio on all, and video on fifteen of them. One of the groups has been identified as the command team. I currently have four of the enhanced drones above them. That team is presently thirty kilometers north of Shanghai."

"Bring the Pod down," Akio ordered.

"It is in the inner courtyard," Abel confirmed.

Akio rushed to his quarters. Moments later, he was in his black armor and sprinting to the elevator at the end of the hall. The doors opened before he arrived, and the elevator was moving before the doors finished closing. When they opened, he stepped out and into the second elevator that would take him to the ground level. He was in the air and screaming toward China three minutes and forty seconds after he left the command center.

The Pod was crossing the China coast when Abel informed him. "Kenjii has engaged one of the teams I am tracking."

"Keep the drone shadowing him and keep me apprised of his location," Akio instructed.

"Acknowledged."

Kunshan-Shanghai border, China

The satellite phone in Cui's pack buzzed, indicating an update from Kun in his command post. Cui stopped and shifted to human form. The others dropped to the ground, panting hard from exertion from the continuous sprint he'd ordered.

"We have him," Cui crowed. "One of the pickets spotted him. He's only a few kilometers ahead of us."

He stowed the phone and was about to shoulder the pack when it buzzed again, this time indicating a call. He answered it, "Cui here."

"Team Six advises that they heard fighting near their location. Team Sixty-Eight's picket was also close, and they aren't responding to calls. Teams Six, Twenty, and Nine are entering the area now. It is only two kilometers south of where he was initially spotted," Kun advised without preamble.

A tiger's roar erupted in the distance. Seconds later, two more followed. Cui's head snapped up, his features clouding with rage. "The teams are announcing their presence. I heard three distinct groups on the hunt," he growled into the receiver.

"I have ordered all teams to engage," Kun stated. "We have the numbers to end him quickly and with little risk if they coordinate their attacks. There are twelve more teams moving to his location as we speak. I suggest you make haste if you wish to take part. This will be over within the next ten minutes."

"Yes, Grand Master." Cui ensured that the connection ended and addressed his team while he stowed the phone.

"Grand Master Peng has ordered the other teams to attack. Three are entering the area where Kun believes the vampire took out another team. We need to hurry before he kills more."

Cui headed south down the expressway and shifted into his tiger form on the run. One second, a naked human pounded down the road on bare feet. The next, a huge orange and black tiger tore down the road, leaving a cloud of dust behind.

Pod over Shanghai, China

"Akio, Kenjii has been spotted. There are multiple hostiles entering his current area. I'm sending the coordinates to your Pod," Abel called as the display screen in the Pod illuminated, showing a satellite view of Shanghai with a pulsing red dot on it.

"Do you still have real-time surveillance on him?" Akio inquired.

"Yes," Abel confirmed. "I have also deployed additional drones to the area where the radio transmission originated. I haven't located the team that's following him, but I have located four more groups that are less than five minutes out."

"Are any of the drones the enhanced model?"

"Negative. All of those are currently engaged. I can divert two from Kenjii if you'd like."

"No," Akio decided. "I will be there in a few seconds. Keep me advised of their locations once you have them covered. Also, utilize the enhanced drones to protect Kenjii if needed."

"I've synced the monitor in your Pod to track the drones covering him. As soon as I've confirmed the additional hostiles, I will sync those locations as well."

Akio studied the screen. "Where is the lead team?"

A blue dot appeared on the screen several kilometers north of the red one. It was obvious that it was moving much faster. While Akio watched, several new markers popped up.

"He has engaged two weretigers, and a second group of four is approaching from the south. They will be there in forty-three seconds at their current pace."

"Put me down on a side street ahead of that team. I want to intercept them," Akio ordered as he touched the dot that indicated the four he wanted to target.

Akio unstrapped himself and stood. The Pod was descending at a comfortable rate for him to do one last equipment check, nothing like the wild ride into Adelaide the last time he had gone into battle.

Miko stopped, his senses flaring as the wind shifted from behind him. *Weres, close behind me.*

He slipped through an open doorway and froze. He pushed his senses out, trying to determine the number of Weres and, more importantly, how close they were.

His body had taken damage in that last ill-advised attack. The muscles around his shoulder were healing, but he'd expended so much energy running during the past two days that his healing was slow. He needed to feed.

The tigers he'd heard after he killed the two in the building were converging on his location. He sensed six nearby and heard many more snarls in the distance.

There were two Weres in tiger form running down the street less than a block from where he'd stopped. There was no chance of getting out of here without them spotting him. Miko grimaced as he pulled the short swords from their sheaths. His mauled arm sent jolts of pain through him when he tested it. It had healed enough for him to use it, but it wasn't going to feel good.

He saw both tigers slow and sniff the air as they approached his location, realizing he was close. He stepped out of the shadows and held his arms out to either side. "Looking for something?"

Both big cats roared and sprinted toward him. The closest leapt at Miko with its claws extended, intending to pull him down. He dodged to the side and brought a sword around, slashing the cat across its front shoulder. The tiger snarled and crashed to the pavement.

The second slammed into Miko, hitting his damaged shoulder, and he twisted to the side, dropping to one knee from the force of the impact. He attempted to lift his injured arm to block a slash, but it didn't respond. The claws ripped across his stomach, parting the flesh in four jagged lines.

Miko tried to move away as his deadly opponent came in for the kill, but the other tiger slammed into him from the side and knocked him to the ground. He was on his back, staring into the open jaws of the enraged Were. The jaws came closer as he tried to bring a sword up to block it, but a weight pinned his functioning arm. The second cat was on him now.

Akio was out of the Pod before it stopped. He drew his katana and darted into the street in front of the four rapidly approaching Weres.

They faltered. They'd sensed the vampire ahead but had no indication that they were facing two. Akio rushed toward them and plowed through the startled group, gleaming steel flashing in lethal arcs. When he stopped, four tigers were dead or dying.

He turned toward Kenjii's battle in time to see the vampire go down, pinned by two tigers, with one moving in to rip out his throat. "*No.*"

Akio growled as he accelerated to vampire speed, knowing deep down that even *he* wouldn't be fast enough.

Miko felt the tiger's hot breath on his face as it moved closer. His arm was on fire as the claws pinning it to the ground cut deep into his flesh. Everything was moving in slow motion as the gaping jaws closed on his head.

The cat's body jerked suddenly and its jaws moved away from his face, then a heavy weight pressed him harder against the ground. He felt something warm run down his face—blood.

Were blood.

The beast was bleeding.

What? How? Thoughts came slowly as Miko tried to make sense of what was happening. One minute, he was dead, no way to escape, and the next, a heavy, limp form weighed him down.

The tiger pinning his arm snarled, then excruciating pain stabbed through his arm as the claws penetrating it were torn free.

Miko pulled his legs close and pushed his body up to free himself from the dead weight holding him down. The corpse shifted slightly and then was gone, lifted and thrown out of his sight. He blinked and looked up to see a terrifying visage—red eyes glowing like fire set in a face twisted with rage.

Akio saw the tiger's jaws closing on Kenjii as he raced toward them.

"Drone deployed," Abel announced as the Weretiger jerked from the impact of one of Eve's combat drones punching through its head.

Akio changed course slightly and grabbed the tiger pinning Kenjii's arm. He lifted it by the scruff, and all four paws raked the air instead of Kenjii's flesh. He didn't hesitate as he brought his katana down, sending a large chunk of the cat's head spinning into the darkness.

He flung the cat away from him and grabbed the limp body pinning Kenjii to the ground. Looking down, he saw the torn and bloody form attached to a face he hadn't seen in decades—one he'd never expected to see again.

"Akio, I am tracking more than eighty inbound Weres. You'll be overrun if you don't leave now," Abel announced as the Pod landed beside him.

Akio didn't hesitate. He leaned down and lifted Kenjii as if he were a child. In one short step, they were in the Pod, and Abel lifted it into the sky.

The frustrated roars of the tigers below ripped through the air as the door slid shut, blocking out the noise as the Pod streaked toward Japan.

Miko looked up into the eyes of the man who gently cradled his battered body in his arms, shocked to still be alive, and equally shocked to see the man who'd haunted his dreams and thoughts for the past weeks. The one who'd watched as Isamu and Ogawa tortured him.

"Who? How? Who are you?" he whispered.

The man's voice was raw with emotion. "Akio."

"Who am I?" Miko asked, his voice barely audible.

Akio pulled him into a tight embrace, face pressed tight to his. "Kenjii. Your name is Kenjii."

Miko's head reeled as memories came to him in a kaleidoscope of images. *Kenjii! My name is Kenjii. Akio? Oh, ancestors...I remember.*

He remembered everything: his parents, the apartment above their store in Chiba, the toughs who had cornered him in the alley...and Akio.

"Akio. What? How? Where have you been?" Kenjii whispered, tears rolling down his face. "I remember the night you saved me, and all the nights we spent talking until you had to flee the sun. The hiding, the danger." His face paled. "The night they came for me—Isamu and that bastard Ogawa."

"*Hai,*" Akio answered softly. "I spent many years remembering it as well. I thought you were dead. I saw you die."

"Heinz. That fucking Heinz did this. He told those animals how to keep me alive, and after they took you away, he gave me his blood. He took my memories and compelled me to come to him anytime they threatened to return."

Akio closed his eyes, feeling Kenjii's pain and betrayal by someone he'd thought a friend through the mental link.

"All of them must die for this," Kenjii growled.

"Shh, it's okay," Akio murmured. "You're safe, now. There will be time once you're healed."

"No. They took my life, my name, and my memories." He pushed weakly against Akio, trying to get out of his grip.

Akio released him, and Kenjii stepped back. Dizziness overcame him, and he would've fallen if he hadn't grabbed the wall. His eyes went wide and dread shot through him when he spotted the red patch with a white female vampire skull affixed to Akio's shoulder. "You? *You're* the Bitch's assassin? The Dark One Heinz and Chang talked about?"

Akio cocked his head to one side, a confused look on his face. "Assassin? Dark One? I serve my Queen Bethany Anne, but those names are not familiar to me."

Abel's voice came over his chip. "The drones in the base obtained that information. Eve thought it best to withhold it. She felt that knowing they were calling you those names would make you unhappy."

Akio snorted and shook his head, causing Kenjii to take a couple of steps back. He held his hands flat, motioning for the man to stop as he lightly tapped one ear. "My compatriot only now informed me. I was not aware I had gained the names."

After a swift, assessing look, he continued, "You're injured. Let me help you." Akio held up a wrist and sliced it neatly, then offered it to him. "Drink. It will help."

He warily reached for the offered arm, trying to reconcile his memories of *his* Akio with the monster Heinz had described.

The blood hit his tongue like an electric shock, and his body began to heal seconds after taking it. He drank greedily, holding Akio's arm tightly as he tried to pull in more of the rich and powerful blood. It was over much too soon.

Akio pulled his arm away. Kenjii held on like a drowning man until Akio pried his jaw open with one thumb.

"I said, enough." Although he'd known Kenjii as a human, he'd been a Forsaken under Heinz's control for many years. Akio couldn't allow him to take enough blood to become more until he was sure the experience hadn't changed him. Granted, he had been the kindest person Akio had ever known as a human, but he had been compelled for a long time.

Kenjii reluctantly stopped, hungrily watching the cut as it healed before his eyes. Akio motioned for him to take a seat against the wall, and he sat on the bench and looked around at the craft, wondering where they were going but too battered and tired to care.

He closed his eyes, feeling at ease in a way he'd never known until his memories of the time he'd spent with Akio returned.

CHAPTER FORTY-TWO

Shanghai, China

Cui couldn't believe his eyes. There were two vampires, one on the ground and the other lifting a Weretiger with one hand and dispatching it with a sword. He watched in amazement as the vampire flung the four-hundred-kilo tiger away like it weighed nothing. The tiger pinning the other vampire to the ground was thrown like the first.

Movement caught his eye as a black object landed beside the vampires. The one standing lifted the one on the ground and stepped into the object. Seconds later, both were gone as the object lifted into the air, snatching the Forsaken from his grasp.

Cui roared in frustration as his quarry fled into the darkness.

"What the fuck was that?" Pan demanded as soon as he'd shifted to human form.

Cui also shifted as he watched the sky where the craft had disappeared. "I don't know," was all he could say.

. . .

Pod, Over Tokyo, Japan

"Abel, bring us down at the base," Akio ordered.

"Acknowledged."

"Akio," Yuko called over his chip. "Will you need the Pod-doc?"

He considered the question. "No."

The trip from China had been made in silence as Akio watched Kenjii, listening to his thoughts as his memories returned. He was happy to have him back, but he was concerned that he wasn't the same man he'd known. The videos he'd seen of Kenjii freeing himself from the destroyed Acheng site, the way he savagely took a man's life that night, and the trail of bodies he'd left across China were concerning, to say the least.

The fear Kenjii had shown when he saw Akio's Queen's Bitch patch, plus his years of living under the control of Heinz and his plans, not to mention the effects of working closely with Isamu and Ogawa, all figured into his decision. He had to remember those as they moved forward. He hoped he had found his lost love, but he was unable to determine if he could be redeemed yet. Kenjii's thoughts were too scattered and his emotions too raw to make an accurate assessment.

Yuko was waiting in the courtyard when the Pod landed. She greeted him with a warm smile and a hug when the door opened and he stepped out into the cool night.

"You found him. Is he..." She hesitated.

Akio answered as best he could. "He is injured but healing. The rest, we shall see."

Kenjii stood in the door of the Pod, cautiously peering at the two.

Yuko smiled at him as she motioned him out. "Hello, Kenjii. I'm Yuko. I've heard much about you. Welcome to our home."

"Your home?" Kenjii asked. "Where am I?"

Akio offered him his hand. "We're in Japan. Tokyo, to be exact."

Kenjii was taken aback. They'd made a trip in only a few minutes that took hours in Heinz's German craft. He took Akio's hand and allowed himself to be guided out into an open area surrounded by what looked like an office building.

"Your home? Tokyo?" he stammered.

"It's a lot to take in, isn't it?" Yuko laughed gently. "Come inside. You can clean up, and then we'll explain everything. Just know that you're among friends and safe."

Safe? I feel like the little girl in the story about the rabbit hole. Alice, I think her name was.

Akio smiled when Kenjii thought that, his first real smile in many years. *You have no idea, my friend.*

Akio and Kenjii walked hand in hand across the courtyard to a door that led inside. Neither knew what the future held, but for now, they were reunited.

It would have to be enough.

THE STORY CONTINUES

The story continues with book three, Retribution.

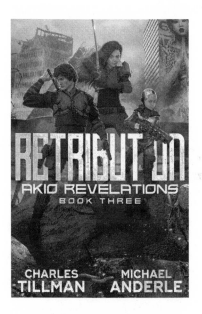

Available now at Amazon and through Kindle Unlimited.

AUTHOR NOTES CHARLES TILLMAN
JUNE 26, 2020

Thank you for reading this book and continuing to read these notes.

WOW! Thank you so much to all the fans who have sent me messages and posted in the Facebook groups about Akio Revelations: *Reprisal.* To say it is humbling is an understatement.

Telling this story has been a wild ride from the start. I knew it would be tough to take Michael's character and tell his story in a way that reflected what Michael, Craig, Ellie, etc... had already established as KGU canon. My biggest fear was and is that I wouldn't be able to do Akio justice.

This second book was a fun one to do. For those in the KGU Facebook family, I'm sure you recognized a name in this one. Yes, she is the inspiration for this character, and knowing her personally, I can sooo see her doing some of the things in this book. Love ya, Kelly!

When I started writing this one, I wanted to show a different side of Akio. While I was reading the other books in KGU, I always wondered why he was so serious. Why does he hate Forsaken so much? Why does he let no one get too close? What happened that made him like he is?

I hope I've answered those questions entertainingly and believably for all of you.

Book Three, Akio Revelations: *Retribution* is complete and will be out in a few weeks. (How's that for the "Where's the next book" questions?) Michael's words at the end of his Author Notes in *Reprisal* go back a few years when my friend and author Ell Leigh Clarke called on fans to ask Michael that question in reviews on Amazon. I did it on every book after that. Well played, Michael. Well played.

Speaking of reviews, they drive all of us who write to create these stories. A review on Amazon or Goodreads, just a few words, makes a world of difference to someone who spends many hours crafting a story.

Again, **thank you** all for reading this book and please drop by my Author page and say "Hi." I respond to messages as fast as I am able.

Thank you all for reading our stories, we can't do what we do without you!

Charles is in the afterglow of his first book release and now he can't pretend anymore.

He did it. *It's done.*

Forever there is an ASIN (and soon ISBN) with his name attached. (The ASIN is a unique id that Amazon provides a book (ebook). If you stay inside the Amazon distribution system you don't have to pay for the ISBN.)

Once we go to paperback (using Ingram POD (print on demand) services an ISBN will be assigned for the paperback version of the book.)

Now, Charles can't feign false humility anymore. He. Is. An. Author. Now, I get to give him all of the crap about fans wanting book FOUR (04) (or a new series etc. etc.) that he provided me over the years, in spades.

So continue doing me the favor of harassing the shit out of him – because he ~~deserves~~ enjoys it.

Speaking of ISBN's (which stands for **International Standard Book Number**) I was working with a database to see what, if any, information I could ferret out of the data just yesterday.

Diary Jun 28th – July 4th

I used to do this for a living. Now? You might be forgiven for wondering if that is true.

In my past life (10+ years ago), I was a professional computer programmer / database guy and messed with different software packages. There was an ISBN file I needed to load into a database was three (3) gigabytes.

Not a big deal anymore. The laptop I am using has 4,000 GBs of SSD storage and 32 GBs of RAM. That means it is MORE than big enough to handle a (fairly sizeable) file.

Well, the file was a RAR (a compressed file; it's smaller than the real file to save on download speed and costs.)

I had to go into Windows (I am typically on a Mac) to play with the file because a partner I'm working with uses Windows, and I didn't think it would be challenging for me vs. the opposite. I'm pretty familiar with the Microsoft Access database program, so no problem, right?

Wrong.

After twenty minutes of screwing around with my Microsoft Office license and downloading Access, I learned it has a 2GB limit.

I'm going to compress this story a little. About four major downloads later of Microsoft SQL Server, MySQL, and Microsoft Visual Studio later…

I finally download SQLite and locate a front-end program to have a look-see into the file I have.

Here are a few interesting facts:

• The 3GB file un-compressed to 32 GB (killing the option of using Microsoft SQL Server personal, which is limited to 10GB.)

• I could not load the latest MySQL to my machine, not because I'm ignorant (maybe that's true as well), but rather because the latest MySQL install *didn't*. Install, I mean.

• SQLite has a 2,000 GB limit to the database (I only need about forty.)

• I found a suitable front end, imported over 18 MILLION records into the file (this took about ten minutes on my super-duper-Mac Pro-running-Windows laptop), and I can now find the +/- 50,000 records I need.

Talk about overkill.

I have NO idea if I will need this data in one (1) month, and I know I'll never get some of those files I downloaded to try off my hard drive. In fact, if this computer is EVER in a museum for Michael Anderle, you will know the latest Visual Studio install is right there in the Parallels Window partition.

Not being used.

The 4th is on a Saturday?

I'm sure for many of you, July 4th (for those here in America, where it is a holiday) being on a Saturday is not news. I just figured this out like yesterday, which is a week from July 4th exactly.

I heard someone call the lack of knowing what day (or time) it is the new "Corona Calendar," and I completely agree. I have a real hard time knowing what freaking day of the week / month / year it is these days.

HAVE FUN! Life is hard enough right now. Take a moment for a few deep breaths and your favorite calming influence, then crack open that next book!

Ad Aeternitatem,

Michael Anderle

BOOKS BY CHARLES TILLMAN

Akio Revelations

Reprisal (Book 1)

Retaliation (Book 2)

Retribution (Coming Soon)

BOOKS BY MICHAEL ANDERLE

For a complete list of books by Michael Anderle, please visit:

www.lmbpn.com/ma-books/

All LMBPN Audiobooks are Available at Audible.com and iTunes

To see all LMBPN audiobooks, including those written by
Michael Anderle please visit:

www.lmbpn.com/audible

Made in the USA
Las Vegas, NV
21 June 2024